soulmates dissipate

<u>BOOK YOUR PLACE ON OUR WEBSITE</u> <u>AND MAKE THE</u> <u>READING CONNECTION!</u>

We've created a customized website just for our very special readers, where you can get the inside scoop on everything that's going on with Zebra, Pinnacle and Kensington books.

When you come online, you'll have the exciting opportunity to:

- View covers of upcoming books

- Read sample chapters

- Learn about our future publishing schedule (listed by publication month *and author*)

- Find out when your favorite authors will be visiting a city near you

- Search for and order backlist books from our online catalog

- Check out author bios and background information

- Send e-mail to your favorite authors

- Meet the Kensington staff online

- Join us in weekly chats with authors, readers and other guests

- Get writing guidelines

- AND MUCH MORE!

Visit our website at
http://www.kensingtonbooks.com

soulmates dissipate

Mary B. Morrison

DAFINA BOOKS
Kensington Publishing Corp.
http://www.kensingtonbooks.com

DAFINA BOOKS are published by

Kensington Publishing Corp.
850 Third Avenue
New York, NY 10022

All Kensington titles, imprints and distributed lines are available at special quantity discounts for bulk purchases for sales promotions, premiums, fund-raising, and educational or institutional use. Special book excerpts or customized printings can also be created to fit specific needs. For details, write or phone the office of the Kensington Special Sales Manager: Kensington Publishing Corp., 850 Third Avenue, New York, NY 10022. Attn: Special Sales Department. Phone: 1-800-221-2647.

Kensington and the K logo Reg. U.S. Pat. & TM Off. Dafina and the Dafina logo are trademarks of Kensington Publishing Corp.

First Dafina Hardcover Printing: June 2001
First Dafina Paperback Printing: April 2003

10 9 8 7 6

Printed in the United States of America

Dedicated to all soulmates

lost and found

Acknowledgments

First and foremost, I give God the glory for all my successes, large and small. I'm blessed to have such a wonderful and loving family.

Thanks to my sisters Andrea and Regina Morrison, Margie Rickerson, and Debra Noel, and to my brothers Wayne and Derrick Morrison, for their undying support for me as an individual and as a writer.

I am eternally grateful to my deceased great-aunt and great-uncle, Mrs. Ella Beatrice Turner and Mr. Willie Frinkle, for my childhood development.

Always and forever, I give thanks to my son, Jesse Byrd Jr. for being such a magnificent young man.

My deepest appreciation goes to my editor, Karen Thomas, my agent, Claudia Menza, and my new friend, Carl Weber, author of *Lookin' For Luv.* Thanks for believing in my work.

Words alone cannot express the love and gratitude I have for my mentor, Vyllorya A. Evans. Her x-ray vision, candid voice, words of wisdom, and words of empowerment have carried me through my most challenging moments.

I'm grateful for the time Carol Taylor devoted from her extremely hectic schedule to candidly critique my work. Her continued support is a blessing.

Thanks to Mr. Joseph F. Smith for his encouragement and infinite wisdom. His reference of Nelson Mandela's words adequately fueled the strength and courage I needed to pursue my dreams.

I deeply thank my publicists, Felicia Polk of Felicia and Associates, and L. Peggy Hicks of Tri-Com, for promoting my work.

Special thanks to my friends Carmen Polk, Michaela Burnett, Marshall Brown, Marilyn Edge, Saul Simington, Tarik Jones, Kenneth Williams, Kendra Hill, the Louisiana Network Group, and my McDonogh #35 Roneagle family for their support.

Thanks to my hero, former vice president Al Gore, for having the courage and tenacity to stand up for the American people. You proved beyond the shadow of a doubt that no matter how difficult the challenge, it's imperative to do what is right.

Thanks to the vast number of reading groups, sororities, organizations, and individuals that have agreed in advance to host signings. Thanks to all of the bookstore owners who are selling my books, and to each and every one of you who are reading and buying my books.

Last but not least, thanks to *my* soulmate.

Chapter 1

The eternal bond of your Soul Mate gels the existence of your life.

She vividly remembered their first kiss. Wellington Jones gently placed his strong caramel-colored hand at the nape of her dark chocolate neck and whispered, "Diamond, I've wanted to kiss you all night. May I?"

Jada Diamond Tanner struggled to maintain her composure, but Wellington was making it increasingly difficult. How was she to respond without seeming anxious to kiss this tall, sexy man she'd known for all of sixty minutes, give or take ten?

She paused, gazed directly into his eyes, and replied, "Only if I choose where you kiss me." The nearby crowd in the noisy garage became silent. Valet attendants dressed in red jackets and black pants hurried to deliver cars. Although the concert was over, *I've wanted to kiss you all night* was music to her ears.

Wellington seductively shrugged his left shoulder, nodded, and winked his left eye. He looked like a pro but not at all like a player. The outline of his black Armani suit highlighted *all* his muscles. The scent of his cologne traveled in the cool fall night breeze, wrapped around all her senses and danced in her hair. The full moon glowed. His bald head glistened. His thick black eyebrows complemented his dreamy midnight eyes.

Ladylike, she extended her left hand, because it was more sensuous and sensitive to touch than her right. Plus, she wanted to see how creative this man was, and whether he possessed qualitative skills that would interest her in taking the relationship to a hotter level. She was cool, calm, and collected, on the outside.

Slowly, he removed his right hand from underneath her dark silky hair, which flowed down to the center of her back. *Beep. Beep.* "Would someone please move this car!" shouted the man in the black Lexus. She focused, as if they were the only two in the garage. Wellington never missed a beat. He placed Jada's left hand into his right. A long steady flow of air quietly entered her nostrils. Their souls gelled. Her spirit danced. Smooth man. Better proceed with caution. Although she wasn't convinced, he was definitely standing in front of the pitcher's mound prepared to bat.

Like watching a video in slow motion, he drew her French-manicured hand closer. He licked his lips and positioned his tongue between her index and ring fingers. His tongue penetrated her crevice while his full caramel lips—with a trace of natural cocoa—warmly encircled her adjoining knuckles. She closed her eyes. Moisture seeped between her fingers and thighs. This man had knocked more than the ball out of the park!

* * *

Unexpectedly, her twenty-six-inch waist moved forward. Her shoulders and thirty-six-inch hips jerked backward, in unison. It was Monday morning. Jada sat at her bedroom vanity and gazed out the window. She daydreamed about that kiss. One by one the treetops came into focus. Lots of tall evergreen trees stood behind her penthouse. They swayed back and forth. Fresh air. Serenity. She loved California. So far, Oakland was the only place she'd lived.

Jada looked at the digital clock on her cherrywood nightstand. It was six o'clock. Time to begin her daily transformation from looking like Sleeping Beauty to becoming irresistibly drop-dead gorgeous. Time to get ready for work.

Photo shooting the finest male models from coast to coast was a tough job. She'd had a passion for photography since she was six years old and an infatuation with great-looking men as long as she could remember.

Unable to move, she sat, thinking about her father. Although he'd passed away three years, seven months, and ten days ago, he'd never left her. She could still hear his deep, Southern drawl. "Diamond." He'd always call her by her middle name. "There's nothing like time off from work with a job, with pay. If you don't have no job, honey, you don't need no time off." Daddy was right; he was always right. Jada smiled. Today was definitely designed with Diamond in mind.

Mr. Terrance Murphy was the new owner of Sensations Communications. He'd purchased the company a year ago when the previous owners liquidated their assets.

The phone rang six times without an answer. Jada's finger curved toward the off button. Then faintly she heard:

"Sensations Communications."

"Hi. Karen. I'm glad you answered. I was just about to hang up."

Karen was Jada's loyal assistant, or so she thought.

"Oh, Jada girl. You know I'm here every morning at six-thirty on the dot."

"Yeah, I know. Listen. I won't be in today, so call Marvin Jackson and reschedule him for Thursday at the same time. Reschedule my Thursday trip to Los Angeles to early Saturday morning. I must arrive no later than seven. And Karen, be sure to call my L.A. client, Terrell Morgan. Tell him he's rescheduled for eight o'clock."

"Consider it done. Will you be in tomorrow?" asked Karen.

"I'll see you bright and early. Good-bye."

"Bye."

Jada pressed nine on the speed dial. Before the phone rang, she hit the off button. Never put off until tomorrow what you can do today. She decided to surprise her fiancé. He had recently moved his financial advisory business, Wellington Jones and Associates, into his home.

Jada cherished surprises. All of them had been good, so far. Her parents bought her first camera when she was seven. It wasn't her birthday. She traveled with her best friend on a cruise to Mexico when she was eighteen. In college, she received four marriage proposals. "No. No. No. No," she replied each time. She "crossed her t's and dotted her i's." She refused to be any man's showpiece. Confidence was a major component of her Lady Leo characteristic.

Perfect. Jada loved most things hot and steamy. She stepped into the shower and lathered her purple scrunchie with strawberries and peaches shower cream. Leisurely she stroked each part of her five-foot nine-inch temple. The water pulsated against her breasts. Her chocolate nipples hardened. Unable to resist, she licked each one. She turned up the water just a notch, parted her legs, spread her lips, and rotated her clit to the perfect beat. Her eyes closed. Knees bent. Quickly she suppressed her flow.

The mist suspended in air. Jada stepped onto the purple, green, and gold rug. It was a gift from Wellington while they were at the Mardi Gras in Nawlins. She wrapped the matching towel around her waist and brushed her pearly white teeth. The combined results of Daddy's money, and the three years she'd worn braces.

Jada's hazel-colored almond-shaped eyes reflected from the bathroom mirror. Her slender fingers caressed her radiant skin with chocolate-flavored cocoa butter lite. She glanced at her ben-wa balls and smiled, knowing she would use the real thing today. Jada loved being a woman. She'd do coochie crunches all day long and the men didn't have a clue. If he was boring, she'd nonchalantly squeeze her gold balls. *"Okay, that's ten sets, ten reps."* On the other hand, if he was interesting, she'd grip so hard she could hear the metal balls grind. She'd mask. And enjoy multiple orgasms.

She looked at the clock. It was 8:00 A.M. Keys.

Purse. Sunglasses. The scent of Zahra and Eunice lingered. The white cotton ankle-length dress with thigh-high splits gently clung. Her diamond anklet—Daddy bought for Valentine's Day before he died—sparkled. She grabbed her FUBU travel bag with lingerie gear intact. Body and Soul was her favorite "gear" store. They catered to women of contour.

The front and back splits bared her chocolate thighs to the sun while she cruised in her red convertible. Through her dark designer sunglasses, traffic on the Bay Bridge flowed. Traffic along the Peninsula was a breeze. Her ponytail dangled in the air. The projected high was one hundred degrees. Thoughts of making love on Wellington's patio by the pool increased her body heat. *Let's get it on. Oh, baby, let's get it on,* echoed on KBLX-FM 102.9. Jada loved to sing ahead of her favorite songs. She adored Marvin Gaye.

She shifted to a lower gear. The engine roared three-quarters of a mile, until she reached the last house up the hill. An unfamiliar car with D.C. plates sat in the circular driveway between Wellington's indigo Mercedes and black Expedition. Oh well, he had thousands of clients. Probably one of his out-of-state's checking on their portfolio.

Jada looked in the rearview mirror. Hair. Makeup. Flawless. Her peripheral vision detected movement on the balcony above. She glimpsed over the windshield. A beautiful woman disappeared inside Wellington's bedroom. Jada's heart raced faster than the hum of the engine.

She tried to shake it off. She rang the bell. Wellington opened the door. His black silk pajama pants—imported from Italy—hung below his waistline. Thoughts of the mysterious woman in her man's bedroom scrolled Jada's mind like it was Judgment Day. His bare caramel-candied chest looked like he'd hired a professional sculptor. Silky-smooth hairs separated and defined his eight-pack.

"Hi, baby." Wellington kissed Jada's coffee-colored lips. A glossy golden-brown imprint remained. "Why didn't you call first?"

Jada slid her sunglasses to the tip of her nose. She felt the hairs on the back of her neck rise. Who was this woman? Where was this woman? And why in the *hell* was she in Wellington's bedroom? She politely said. "I didn't know I needed to call first."

"It's not that you need to. It's just considerate. You know, like I do."

In one swoop, Jada braced her Ray Bans on top of her head and released her ponytail. "Let's skip the preliminaries. Who's your houseguest?" She was cool. But she really felt like acting a damn fool.

"Oh, that's Melanie, from D.C. She had a break from the studio, so Mom invited her to visit and insisted she stay with me. You know how my mother likes showing me off to her friends. Remember, I told you Mom and Dad are in D.C. They'll be back Friday." Wellington flexed the right side of his chest and smiled. "Just in time to host the Jones family's thirty-fifth annual barbecue Saturday." Jada tasted the scent of his Wintergreen Altoids. She inhaled. Wellington's breath was always fresh.

"Yes, Wellington, you've told me how your parents' annual barbecues started on your first birthday. Now it's not only a family tradition but also a

societal affair where prestigious folk gather to let
down their hair. And let the good times role." Jada
spoke so fast, she could hardly hear the words
coming out of her mouth. Wellington clamped his
hands behind his back.

"I clearly remember you saying no matter how
successful we become, we still know how to throw a
great barbecue. I've heard the story time and time
again. And you didn't invite me last year because
we'd just met and you didn't know what I'd think
of your parents' tremendous sociopolitical involve-
ment with numerous affluent organizations. *Now,*
let's get back to Melanie." By the time Jada got to
her point, she had to take a deep breath to regain
her composure.

Wellington never shifted his dreamy eyes away
from Jada's. She stood in the foyer. Peeped over
his shoulder. He lovingly stroked the left side of
her face. Wellington's six-feet four-inch, two hundred and twenty-pound frame obscured her view.
Jada's temperature must have been well over the
today's projected high but for all the wrong reasons.

"Look, sweetheart. I know this is the first time
I've had a female houseguest since we've been together. But you have to trust me. She's just a
friend. She's leaving next Sunday. Mom invited
her to the barbecue and Melanie volunteered to
help prepare the food. She's an excellent cook.
Get to know her. You'll like her."

Damn! Jada wondered how *well* Wellington
knew Melanie. He hadn't budged since he opened
the door. Maybe he was stalling while she freshened up.

"Melanie and my mom have a lot in common.

They're affiliated with most of the same *prestigious* organizations. You know how important that is to my mom. It's been a long-standing tradition in Melanie's family. That's why my mother respects her so much. You really should join *at least one.*"

Well, don't we just know her whole life history? Isn't that cute. "Wellington, we've had this discussion before and you know I *refuse* to join any of those organizations. Getting back to the subject at hand. If she's just a *friend,* why was she on your balcony and not the guest balcony?"

"Look, Diamond, I don't have to prove myself. It's too hot and too early for ninety-nine questions. You show up unannounced and now you want to interrogate me. Baby, please come in. Have a seat in the living room. I'll prepare breakfast for both of you."

Wellington's foyer was larger than most. Consuming approximately two hundred square feet, the floor was made of crystal clear marble. His favorite color black was swirled in an abstract pattern. Jada had never seen this type of marble anyplace. London. Paris. Italy. China. Two black pillars—ringed with twenty-four-karat gold accents around the top and bottom—stood twenty-four feet high, twelve feet apart. The custom-designed silk African drapes, spiraled each pillar from ceiling to floor.

Convinced he wouldn't tell her the *real deal,* Jada entered Wellington's spacious sunk-in living room like Inspector Clouseau. The furniture was strategically situated near the sliding glass door leading to his main patio. Step by step. Thump. Thump. Thump. The pulse in her throat kept pace.

The tailored winter-white drapes were drawn to prevent glare on the seventy-inch television. Ah ha! Melanie appeared right at home. The world news was on the big screen. An X-rated film featuring Vanessa on the other. Melanie's French pedicure blended with the off-white chaise longue. Jada's heart and feet sank into the tan carpet's thickness. She noticed how Melanie's bright teeth shined through the cherry-red lip gloss. So this was what high-society women did on vacation.

"Oh hi, I'm Melanie." Melanie resumed watching TV. "Wellington has told me so much about you."

Before today, he'd never mentioned Melanie. Jada had the inside scoop on D.C. women. They didn't have a problem sharing a man. In California, if women shared, it was strictly for the moment. Do not get attached. For the moment, Jada ignored the video and lay on the couch parallel to the chaise longue.

"Hi, Melanie, I'm Diamond, Wellington's *fiancée.*"

Eyebrows arched. French manicure. Perfect size ten. Small waist. Bigger breasts. Smaller butt. Shoulder-length hair, brown. Teasing tan. Gorgeous. Five-nine. Five-ten. One forty. One forty-five. High cheekbones. Piercing light-brown eyes. Thick lips. Soft shoulders. Lustrous skin. Melanie was too sexy for comfort.

"So, *Melanie,* what brings you *all* the way to California, *in your car?*"

Melanie's light-brown eyes were fixed on the video.

"I needed a break from the studio. I'm a photographer for *Vibrations Magazine.*"

Jada's body went from horizontal to vertical in three seconds. "Excuse me for a moment. I'll be right back."

Wellington had gone upstairs to his bedroom. The Road Runner couldn't have gotten to him quicker. He stood naked. She stood still. He flexed in front of his wall-length mirror. Needless to say, Ms. Melanie could prepare breakfast her damn self.

She entered his suite-size bedroom. "Hi, baby." Her tongue traveled three hundred and sixty degrees around her lips. Jada lusted for Wellington's six-foot-four, two hundred and twenty pounds of succulent, caramel flesh. She felt her heart beat against her thong.

"Hi, precious, you have perfect timing." Wellington did three quick dick curls. "I was just about to shower. Join me."

"You said you were going to prepare breakfast."

"What's the rush? I'll do it later."

Jada realized she'd just gotten out of the shower, but what's a woman to do! White cotton cloth circled her feet. Wellington never could resist her tasty chocolate mounds with nipples that tasted like Hershey's Kisses. It was her favorite flavored cocoa butter lite.

He did an erotic strip-tease move. Spun around. Glided close behind. "You know I love the way you smell, baby, but I can never figure out exactly what you're wearing." The wetness of his tongue invoked a trail of coolness up her spine. His smooth masculine hands caressed her voluptuous thirty-six Ds. The view in the mirror turned Jada on. The flow she suppressed earlier welled up inside her pulsating walls.

Gently, he turned her around and palmed her firm ass. Wellington's winter-fresh tongue invaded Jada's mouth. She greeted it like it was opening day at Disney World.

A video scene flashed across Jada's mind. Vanessa blew softly and feathered this handsome young guy. Absent her touch, his body trembled. He climaxed. Jada had acquired most of her sexual skills from reading. But one day soon, she'd have to try that on Wellington.

They stepped into his 150-square-foot custom-made shower. It was large enough to accommodate six people standing, or one person lying on the shower bed. The walls were pallid with beautiful African American art originals strategically displayed on every accessible wall. Wellington's fetish for fine art ran deep. Art was exhibited on easels and hung on walls in every single room, including the thirteen-person Jacuzzi room.

Wellington's parents, Mr. and Mrs. Christopher Jones, worked extremely smart to achieve their wealth. They taught Wellington how to track his mutual fund at five years old. Now he maintained his lifestyle on interest from his investments and fees from his clients.

"Baby, I've got an idea. Set up the shower bed."

"Precious, this is why I love you so much. Because you're a freak girl, but only for me, and I love it! You know every man wants a little trash in his woman but no man wants a trashy woman."

"Wellington, set up the shower bed." Jada whispered, *"Now."* Inconspicuously built into the wall for convenience and safety, it unfolded horizontally.

"Lie down. Relax. And allow me to give you the

most exotic and erotic massage of your life. Today you'll experience cosmic ecstasy."

The four-by-eight-foot bed was crafted with genuine Italian waterproof leather and tailored to suit Wellington. Traditionally he gave Jada full body massages. Not today.

She inserted the attachable pillow. Jada wanted him to watch. Then she positioned the six showerheads. One each above his chest, abs, feet, thighs, one over his throbbing nine-inch penis, and the last underneath his firm ass. A structurally designed opening exposed Wellington's ass. "Now relax and observe *Mama* at work."

Jada lathered up his black scrunchie. Wellington was so clean he almost squeaked. She believed cleanliness was next to Godliness. If it wasn't clean, Jada refused to get close.

The warm water flowed over Wellington's body. She rubbed Karma Sutra oil all over his body. Teased his hardened nipples. Massaged his chest and abs. And stroked his circumcised penis. He moaned in a deep passionate voice.

Jada's vagina snapped. Released. Contracted. Her hot watery tongue raced up and down Wellington's shaft. His muscle slapped her right cheek several times. She kissed, licked, and then sucked him hard—so hard she felt the walls of her mouth cave in and tighten around *The Ruler.* With each deep suck, her nose and lips pressed against his pubic hairs. She never disclosed how she'd learned to deep throat.

"Ow, girl."

"You taste so good, baby." Jada drooled.

Her lips explored his inner thighs. Voyaged to his jewels and slowly continued to his knees, his feet. She embraced his toes with her lips. He shivered and muttered, "Come back up."

"In a minute." Jada slid her slippery breasts against Wellington's smooth feet and fondled them. He wiggled his toes as if to say "Fuck the feet!"

The thought of blue balls convinced her to switch. She started performing her special lemon twist. With oily hands she twisted his dick. Left and right. Up and down. The palm of her hand occasionally covered his head to prolong his ejaculation. Wellington watched *Mama* work.

"Whose is it?" She slipped his hardness into her hungry mouth.

"Da-Da-Diamond ru-rules *The Ruler.*"

Each time his head touched the back of her throat, her juices flowed. This time she held her lips and nose against his pubic hair so hard she could hardly breathe. She didn't care. She had to reach her other G-spot. She knew Wellington's excitement heightened whenever she did this. Jada intentionally limited her oxygen supply to intensify her orgasm.

Jada slid her hand under the table and gently penetrated Wellington. Her oily index finger glided in and out of his rectum. His toes curled. "Damn, girl. You sure know how to make me feel good. Don't stop. Please! Don't stop."

She loved it when he begged. Jada's finger test was pass or fail. If a man became paranoid and rejected the gesture, he was too damn conservative. An experienced man who was secure with his manhood understood that dual sexual stimulation was cosmic.

Steadily, she increased the pace. Not too fast.

She wanted her man to enjoy every second. Wellington could no longer hold back his powerful explosion. He released the loudest and deepest groan she had ever heard.

As he reached his orgasmic peak, he shivered, epileptic-like. She wasn't finished just yet. Her mouth welcomed the thick creamy fluids that flowed like lava oozing over the top of an erupting volcano. Little by little his sweetness flowed from her mouth while she kissed, licked, and sucked him.

Wellington could barely move. He stumbled to his king-size bed, dripping wet. He fell backward on the brown silk comforter. His arms spread east and west. "Damn, girl."

"Mission accomplished," Jada whispered as she kissed Wellington's forehead. She slipped into her dress and went downstairs.

Melanie was preparing a vegetarian omelet. She held the blue plastic ladle in her hand and asked, "Would you like to have breakfast *again*?"

"That depends on what you're serving."

"Omelet. What else?" Melanie's cherry-red lips curved. The flawless arch in her eyebrows extended upward.

"Sure. Why not?" Jada sat at the breakfast nook near the window and admired the architectural design of the kitchen. Wellington's kitchen was designed as if he were a chef. Pots and pans hung from the ceiling. Most of them had never been used. His double stove with eight burners and customized grill rested in the center like a huge island.

Melanie cracked three eggs. She moved about the kitchen like she was right at home. She knew exactly where everything was located. Melanie held the bowl of diced ham and said, "I'm having a vegetarian omelet. Would you like me to add meat to yours, or have you had your fill today?"

Her sarcasm had grown old. Jada crossed her arms and pivoted in her seat. "Look, Melanie. I really don't know you. But the way you're making little snide remarks leads me to believe you're lacking sexual gratification in your socioeconomic and politically correct environment."

She delicately folded the omelet. "No, Diamond."

"Stop right there. Only my father—may he rest in peace—and Wellington use my middle name. *Please,* call me Jada."

Melanie sighed. She quietly placed the ladle in the sink. "I'll call you whatever you prefer. But you shouldn't introduce yourself as Diamond if you don't want anyone other than *your men* calling you that. No, *Jada*—as you prefer—to answer your question, I'm not lacking at all. I was simply trying to break the ice. So let's try this a different way."

Melanie sat perpendicular to Jada, crossed her legs, leaned forward, and said, "My name is Melanie Marie Thompson. I graduated from Howard University in 1987. I'm thirty-two years old. Never married. No kids. My grandmother is a Greek. My mother's a Greek. And I'm a Greek. Are you a Greek, Jada?" Melanie returned to the stove and flipped the omelet with ease.

Jada unfolded her arms. "No, my mother never believed in affiliations and I feel the same."

"Oh, so I see. Well, my family has a long-standing history with many *affluent* organizations. Just like Mrs. Jones."

The omelet was almost ready. The aroma made Jada hungry.

"So I've heard."

"Would you like me to add any spices to your omelet?" asked Melanie.

"No, thanks. I've had enough *spice* this morning." Jada tossed her wet hair over her shoulders.

"See, now you're the one bringing it up so I'll just ignore that statement. Here's your omelet."

"Thanks. Let's sit outside by the pool," suggested Jada.

"Sure."

Wellington's Olympic-size pool resembled the number zero on a football jersey. The elevated oval-shaped hot tub—with four diving boards—could accommodate eight people.

It was close to eleven o'clock and closer to one hundred degrees. Jada swooped up her damp hair, wrapped it in a ball, and tucked the ends for security. She looked directly into Melanie's piercing eyes. "So what's the real reason you're here?"

Melanie proceeded to say grace and picked up her fork. "That depends."

Jada almost choked. *"On?"*

"Are you insecure?" Melanie stayed unruffled. "Don't answer that. I'm just kidding. Loosen up. With a man as fine as Wellington, I *do* understand. Mrs. Jones is my godmother. We hadn't seen one another in several years. She invited. I accepted."

Melanie must have graduated head of her class in charm school. After three bites of her omelet, her cherry-red lipstick hadn't smudged. For Jada, Friday could not come soon enough. Insecure? No. Concerned? Definitely.

Jada's mama taught her how to love and treat a

man but she never taught her how to *find* a good man. Jada searched all her life for a man like Wellington. He was hers—*only time would tell*—forever.

"So, when's the wedding?" Melanie dabbed the corner of her mouth with the white cloth napkin.

"Valentine's Day next year. Since it falls on a Saturday, and Wellington is my soulmate, timing couldn't be better."

"One day I want to get married and have two children, maybe three, but living in D.C. makes it a challenge."

"Why?"

"Because most D.C. men want to unwrap the package, use it, and then return it—not for a refund—for an exchange. They move from woman to woman, like it's open season year-round. You open. They season. You can get Classic seasoning, Charley seasoning, and if you really want some old spice, you can get yourself some **Channel seasoning**."

Jada laughed so hard it hurt. Her hands held her stomach. A cute laugh bellowed from Melanie as she stared directly into Jada's mouth.

"Anyway, girl," Melanie continued. "You've got a good man, and when you guys get married, I want to be in your wedding."

"Really, girl!" Maybe Wellington was right. If she got to know Melanie, maybe she would like her.

"Yes! Really. My mother's friend plans weddings for the rich and famous from D.C. to L.A. So I'll be happy to assist you any way I can."

"Thanks." Jada paused. Looked into Melanie's eyes. "Why do you keep staring at my mouth?"

"Because the way you speak reminds me of this

woman I went to college with. We were partying late one night in my apartment, when—" Melanie swiftly responded.

Jada thought she would sunburn before the story ended. "I'd love to stay and chat but I've got errands." She carried her plate inside. Melanie followed. Jada turned and noticed Melanie staring at her ass.

Melanie shifted her eyes. "I'm going to get dressed and go over to my godmommy's house. I promised to water the plants and feed the tropical fish. Maybe we can get together before I leave. I want to shop and party 'til I drop."

"Sure, let's do that, girl. Before you *leave.*"

Jada strolled out the front door. Melanie walked into the kitchen and restored it to its original state of cleanliness. Thoughts of Wellington crept through her mind. Melanie went upstairs to Wellington's bedroom, but she was not prepared for what she saw. Wellington was sound asleep on his back naked. His erection was fully extended.

Melanie boldly walked into Wellington's bedroom and stood over him. She zoomed in closer. Wellington snored. Melanie took his penis into her hand and began to fantasize. Damn, he looked so good she could devour him in one gulp. Melanie wanted to experience Wellington for herself. Melanie concluded she would give Jada all the help she wanted but none of what she needed. Wellington was the man for her. Melanie decided there was no need to make a return visit to San Francisco. She simply wouldn't leave.

* * *

Jada Diamond Tanner came across classy and confident. Whenever she became insecure, she masked. Growing up with dark skin hadn't been easy. It wasn't until tenth grade that she became popular. The birthday makeover that Henry Morgan and Ruby Denise Tanner surprised her with increased her self-esteem. Prom queen, college queen, she was exquisite. She could have any man she wanted but she was in search of her soulmate. Jada believed her search had ended the night she met Wellington Jones . . .

Life for Wellington Jones had been predominantly mapped from day one. The private schools he attended. The long-term buddies he had. The career he chose. He believed he was in control but nothing happened in Wellington's life unless his mother, Cynthia, deemed it.

Cynthia Elaine Jones controlled everything and everyone around her. She knew one day she'd have to account for her wrongdoings. Until then, the show must go on. Her dance with the devil would last longer than she'd anticipated. The only person she truly adored was Melanie. Melanie was the one child she'd wanted but couldn't bear.

For Melanie Marie Thompson, life was never a dull moment. Money. Sex. Men. Sex. Women. Sex. There was nothing in her life she wanted to do and didn't. Life was great but she knew her biological clock was ticking. She wanted a family. She wanted Wellington Jones.

Chapter 2

Jada reflected on the commencement of her relationship with Wellington. It was like a dream come true.

Her impromptu decision to paint the town red that night—the night she met her soulmate—had been the best she'd made in years. It was a hot Friday, Indian summer night. One of the few she could enjoy in San Francisco without needing to wear a jacket. This time Jada concluded a bird in the hand wasn't better than two in the bush. Maybe she'd get lucky. Perhaps Mr. Right wouldn't end up Mr. Right Now. Her workday was about to end and party time was getting ready to begin.

"Jada, Candice is on line one," said Karen.

"Thanks. I'll take the call." Jada propped the phone between her shoulder and ear. She casually fumbled through her purse. "Hey, girl. I have my car keys in hand. What's up?"

"What are you doing tonight?"

"Going to dinner with Darryl. He made eight o'clock dinner reservations at Cityscape Skylyne. You know the restaurant on the fortieth floor of the Cityscape Hotel." Jada jingled her keys.

"You mean Mr. Darryl, NBA, sexy-as-he-wanna-be Williams?" Candice's voice raised five octaves.

Jada looked at the small gold and crystal clock on her maplewood desk. It was five o'clock. The salad she'd bought for lunch sat in the miniature refrigerator in her office. "Yeah, that's the one."

Jada sat at her desk and flipped through the photos from her prior day's shoot. Candice thought Darryl was fine, but the pictures of the guy spread in front of her face were sinful.

"Girl, he has a body to die for and you know it." Candice whispered like she'd just told a secret.

"I can picture him now," she continued at a normal tone. "Six-nine with his spicy golden complexion. Handsome. Suave. Debonair. I thought you stopped going out with him last year." Candice must have been born a flirt. She drew attention even when she wasn't trying. Her get-back booty demanded at least three feet of space.

"How many times do I have to explain? Darryl is on my *Active Reserve* list. Write the categories down this time, Candice. There's Active, Active Reserve, Inactive Reserve, and Inactive. Besides, Darryl's still the best fuck I've had on the West Coast." Darryl had been on Jada's Active Reserve list since twelfth grade.

Women practically threw themselves at Darryl's feet. The panties and the pussy flew so fast he had to wear two catcher's mitts. Candice was right. Darryl was handsome and the fact that he was a multimillionaire didn't hurt. His mother was African American. His father was Native American. Darryl's ponytail was kohl black and wavy. The two-carat diamond earring in his left ear turned Jada on. She liked a taste of *bad boy* in her men. She avoided rich boring men like the plague. Jada loved Darryl's gray eyes, long curly eyelashes, and well-defined cheekbones.

"Well, I can't fuck you," replied Candice. "But if you're interested, I've got two tickets to see Will Downing, Rachelle Ferrell, Gerald Albright, and Kenny Latimore at Top of the City Jazz and Supper Club. The show starts at eight."

Candice had been Jada's best friend since elementary school. She was the one person—outside of Jada's parents—who knew almost everything about her.

"What kind of question is that? Am I interested? I'll have Karen reschedule with Darryl. Pick me up at seven."

"Seven-fifteen."

"Great. Bye."

"See you later. And Jada, be ready when I get there." Jada put her salad in the refrigerator and pressed the intercom button.

"Karen."

"Yes?"

"Would you please call Darryl? Ask him if we can reschedule for next Friday at the same time." Jada gathered the photos and put them in her desk drawer.

"You mean you want to reschedule with Darryl Williams?"

"That's right." Every woman just loved Darryl. Although he was no longer on Karen's speed dialer,

Jada knew Karen had his number etched in her brain.

Jada checked again. Her makeup and hair still looked impeccable. After Jada's tenth grade makeover, image became everything. With all the fine men in her building, she refused to check her mailbox unless she looked good. The ginger-colored pantsuit she wore replaced the tea-stained pale-yellow dress she'd worn to work. She always kept a pair and a spare—shoes and an outfit—at work. Jada sashayed out of her office.

"Ms. Tanner, Mr. Williams said he'd call you next Thursday to confirm."

"Oh great, thanks, Karen. You've worked hard today. Don't work the extra hours. I'll pay you for them anyway. Go home. Enjoy your weekend and tell Damien I said hello."

"Gee. Thanks!"

Karen's son was her pride and joy. For eleven years in a row, Damien had earned a 4.0 grade point average. Two more years and he'd become valedictorian of his senior class. Karen's GPA had been closer to 0.4. She'd graduated by the skin of her . . . But once she had Damien, she'd strived for perfection.

Jada headed straight for her stereo. Popped in Will Downing's *Mood* CD. Went to the kitchen. Poured a nice cold glass of Moët. She hung her imported designer suit in the closet. Left side. Everything on the left had already been worn and needed to go to the cleaners. Everything on the right was ready to wear. She pulled out a fuchsia silk minidress. Put it back. The black satin dress with pearl straps was too formal. The choices narrowed to her red double-breasted pantsuit with matching bustier or her leopard diva dress with the split that just wouldn't quit.

Long dresses with high splits were her trademark. She treasured the way they showed enough but not too much. Men noticed her long sexy chocolate legs. Her seductive walk—stride—with hips swaying methodically from side to side drove them nuts.

Jada couldn't thank her mother enough. Mama taught her a long time ago that all women were sexy. Mama would say, "Simply accentuate the positive and eliminate the negative. God gave each of us talent and beauty. Never apologize for your heavenly gifts."

Jada showered and napped for twenty minutes, so she'd look refreshed. Not refurbished. Slipped into her exotic leopard dress with spaghetti straps, front split, and backless swoop that stopped right above her ass.

It was seven-fifteen. Jada greeted Candice in the lobby.

"Hey, girl! I have one question for you," said Candice. "Are you ready to have fun tonight?"

"Hell, yeah!" Jada put her hands in the air like Diana Ross and blew kisses to the wind. When Jada masked, even Candice couldn't tell. Deep inside she'd grown tired. Countless men. Rich. Sexy. Fine. Unattached. But where was her soulmate? She figured at thirty-two surely she should have found him by now. If it took much longer, her knight in shining armor would need Geritol and ginseng.

Candice had recently bought a white Lexus sports car dipped in gold. Jada strapped on her seat belt. "I have to be in L.A. at seven in the morning. This new guy, Terrell Morgan, is fresh. I've already heard through the grapevine, he has a body to die for and a face to match."

"Well, if he's all that, let me know. Maybe *I* can throw some action his way." Candice commented and shifted into fifth gear.

"No, you are not trying to throw your thirty-one-year-old coochie on a twenty-one-year-old guy." Jada laughed so hard her stomach ached. Her thoughts instantly reverted to having a family.

Candice turned down the radio. "Women have always had the advantage over men. In this day and time our position has improved. Think about this. When a woman is twenty, she can have any man she wants from twenty to one hundred and twenty. When a woman is thirty, she can still have any man she wants. When a woman is forty, younger guys are impressed because they know she's experienced and older men are blessed because she's still younger than them. There is *nothing* finer than a physically fit fifty-year-old woman because *she* can have them *all*. And girlfriend, when a woman is seventy and older, she can buy that new drug on the market overseas. You know the one that'll make a man faithful *forever.*"

Jada laughed on cue. Her psychological noise drowned out Candice's words. But the cool breeze, full moon, and bright stars did not go unnoticed.

The express elevator doors closed. Candice pressed the button for the forty-second floor four times.

For a split second, Jada's forehead wrinkled. "Why did you do that?"

"You won't believe who I just saw."

"I probably would. Try me."

"It was Mr. Darryl, B-ball six-nine, superfine Williams and he is looking good tonight!" The ears of the women on the elevator stood like dogs listening in the night.

That was good Darryl had come. Maybe she'd bump him up to *Active* if she didn't get a better offer. Jada didn't bother to respond.

When the doors opened, Jada and Candice stepped into a room filled with partygoers from just about every nationality imaginable: Asian, Caucasian, African American, Puerto Ricans; you name it. Jada appreciated the cultural diversity in the Bay Area.

At five feet eleven inches, Jada definitely stood out in the crowd. Five inches shorter than Jada, Candice still held her own. Her peach lace mini-dress showed off her soul-sista track star thighs. Most people had to request three feet of space but not Candice. Her *butt* demanded it.

The three-foot-high brass rail separated the dining, dance, and stage areas. Not quite front and center, but Jada and Candice could see almost everything from their seats. Jada's eyes viewed outside the window. The Golden Gate Bridge twinkled over the San Francisco Bay. The Oakland Bay Bridge dazzled with thousands of lights shining as bright as a million stars. The full moon illuminated the sky between the bridges.

Jada scanned the room for prospects. "Damn! Don't look now. But there's a handsome brother that just stepped in the room." Her extraterrestrial senses told her he was with the guy walking behind him.

Candice automatically turned.

"I told you *not* to look now."

Candice faced Jada. Gave her a devious diva wink with her big brown eye. Flashed a cynical smile. And immediately took a second look.

"Damn! He *is* fine. Why do they travel in pairs? His friend is a dud."

The hostess escorted Jada's prospect. Jada's eye trailed him from the door until he was out of view. "No. Come back."

Candice sang. "He can't hear you." Then very matter-of-factly, she said, "But if he resurfaces, he's all yours. I've already booked my reservations for tonight." Candice was a confident woman, most of the time.

Jada inconspicuously glanced around the room. "Great! You can have his friend." *Where did he go?*

"He's not my type! And no. I won't double date with you if ya'll go out. Not for all the tea in China. Now the guy with Darryl, he's all that and a bag of chips." Candice put the tip of her acrylic nail on the edge of her tongue.

Candice had a good point. After Jada became popular in high school, she'd hook Candice up with blind dates. One guy had halitosis. Another couldn't speak English. And the last dressed like he was stuck in the seventies. How was she to know? Jada always met them at the same time.

"Double date or not, I'm going to get noticed by Mr. Wonderful before he sets his eyes on *anyone* else."

"Strut your stuff, girl." Candice flicked her peachy cream nails twice.

Jada orchestrated every move.

Plan A. Jada ran her well-manicured fingers through her hair. Men parted like the Red Sea. She heard one woman say, "Bryan. Bryan. Bryan!" Mr. Wonderful was nowhere in sight.

Plan B. She ordered a drink at the bar, even though she already had one at the table. Before she could pick up the tab, an unidentified stranger had already paid it. She perused. Took a sip. Searched again. Then sat the Tres Generaciones tequila on the counter.

Plan C. The line in the rest room was long. It didn't matter that she wasn't there to use it. She required a temporary haven so she wouldn't seem like a raven. She teased and fluffed her hair. Refreshed her favorite fragrance, Zahra. She washed her hands and did a quick check in the mirror. The women acted as if they weren't watching. She departed and resumed her hunt.

The band had started. Couples held hands. Jada heard Will Downing's voice fill the room. At first she couldn't believe her ears. How ironic. His first song was "Don't Wait for Love." *"I know you're sad . . ."*

The men parted again. Jada smoothed her hands over her hips.

"Give me the four-one-one," Candice said.

Jada sat. "How about nine-one-one?" She sighed. "But all is not lost. I still have three hours to find him."

At that moment, *the rose man* put a red rose on the table. Jada and Candice's eyes met.

"The rose is for you," he said, pointing at Jada. His Puerto Rican accent was heavy.

"Why, thank you."

"No. It's not from me."

Rows of flesh buckled along Jada's forehead. "Then who?"

Will Downing started to sing "Just to Be with You."

"I gave my word. I can't tell you. This rose is for you too." Another long-stem red rose.

"Wait. Don't leave," said Jada, reaching out to the stranger. But he kept walking.

"I think it's Darryl," said Candice.

"I have no idea." Jada hadn't seen Mr. Wonderful since he walked in. She doubted if Candice was right. Darryl had class and pizzazz, but he lacked creativity outside the bedroom.

When Will sang his last song, "Fall in Love Again," a yellow rose was delivered. During Kenny Latimore's "For You," and Gerald Albright's "Mr. Right," red roses were delivered.

"Stop!" Jada's fingers wrapped around the rose man's wrist and tightened. "Either you tell me who's sending the roses or stop bringing them."

"Sorry. I told you. I gave my word. Julio Ramirez's word is his bond."

At a snail's pace, Jada's fingers gave weight. With each remaining song, Julio delivered a red rose. From that point forward, Jada and Candice pretended it was part of the show.

Candice sucked cocktail sauce off the same shrimp all night long. The waitress brought Darryl's friend's business card to Candice. The name on the card read TERRELL MORGAN. He also asked the waitress to replenish Candice's sauce.

When Rachelle Ferrell announced the last song of the evening, Jada heaved. "Finally. Now maybe he'll reveal himself." "With Open Arms" had everyone grooving in their seat.

"What if it's a woman?" Candice laughed.

"Hardie-har-har-har. Candice, you play too much, girl."

Out of the blue, Mr. Wonderful appeared holding a sterling silver platter covered with rose petals. "So, I take it you didn't like the drink?" he asked Jada.

His Barry White–like voice sent chills through Jada's body. He was handsome. Thick eyebrows. Dreamy eyes. Bald head. Goatee. Jada gasped. Swiftly she composed herself. His upper lip was slightly larger and darker. Sexy. He kneeled before her. Yellow and red petals floated to her feet. "May I have the last dance?"

Jada's lips mouthed yes. She tried to move her feet, but couldn't. He reached for her hand. His was warm. Hers cold. She froze.

"Allow me to introduce myself. I'm Wellington Jones."

Faintly she said, "Hi, I'm Diamond."

Darryl walked up behind Wellington. "She saved the last dance for me. I'm Darryl Williams of the NBA." Darryl extended his hand.

This is not *happening*. Jada stared at Darryl. Candice sat back and crossed her legs as if she had a ringside seat to see Mike Tyson vs. Evander Holyfield. *Not now, Go away! Disappear!* Jada shouted silently.

Wellington grasped Darryl's hand and didn't let go. "I'm Wellington Jones of Wellington Jones and Associates, financial advisor. Here's my card. Call me. I'm *sure* you could benefit from my expertise." He released Darryl's hand.

Then he turned to Jada and said, "Perhaps

there'll be another opportunity for us to dance. Here's my card."

Oh hell no! He was not the one leaving. Jada eased to her feet. Wellington's bicep was solid. She squeezed gently. "Give us just a moment, please."

"I like a woman who's not afraid to take control." Wellington smiled captivatingly. Winter-green freshness escaped his kissable lips.

Darryl looked at Wellington, then at Jada. "Call me next week if we're still on for Friday night. *Baby.*" His lips traveled in slow motion toward hers and landed on Jada's cheek. Not tonight. Darryl walked away with his shoulders squared and chest stuck out. Damn! What bad ass timing.

"Ladies and gentlemen," Rachelle announced. "It's been our pleasure to perform for you tonight. This *was* the last song but I am making a special dedication. This is for the gentleman who showered the lovely lady with roses *all night long.*"

As Rachelle began to play "Nothing Has Ever Felt Like This," Wellington escorted Jada to the dance floor. He held her so close, the creases in their stomachs fit like pieces to a jigsaw puzzle. His hand traveled down her spine. She laid her head on his chest and melted in his arms. For the first time in Jada's life, time stood still.

Chapter 3

A week had past. Nine days to be exact. Jada undeniably concluded that Wellington Jones was Mr. Right Now. Probably another spoiled rich guy who strived for attention. Fortunately Sunday morning church service was only an hour away. She needed all the prayer she could get. Jada picked up the phone and dialed Candice's number.

"Hi, Candice. I need to talk." Jada explained her dilemma in detail.

"Candice, what would you do?" Jada couldn't drink the goblet of chilled orange juice on her nightstand. She rolled over on her back and tucked the red silk pillow under her head.

"I don't know why you keep asking my opinion. Besides, your daddy always insisted that you make your own decisions. Now if it were me, I would have called him Saturday morning."

Jada felt nauseated. One of two signs that revealed

she cared more than she'd admit. At least the migraine headaches hadn't kicked in. When she was a little princess, Mama called them growing pains.

"But that's what he expects. Just because he's good-looking—"

"Stunning!" interrupted Candice.

"He has a nice body—"

"Glorious!"

"Candice, would you stop doing that. I've made up my mind. If he doesn't call by this Friday, he can forget it." Jada's red manicured nails covered her abdomen.

"That's why so many women miss out. You're expecting to receive more than you're willing to give. Darryl is a prime example. You took his number. Refused to give him yours. And you didn't call him for over a month."

Candice was right. "Bye, Candice. I've got to get dressed so I can pick up Mama. I'll call you later."

"Bye, Jada. And remember, girlfriend, nothing from nothing leaves nothing."

Jada showered for five minutes. She put on her sleeveless sapphire silk designer dress with matching long-sleeve double-breasted jacket. Her genuine pearl necklace with matching earrings was a gift from Daddy when she turned thirteen. A dab of Vanilla Cream behind each ear functioned as an all-day aromatherapy. As soon as the elevator door inside her condo opened, the phone rang. She didn't wait for it to close. Jada grabbed the kitchen cordless.

"Hi, Mama. I'm walking out right now."

"Big Daddy might be more appropriate if I knew you better."

"What! You need to be on your way to church to praise God, Big Daddy. Or whoever you are."

"As a matter of fact, I *am*. Would you care to join me? This is Wellington Jones."

Jada's fingers touched her forehead, chest, left, then right shoulders. "I'd love to but I have to pick up my mother for church by ten-thirty."

"Well, I don't want to impose on your spiritual time, so why don't I call you tonight," he said.

Jada ran her fingers through her hair. "I'd really like you to fellowship with us soon. But Mother should meet you first. That way she'll have more answers than questions for her inquisitive friends. They're persistently asking when am I going to get married and have babies." Shit! She softly stomped her foot and wished she could eat her words.

"Marriage *and* babies." Wellington laughed. "Say a prayer for *me*. I'll call you later. Good-bye, Diamond." He blew a kiss into the receiver.

"Anytime after six is good. Bye." Jada pulled out her electronic calendar and scheduled an extra half hour of meditation and prayer before six o'clock. Wellington was truly Mr. Right.

On her way to pick up her mother, Jada reflected. How perfect—a twofer—Wellington was a churchman and a gentleman.

The scenic drive along Interstate 580 was beautiful. Above MacArthur Boulevard there were evergreen trees leading from the highway to the top of the Oakland hills. From the freeway, homes appeared sporadically spaced among the evergreen. But the Mormon Temple always stood out, especially at night with all the lights. Luckily Jada's cellular had caller ID.

"Hello, Mother. I'm exiting off a Hundred and Fiftieth Avenue right now."

"Okay, baby. I'll wait outside."

Jada cherished the moments they shared. She never understood why so many people didn't enjoy quality time with their parents. "Look at you, Ms. Lady, all decked out in your Sunday best. Let me open the door for you, Mama. Give me just a minute." Jada's curls dangled in the breeze.

"You're so kind to me." Her hazel eyes softened.

Jada kissed her mother's buttery smooth cheek. "Where did you get that jazzy lavender suit?"

"Sacramento," Ruby said.

"Sacramento? When did you find time to go to Sacramento?"

"Baby, you know Mama can't tell you all her secrets."

"What secrets?" Jada snapped her head in her mother's direction. "I'm thirty-two years old, and if I can't have secrets, neither can you, Ms. Lady." Jada had her share. She preferred to label them untold stories. Most generated from the temper tantrums she had never outgrown. Mama never knew she left the bathtub water running on the third floor in Stanley's townhouse. That gigolo deserved worse.

"So, answer the question."

"Well, if you must know, Mr. Hamilton had business at the State Building, and he asked if I'd take the ride. So off we went in his brand new 1998 red-hot convertible. We listened to Coltrane, Billie Holiday, Nat King Cole, Diana Ross, and Bobby Blue Bland. Child, we had ourselves a grand old time. Can you believe his CD player holds *twelve?*" Ruby smiled.

"That's great, Mama." Jada smiled back. It felt good to see her mama happy again. The church parking lot was full. Jada got out of the car and opened the door for her mother.

"Now don't park too far away. I don't want you to have to walk a long distance in these three-inch heels." Jada remembered how her father always opened the door for them. She missed her daddy.

"Good morning, Sister Simon and Sister Brown," Pastor Tellings said. He refused to cut his miniature Don King Afro.

"Good morning," they responded together.

"Good morning, Jada. Your mother's waiting for you."

"Good morning, Pastor." Jada hugged her Bible to her chest and shook Pastor Tellings's hand.

The congregation had doubled in membership over the past five years. The pastor had added two additional services: one at seven o'clock in the morning and the other at seven o'clock at night. Jada and her mother still attended the eleven o'clock service. Stained glass covered every window, and a picture of Christ on the cross hung high upon the wall behind the pulpit.

Jada enjoyed when Pastor Tellings opened his sermon with a poem. This morning he recited "Ask Why," which was one of her favorites.

> *Heaven on earth*
> *Hell for some*
> *depends on whether*
> *you're smart or dumb*
> *depends on whether*
> *you're rich or poor*

or whether you're four feet
or six feet or ten
from the floor
depends on whether
you're white or black
skinny or fat
depends on whether
you're ugly or cute
bony or brute
funny or shy
please ask why
Heaven on earth
is Hell for some
most smart people
are really dumb
Heaven should be for all
and Hell
for NONE.

"Pastor is really hitting home this morning," Mama whispered.

Pastor Tellings continued with his sermon topic: "Heaven Should Be for All and Hell for None."

"God is the only one who can judge us. Therefore, it matters not what material gains you've acquired, or what size you are, or the color of your skin. Christians help those in need. How can you leave your nice cozy home and walk right by a homeless person. Then you walk through the doors of the church, praise God, and ask him to bless *you.* You walk out of the church, pass the *same* homeless person, and walk into your home *without a conscience.*"

Pastor Tellings hardly resembled Don King. Sister Armstrong always called him Reverend

James. He was fifty-five and single. His high-yellow complexion, flat nose, and slender face clashed with his hair. He sparingly accepted dinner invitations from married couples and never from single women in the church.

"You need to hold yourself accountable and *ask why*. Don't you know that if each one teaches one to be self-sufficient, Heaven on earth would be Hell for none?" Pastor picked up his white handkerchief, dried his forehead, then took a sip of water.

"In closing, I ask each of you to *ask why*. Ask yourselves why, and the next time you pass a person in need of help or in need of prayer, take a moment. One day it might be you standing in the need of prayer." He sang. Pastor Tellings had begun to sing and not a soul in the church reached for the hymnbook that sat in the pew's bookcase facing them. The choir and congregation joined in.

Afterward, a lot of the congregation wore guilty expressions. Jada commented on the mother and two children living on the corner of Ninety-eighth Avenue and East Fourteenth Street.

"Baby," Mama said, "do you think we can really help them?" Mama's eyes were slightly red.

"Well, we can definitely try." Jada felt obligated.

They approached the woman. A large-brimmed navy hat and sunglasses hid her face. A scarf was tied around her cheeks and under her chin. She sat on an old blanket with holes. The cardboard sign in her ashy hands read LOST OUR LEASE ON LIFE PLEASE HELP. Tears formed in Jada's eyes. She felt ashamed for having so much and sharing so little.

"Hi, my name is Jada Tanner and this is my

mother, Ruby Tanner." The story they heard changed their outlook.

"My name is Jazzmyne. These are my children. Brandon is three and Shelly is eight. I'm not looking for a handout. But I do need help."

The normally busy intersection was fairly quiet. Sister Brown with Sister Simon drove by and tooted her horn. The overcast sky hung low but there was no rain in the forecast. Jada and her mother were shocked to learn Jazzmyne had a master's degree in social work.

"My husband almost broke my collarbone and fractured one of my ribs. I know you're confused, but it's more commonplace than most folk can imagine. Working in a profession is no guarantee you won't be the victim."

Jada looked at her watch. Only three hours left before Wellington would call. She didn't want to appear self-centered. A ray of sunshine peeped through the clouds.

"I promised God if He allowed me to recover, I'd renew the lease on the life He'd given me. I'm glad the Lord opened my eyes. I was putting my husband before all of us. I loved Franklin more than life itself or so I thought until he tried to kill me."

The beam of sunshine disappeared. Jada's feet ached from the three-inch heels. With two and a half hours left she had to take control. Jada and Ruby paid for Jazzmyne and her children to spend two weeks in a hotel. They promised to take the family shopping and help Jazzmyne get back on her feet. Jazzmyne agreed to meet with Pastor Tellings on Wednesday. Before leaving the front desk, Jada noticed the last name on Jazzmyne's registration was Jones.

Jada made it home in record time. The meditation and prayer helped her unwind. When she finished, the digital clock read six o'clock. Jada reflected on how Wellington had kissed her hand after the show. She waited. Eight o'clock. No call. She watched reruns of *In the House* and *Fresh Prince*. At ten o'clock she watched the news. She double-checked for an interrupted dial tone but it was flat. The lampshade on her nightstand dimmed with each touch. One. Two. Three. Surrounded by darkness and silence, Jada wept.

Chapter 4

Wellington picked up his cordless and dialed Jada's number. He stepped onto the deck outside his bedroom. Below, the Friday morning sunrays glistened atop the water in the pool. Two weeks had passed since he'd promised to call. He dipped his finger into the maple syrup that flowed over his pancakes and sucked it off. His enthusiasm about marriage didn't match hers. Typically, he dismissed women that dropped hints or spoke in code about having a husband or kids. But Jada intrigued him. Wellington smiled. Jada answered on the first ring.

"Good morning, my Nubian Queen. How are you?"

"Who is this?"

"Wellington Jones." The dial tone indicated she might have been pissed. He hit the redial button.

"Hello!" Jada answered.

"You know, I deserved that. Please don't hang up again. *Mmm.* These hotcakes are delicious." He hoped the sound of his voice would turn her on. "Do you like surprises?"

"Yes, but not yours. Look, why don't you stop playing games." Jada's frustration lingered.

"Diamond. I've spent the past couple of weeks thinking about you. I apologize for not calling sooner."

"I don't know if I want to accept your apology. I've got to go to work. Good-bye, Mr. Jones."

Wellington could tell she wasn't going to make it easy. He sat up in his lounge chair and placed his plate on the tinted rectangular-shaped glass table. "Wait! Don't leave! Let me pick you up at noon."

"Pick me up?" Jada paused. "And?"

Wellington removed his cerulean Versace robe and laid it across the chair. "If I told you it wouldn't be a surprise. But I will tell you this much. Pack enough clothes for the weekend. And you need to bring and leave something." Wellington hoped at a minimum he'd piqued her curiosity. No woman had ever refused his all-expenses-paid weekend getaways.

"I'm listening."

Wellington cleared his throat. He spoke seductively. "The one thing you must bring is your imagination. Then you must leave all inhibitions behind. The rest"—he paused—"is up to me. But I have to warn you"—he paused again—"there is one requirement."

"What's that?" Jada asked flatly.

"This outing is a mandatory good-time excursion. You are welcome to bring your luggage but please leave all baggage behind." Stillness lingered. Wellington patiently waited for Jada to respond.

"I can handle that. But don't call the game if you can't bring the same. I'll see you at twelve o'clock sharp."

Wellington walked inside to his nightstand and wrote down the directions and address. "On that note, my Nubian Queen, I'll see you at high noon."

Wellington hung up the phone and proceeded to bust a move like Chris Tucker in the opening scene of *Rush Hour.* He showered for twenty minutes. Shaved. Flossed. Brushed. He put on his black denim shorts with matching FUBU 05 jersey. With his baseball cap turned backward, he packed two bottles of Dom Perignon on ice. He grabbed his prepacked leather bag and set his home security alarm.

The digital clock in his Mercedes said tenfifteen. He promised his mother he'd stop by before he left town. It was a perfect day in the Bay Area. The morning rush hour had ended. He zipped across the Golden Gate Bridge and took the first exit into Sausalito. The zigzag hill resembled Lombard Street. With each curve, he plunged his accelerator uphill as if he were test-driving for a commercial. He parked behind his mother's silvery Jaguar.

The house had looked the same as long as he could remember. His friends called it the White House. It was three stories high with six thousand square feet. Often he wondered how it survived the earthquakes. The sunroom on the third floor was where he'd spent countless hours meditating. Wellington walked in and followed his nose. The aroma of bacon trailed from the living room, through the dining room, and into the kitchen. He tiptoed behind his mother and wrapped his arms around her waist.

"Boy! You almost scared me to death."

"Nothing could scare you to death, woman. Give me a kiss." Her cold thin lips pecked his cheek.

"Have a seat. I just finished cooking breakfast. And take that cap off in my house."

Wellington held the cap in his hand. "I can't stay. I've got to pick up Diamond by twelve. I'm taking her on a surprise trip. We'll be back Sunday. Where's Dad?" Wellington sat on the bar stool nearest the stove.

"Christopher is at the Forty-niners game." Cynthia paused. "Who's Diamond? And *where* are you taking her?"

"I think she might be the one, Mom. But I'm not sure yet. That's why I'm taking *her* down the coast. She's the most beautiful Black Nubian Queen I've laid eyes on." Wellington grabbed a piece of bacon off the plate. Wellington admired his mother's beauty and brains but her personality was harsh.

Sternly she commented, "Well, just don't forget to ask what organizations she's in. That way I can do my own research. You're the only one who can carry on the family name and tradition. I've told you—I don't want you thinking about marrying someone who doesn't fit. And besides, how black is black?" Cynthia removed her Oakland Raiders apron. Wellington's mother was still crazy about them. But everyone knew Cynthia liked the team best when they were the roughest in the NFL.

Wellington stood. He leaned over his mother's shoulder and kissed her on the cheek. "She's radiant!"

"I can't see radiant. Keep going." She opened the oven and removed the tray.

"Okay. She's Blacker than Whoopi and more beautiful than Angela Bassett."

"Nonsense. No one is more beautiful than Angela or Blacker than Whoopi. How are Walter and Deon?" Cynthia placed the hot buttery homemade biscuits next to the bacon. "Oh, did I tell you Melanie called?"

"Walter's fine. We groomed his lawn last weekend. Deon and Gina are doing great. And Mom, Melanie's just a kid. I haven't seen her in almost twenty years." Wellington hugged his mother and shouted from the dining room, "You're gonna love Jada, Mom! Trust me."

With his cap turned backward, Wellington flew down the hill. His Byron Lee Soca Frenzy CD bumped hard against the SurroundSound speakers in his Benz. "Who let the dogs out! Ruff. Ruff. Ruff. Ruff. Ruff," he barked. He chose the back route through Richmond and Berkeley into Oakland to avoid tourism and lunch-hour traffic on the Golden Gate and Bay bridges. His whole body grooved to the Caribbean beat. He sang, "A doggie is *nothing* if he *don't* have a *bone*. All doggies hold your bone!" Wellington arrived precisely at eleven fifty-nine. He parked his car in one of the spots marked VISITOR. The doorman greeted him. Wellington read the name on his tag.

"Hello, Edward." Wellington firmly shook his hand. "Would you kindly let Ms. Jada Diamond Tanner know Wellington Jones has arrived?"

"My pleasure, sir."

Wellington watched the elevator light move. Twenty-one. Twenty. Nineteen . . . All the way down to the first floor without stopping. When the doors opened, he instantly realized Jada lived in the penthouse. She looked more striking than he remembered.

Jada was dressed in a simple tropical ankle-length skirt with thigh-high splits on each side. Her pierced belly button wore a small ruby circled by miniature diamonds. The matching exotic scarf wrapped around her protruding breasts. Her hair flowed over her bare shoulders down to her waistline.

"Hi. You look great," Wellington complimented her.

As Wellington carried Jada's bag and basket, "Doggie" replayed in his head. *Ruff!* He felt so good; he slipped the bellman a fifty and winked.

"Thanks. Hi," Jada responded. "I'm really curious. Can you at least give me a hint as to where we're going this weekend?" Wellington opened the door and waited until Jada was comfortably seated.

Once they were both inside, he said, "Relax. I could but that would spoil the surprise. Patience, my Queen . . ."

Jada reclined in the passenger seat and put on her sunglasses. "Okay, Mr. Wonderful, I'm relaxed now, and since you won't tell me where we're going, at least allow me to ask you a few *personal* questions."

Wellington learned the hard way how women could get your whole life history in one conversation and use it to their advantage. So he devised his own strategy. "Under one condition. We trade one for one."

"I can handle that." Jada leaned forward, flipped her hair over the headrest, and leaned back.

"Ladies first." Wellington switched to disk eleven, Kenny G, and cruised south along Highway 1.

"Okay. If you could change just one thing about your life, what would it be and why?"

Wellington premeditated. "That's an easy question with a hard answer. The absence of my real parents has created an irreplaceable void in my life. I often wonder if they're alive." Everything around Wellington was a blur, except the road ahead. There was less than two feet of space where the shoulder ended and the steep cliff began. Below, Wellington could see waves washing ashore, children wading, and lots of people sunbathing. "I love my adoptive parents but . . ." A lump formed in his throat.

A moment of silence passed. "You can just hire an investigator to find them. At least that way you'll know," suggested Jada.

"Unfortunately, it's not that simple." Wellington shifted in his seat. "It's like, I really want to know, but then again I don't. If they're alive and choose not to acknowledge me, I'm not sure how I'd deal with the rejection." For the first time in years, Wellington openly discussed the subject. He sighed and tried to enjoy the view. "I have pictures of both my mothers hanging in the living room. I'd like to show you when you visit. I'm not sure what my old man looks like. Perhaps one day, I'll seek them out. Who knows?" Wellington paused. "Okay. That's enough. Now it's my turn to ask you a question."

"Go for it." Jada propped her hands behind her head.

Her fragrances enthralled Wellington's head. He contemplated, then asked, "If you could change just one thing about your life, what would it be and why?"

Instantly Jada leaned forward and looked over at Wellington. "Now that's not fair. You're asking the *same* question."

"Life isn't fair. So answer it." He was thankful his big head dominated and put the little one in check.

First she repeated the question. Then Jada hesitantly began to speak. "I would change the color of my dark skin." Wellington's forehead wrinkled and his eyes cut to the right. He listened attentively. "As a child, I was constantly teased. What hurt most was it wasn't the whites that tortured me. It was the blacks. Some were my so-called friends. I can picture their faces. I can still hear them chanting: 'Don't! Don't! Don't come out at night because you'll grow wings like a crow and take flight.'" Jada took a deep breath. Her fingers interlocked and rested in her lap.

Wellington interrupted. "You're the most striking woman I've laid eyes on. Your jet-black skin radiates. You have a Ms. Universe smile. You're tall, sexy, gorgeous, intelligent, warm, and lovely for all to see. Why do you think I laid rose petals at your feet? Why do you think I call you my Nubian Queen? Diamond, you are beautiful. Absolutely beautiful."

"Thanks. Don't get me wrong—I love myself more than anyone else. But I hated those kids."

Wellington tried to understand although he

couldn't relate. People had envied him all his life. There was nothing he'd wanted to do but hadn't had an opportunity. But he was glad the questions were over.

"Okay, my turn to ask another question," Jada said.

Wellington's foot plunged the accelerator.

"Are you the type of man who will commit to one woman? And before you answer, let me say that fidelity is extremely important to me."

At least this was an easy question. "Well, I had a wife once but her husband came and got her." Wellington slapped his leg and nudged Jada's shoulder. She laughed too. "I'm happy you have a sense of humor. You just passed your first test."

"What do you mean?" Jada inquired.

"If you had taken me serious, I would have known you weren't comfortable with the subject even though you asked the question. Therefore, I wouldn't have discussed my personal relationships with you. It's a major turnoff when a woman gets defensive about my past experiences. I'm not perfect and I don't try to be." Wellington glanced down at Jada's thighs. The front flap of her skirt had formed into a V at her crotch.

"Now seriously, I have no problem with dedication. However, I'd commit myself before I'd be faithful for the sake of making someone else happy. Society dictates so much that people have subconsciously bought into—what I call the unwritten rules. Any man can have a wife; I'm going to marry my soulmate." Wellington exited off the freeway. White sand. Blue water. Seventy-eight degrees. "Welcome to Carmel," he announced.

Jada's hazel-colored eyes beamed with excitement. "Oh my gosh! This is one of my favorite hideaways."

"This is only the beginning," Wellington reassured her.

"Yes! I am living for this weekend. I'm ready to have a mandatory, downright, outright good time starting right now. Stop the car! I want to get out here." Jada bounced in her seat.

Wellington pulled the car over to the parking area near the beach. "Actually, this is where we start. Let me open the door to more than just the car."

He got out and walked around to the passenger side. Jada was so excited she jumped out and planted a kiss on his lips.

"Wait right here." Wellington removed his goody bag, picnic basket, and CD player from the trunk. "You may have brought your own bag but did you bring the *funk*." He held the portable in one hand like a trophy.

Jada threw both hands in the air. "Hey! I've got to get up just a little bit earlier in the morning to keep up with you, my brother. But let's see if you can beat Mama to the beach. *Baby*."

Wellington admired Jada's spunk. She ran toward the water like Flo Jo. Wellington tried to keep up. He came in a not-so-close second. He placed everything on the dry sand. Jada took off again. This time he trailed right behind her.

"You're a little frisky. I like that." He grabbed her from behind and wrapped his arms around her slender waist. "This is a great beginning to a beautiful friendship." Then he reached into the crystal blue water and drenched her hair.

"Hey! That's not fair!"

"Life isn't fair." Wellington smiled. "Come with me."

Wellington led Jada by the hand. She followed him back to their place on the beach. He spread out a blanket with exotic tropical designs.

Jada inhaled. "Do you think this blanket is large enough?"

"It's perfect." Then Wellington commanded in a deep sexy voice, "Lie down. Turn over on your stomach. Now, you have to trust me. Let *me* do *my* thing."

Wellington unwrapped the back of Jada's scarf.

"What are you—?"

"*Ssssshhh.* Don't speak. Just listen and bond spiritually with the sounds of the ocean, and the setting of the sun. Soon will come the full moon, and the twinkling of the stars." Wellington turned the volume low and popped in a CD with all the songs played from the night they'd met. "Let the music feed your soul. This is the ideal time to be on the beach. Within a few hours, we'll experience it all."

Jada turned her head to the side and closed her eyes. Wellington pulled out the oil and began to massage her back. Deep, strong strokes glided along her soft skin. He rolled up Jada's skirt as high as he could. His hands journeyed up her sexy chocolate thighs. His thumbs rested in her arch. He pressed along the outer sides of her lips. She responded with mild convulsions. He slid his hands under her skirt and massaged her ass. Damn! Her pussy smelled like Lady Godiva. His body ached. She moaned. His penis expanded. He thought how nice it would be to make love right there on the beach. He tied Jada's scarf.

"Turn over," Wellington insisted.

Slowly she revolved. He lay beside her. Gazed at the sunset. "Did you just have an orgasm?"

"That's one for me." Jada smiled.

"And James Brown said 'It's a Man's World.' Now that shit turned me on." Wellington nodded. "Changing the subject, I want a spiritual woman who's connected with the *universe*. You know most people never take time to embrace different forms of life. I'm vibing with you right now. I feel your spirit moving. Close your eyes and listen to the waves wash upon the shore."

"Okay," Jada whispered.

"Now open your eyes and gaze at the stars above. Can you feel the twinkle inside your soul?"

"Oh, yes. I feel *more* than a twinkle." Jada's cheeks tightened. Wellington watched her hips rise and fall.

"We've only just begun." Wellington spoke softly in Jada's ear. "Well, it's getting late but the night is still young." Wellington outlined Jada's lips with his tongue. "I reserved two rooms at Carmel's Beachfront Inn."

Jada's eyes flashed open. "Two rooms?"

"Yes, two adjoining rooms, my Queen." Wellington knew she'd respect him even if she didn't like the idea.

Once Jada was settled in her room, Wellington went to his and hit the shower. He cleaned everything, twice. Wellington had discovered in the ninth grade that sexually adventurous females would cut your game short if your ass wasn't clean. Naked, he went to answer the phone.

"Hello," Wellington said.

"Hi. This is Diamond. Videos in my room at ten. Bring the music and don't be late."

"I'll be on time and I'll bring the champagne."

Instead of knocking on the adjoining door, Wellington went into the hall. "Knock, knock."

When Jada opened the door, Wellington's bottom lip hit his chin. He almost lost his grip on the bottle. She stood dressed in a silk safari nightgown with spaghetti straps. Titties. Damn! Ass. Bam!

"Come in," Jada whispered. "I've been expecting you." Then she braced her hand against Wellington's chest. He felt her squeeze his nipple. "Did you bring your imagination?"

"That's not fair." He drooled. His backhand wiped the corner of his mouth. "You're standing here looking sexy and smelling edible. You didn't give a brother any advance notification."

Jada extended her tongue inside his ear. "Life isn't fair," she whispered. Wellington shivered and shook his head as if he were trying to wake up.

Jada closed the door. "I've selected two of the hottest movies. I hope you like comedy and love Chris Tucker because he's *my* man."

Wellington observed how Jada set the mood with aromatherapy candles strategically lit around the room. "I love comedy and Chris is definitely *the* man!" He wondered what else she'd packed. Wellington popped the cork. Poured two glasses of chilled Dom. "A toast to the spiritual unity that bonds us together."

"Forever," replied Jada as she clinked her glass against his. "Now let's lie on the floor and watch TV."

"Why the floor?" Wellington's eyes focused on the bed.

"Because I enjoy fucking on the floor. Hey, just go with the flow." Jada lay on the puffy pallet. Wellington followed her lead.

It was difficult for Wellington to concentrate on the movie. He tried to be inconspicuous but his peripheral vision of Jada lying parallel to him was distracting. Her thighs, cheeks, and safari thong were slightly exposed through the splits in her gown.

Suddenly Jada stopped the video.

Wellington shifted his eyes from her ass to the TV. "Why did you do that?"

"Because it's intermission. What would you like?"

"I'll have one healthy order of whipped cream!" Wellington joked.

"Coming right up." Jada went to the refrigerator and popped open the can.

"Where on earth did you get—?"

"Oh, weren't you the one who said *bring your imagination.* Well there's more where that came from. Would you like ice cream, ice, sprinkles, nuts, cherries, caramel, fudge, hot or cold?"

As bad as Wellington wanted to taste Jada, he wasn't going to let this opportunity go. "Well, since you opened the door, I'll have two scoops of chocolate D's with sprinkles on top."

"What about the whipped cream?" Jada asked.

"Oh, yes. Definitely. *Squirt* it on."

Jada stood four inches from Wellington's face and oozed strawberry whipped cream all over her chocolate breasts. Wellington licked the excess off her fingers the same way he'd done the night they met. She added sprinkles and two cherries to top it off: one on each nipple. "Come and get it, Big Daddy."

Wellington led Jada to the bed. The cherries rolled onto the floor. He propped three pillows against the headboard and leaned her back. He straddled her. He pressed her breasts together and bit her erect nipples. Jada buried his face deeper. His erection screamed for release.

Jada slid his sweats over his ass and down to his knees. Wellington's dick broke through the opening in his black silk boxers. Her eyes widened. He prayed the size didn't frighten her. "Say hello to *The Ruler.*" Wellington smiled.

Much to his delight, Jada positioned two pillows under her lower back. She wrapped her thighs around his waist and guided him into her moistness. His back arched when her walls compressed. Again. Again. Again.

With well-calculated movements, he explored paradise one stroke at a time. The passion continued to grow and the strokes came closer together. His rhythm increased. She locked her legs around his waist.

Jada's head hung over the edge of the bed. "Don't move. Let *Mama* handle this!" Wellington was in pussy paradise. She placed her hands on the floor and braced herself. Her legs restricted his movement. She rode him like an underground roller coaster, inside and out. Jada's flexibility reminded Wellington of a slinky. He allowed her to take complete control. Her muscles sucked up his cum like a dental vacuum. He felt her climax several times.

Wellington strolled to the kitchen. He refilled their champagne glasses. Jada hit PLAY on the VCR and laughed. "Now that's what I call half-time entertainment!"

Chapter 5

Over six months had passed since Jada and Wellington's first date. Their relationship had
grown by leaps and bounds. This vacation was as
perfect as the first and each in between. But this
past weekend had Jada glowing. It was Sunday
morning and as usual Jada's phone was ringing off
the hook.

"Hello," Jada answered.

"Hi. I'm in the mood to fellowship with my best
friend this morning," Candice said. "Why don't I
pick you up for church? And you can tell me about
your weekend with Wellington."

Jada modeled her Body and Soul underwear in
front of the stand-up mirror in her bedroom. The
three-carat studs in her ears matched the solitaire
on her finger. "Girl, you know I've gotten really
good at summing up our weekend activities in
twenty minutes or less. But I have to tell you the

details of this weekend over lunch. I would have called you last night except I was too exhausted to pick up the phone." Jada sat at her vanity and painted her lips spicy brown. "Lunch is on me, so I'll make reservations at our favorite restaurant in Sausalito for two o'clock."

"This must be really important if we're going to the Seafood House. I can hardly wait."

"Listen. Sorry I can't pick you up. I promised to pick up Jazzmyne and the kids." Jada penciled over her arched eyebrows.

"How are they doing?" Candice asked.

Jada stepped into her purple skirt and zipped it up. She opened the blinds. The sunlight was blinding so she closed them. "They're doing fine," Jada answered. "Jazzmyne is looking great! She got her hair cut into a sophisticated short style. The sides and the back are tapered. You have to see it to believe it. She's the lead counselor at the women's shelter in Oakland. She even said her experience made her a better counselor, *and* some of the church members are her clients. But of course, she wouldn't disclose which ones."

Jada started to sip her cranberry juice, but quickly remembered her lips were already painted. "It's hard to believe women in the church experience physical abuse at home. Their husbands come to church on Sunday and act like *perfect* gentlemen." Jada pulled her black lace camisole over her head.

"Well, you know how our people *mask* and un-mask very well," Candice chimed in.

Jada paused for a moment and wondered if Candice knew her well enough to tell. "Yeah, that's true. But this abuse thing isn't even about black and white. It's about wrong and right. It's about black and blue emotional scars on your heart and spirit. Generally, the physical scars heal, but the emotional ones remain in the blood that flows through your veins. I cannot imagine loving anyone else more than I love myself." Jada buttoned her purple blazer and blew kisses to herself in the mirror.

It was closer to ten o'clock than Jada had realized so she gave Candice a condensed overview of the remaining events. "Shelly is making straight A's at Shelton. Brandon is still Brandon, happy go lucky. Brother Calvin Dupree has been trying to take Jazzmyne and the kids out for dinner for the past two months, but Jazzmyne tells him enough to let him know she's interested, but not ready for a relationship. I'd better get off this phone and out the door before Mother calls."

Jada drove her BMW 735I like a bat out of hell. The scenic view along Interstate 580 was a blur. Before she could get her key in the door, her mother had already opened it.

"Hi, Mama."

"Hi, baby, I was just about to call when I saw your car. We'd better get going so we're not late picking up Jazzmyne and the kids."

"Yes, Mama." Jada opened the car door and waited for her mother to get in.

The sunlight danced on the diamond. Jada removed her right hand from the steering wheel and placed it on her thigh.

"Is there something you forgot to tell your mother?"

"Like what?" Jada's mother eyed the ring. "Oh.

No, I didn't forget. I haven't had time to tell you because Wellington just gave it to me yesterday. And since it's *not* an engagement ring, I didn't want you to start talking about grandchildren again. That's all." A decade had passed since Jada's last proposal. Jada often wondered why Darryl hadn't asked her to marry him.

"Well, you know Mama still wants her grandchildren. But I have to admit, I really like when Jazzmyne brings Shelly and Brandon over on Saturday mornings. The three of us play games and I'm teaching Shelly how to cook. And Brandon has learned how to set the table Brandon's way."

Jada and her mother laughed. Brandon could brighten anyone's darkest moment.

"I just want what you and Daddy had." Jada's parents never fought or argued, at least not in front of her. "Marriages don't last like they used to. People divorce for convenience these days and call it irreconcilable differences."

"Well, you know your father and I had our ups and our downs, but I knew Henry was my soulmate when I first laid eyes on him. That's not something Mama can explain to you, baby, but if Wellington is that person for you, you already know it in your heart and, more importantly, you feel it in your soul."

"I love you, Mama." When Jada drove up, Brandon jumped with joy. His tie flapped haphazardly and bounced off his head.

"Good morning," Jazzmyne said. She leaned over and kissed Mama on the cheek.

"Good morning," Jada and her mother responded at the same time.

"Good morning, everyone," Shelly sang. She

had the brightest brown eyes and prettiest smile. "Aunty Jada and Grandma, I got all A's again this week."

"Wonderful!" Jada said. "We're very proud of you."

Mama slipped Shelly a five-dollar bill.

"My mother tells me that the nice gentleman who helps pay my tuition and Brandon's child care is your very good friend, Mr. Wellington." Shelly buckled her seat belt. The yellow satin ribbon in her hair locked around her ponytail of spiral curls.

"That's true." Jada parked in the last space in the church lot.

"Do you think maybe one day I could actually meet him?" Shelly asked.

"I don't see why not." Jada smiled.

"How's everyone doing this blessed Sunday morning?" asked Pastor Tellings as he greeted each member of his congregation. The pastor opened his hand. He and Brandon exchanged five.

Jada joined Candice. Mama took her usual seat.

The pastor opened his sermon with a prayer poem entitled: "When This Earthly House Is Dissolved."

Until then . . .
Dear GOD,
You know I will give my very best
And when I am weary
I will take a moment to rest
But not too long because I must run Your race
And while I run I will keep the faith
And yes—Dear GOD—I will keep a smile on my face

When this earthly house is dissolved

Until then . . .
Dear GOD I will help my fellow man
Because I truly understand
I must let Thy will be done
And while I run this race
I will keep the faith
And yes LORD I will keep a smile on my face

When this earthly house is dissolved

Until then . . .
I will make my earthly house a HOME
And my family—Dear Lord—I will never leave them
    alone
I will run this race
I will keep the faith
And yes—Dear GOD—I will keep a smile on my face

When this earthly house is dissolved

Until then . . .
Dear GOD
I will continue to pray
That You continue to bless me in Your HOLY way
So that my light will continue to shine
And I will never have to tell anyone that I am a
Christian
Not one single time
Because LORD I will run this race
I will keep the faith
And yes—Dear GOD—I will keep a smile on my face

Until I leave this place
Until I can see You see the smile on my face

When this earthly house is dissolved

I will be gone from it, LORD
But I won't be gone at all

And thank you, Dear GOD
Because when this earthly house is dissolved

I will never—ever—be alone

Amen

"What will you do until your earthly house is dissolved?" Pastor Tellings preached. "Are you giving the Lord your very best? Are you helping your fellow man? Are you making your earthly house a home? Do you complain about the things you do for others or do you thank GOD that you are able to do for others? If you don't make your *earthly* house a home, what kind of home do you *think* you will have in Heaven? Will your house be in Heaven? Christians. You've got to run God's race. You've got to keep the faith and keep a smile on your face. Everything I just preached would cost you time but it won't cost you a dime. Remember, the *best* things in life are still free.

"Next week we're going to partnership with a male and female correctional facility. So come prepared to sign up to be a pen pal, a mentor, a Christian. We as a congregation will start communicating by writing to inmates. All letters sent and received under the program will go through the church for two reasons. One, every inmate who requests a pen pal will receive one, even if I have to write them myself. Second, the church will measure the success of the program by the number of participants, the volume of letters, and partnership testimonials given by inmates and by you.

"I want additional volunteers to accompany me to the prisons when I visit to minister to God's people. The first group will be from ages twelve to twenty-six. I strongly encourage you to allow your children to witness what prison life is like. It may make your jobs as parents easier. This experience will open your eyes and your children's to a whole world that most are oblivious to.

"Brother Calvin Dupree volunteered to sign up the men and Sister Jazzmyne Jones agreed to sign up the women. Spread the word and let others know they don't have to be members of the church to volunteer."

After church was dismissed, Candice said, "Girl, I see how you stay so busy. I like your pastor. If we had more ministers like him and congregations like this, we could really make a positive change."

After the service Jazzmyne walked over to Jada and Candice.

"Candice, this is Jazzmyne Jones. Jazzmyne, this is Candice Carol Jordan."

"Pleased to finally meet you," Candice said as she shook Jazzmyne's hand.

"My pleasure," Jazzmyne responded. "I've heard so many wonderful things about you."

Then Jazzmyne faced Jada and said, "B
Dupree is taking us home. We need to work
plan to sign up volunteers for the pastor's ne
gram." Jazzmyne's mannerisms and look
minded Jada of Loretta Devine.

"Do you think he'll take Mother home? That

way Candice and I can make our two o'clock lunch reservation."

"Oh sure, Calvin's a sweetheart," Jazzmyne said with an innocent smile on her face. She batted her long black eyelashes.

Candice tapped Jazzmyne on the shoulder. "Please put my name on the volunteer list. I did hear Pastor Tellings say you *didn't* have to be a member. Right?"

"Yes, and thank you. I'll be sure to add your name," Jazzmyne confirmed. "I've got to go now. I won't keep this man waiting another minute." Jazzmyne's emerald two-piece skirt suit softly hugged her full figure. Her hat and shoes were a lighter shade of green.

"It's so amazing how she turned her life around so fast," Candice said.

"She was down but never out," Jada commented. "We have to remember each of us will be down at some point in our lives but we're only out if we give up. Although it's not wise, most people are only a paycheck away from being homeless. Jazzmyne's circumstances were different but her end result from not saving money was common.

"So how is Mr. Terrell Morgan doing these days?" Jada asked as she looked over the San Francisco Bay.

"Well, let's see. We still talk at least once a week and I am so tempted to have a serious relationship with him but long-distance never works out. Someone eventually ends up having to move and I don't envision moving to Los Angeles and he's at the peak of his career. *Every* modeling agency wants him."

Jada nodded. "We get at least three inquiries

per day." Terrell was labeled the new Tyson on the block.

"I just don't know."

"You don't know what?"

Candice sighed. "I know, girl, it is so unlike me. My heart says yes but my head says no. So until one or the other gives in, I'll just be in limbo."

"As long as you realize he may not be in limbo as long as you, it's cool." Jada recognized this was the first time Candice was concerned about dating a younger man.

"Oh, I know he's not monogamous. We talk openly about everything."

"I'm not speaking of him being intimate with other women. I'm talking about him giving his heart to someone else." Jada stopped in front of the valet sign. The parking lot was half-empty, a sign that most of the early-morning brunch goers had already left.

"Hi, Jason. How've you been?" Jada asked as she gave her preferred host a warm hug.

"I'm doing great. I'll validate your parking ticket. Right this way, my favorite ladies," Jason said. He still walked like a Marine. Jada and Candice mimicked him behind his back. He seated them at their favorite table overlooking the bay. Sailboats were docked right outside. Dozens more sailed by.

Jason sounded like Jeffrey on *Fresh Prince*. "I saw that. The usual, ladies?"

"Yes. Thanks, Jason." Jada sat and watched the couple dock their boat and enter the restaurant.

"Gosh, it feels great to be here. It's been a long time," Candice said with a warm look of endearment.

Jada nodded slowly. "Too long."

"So tell me about the ring." Candice held her mimosa like she was posing for a picture. Her pinky finger was extended.

"Well, let's see, where do I begin? Wellington made reservations at Bellagio in Las Vegas. The entire weekend was exhilarating. We arrived early Saturday morning. The limousine took us directly to the hotel." Jada stared into Candice's eyes.

"We played blackjack and slots. Then we walked over to New York, New York and rode the roller coaster, three times!" Jada fanned herself with one hand while she held her champagne glass of mimosa in the other. "I got dizzy just thinking about the roller coaster zooming around the top of the hotel. The first two times were a breeze. But by the third, Wellington and I both were holding on to one another."

Jada paused for a moment. Candice sat on the edge of her seat. "I just like being with him so much. I'm free to be myself. I don't have to pretend. We like a lot of the same things. He's caring and carefree at the same time."

Candice interrupted. "Get to the ring. Today is not the day to keep me in suspense." Candice motioned to Jason and held up two fingers.

Jada flattened her voice. "Okay. I was trying to set the mood for you but if you insist. Later that evening the orange, red, and yellow sunset was breathtaking. Wellington and I walked over to the Stratosphere and went to the observation deck."

Candice's eyes widened.

"He said I have something very special I want to give to you. He didn't get down on one knee so I immediately dismissed the thought of an engagement ring. Actually, I didn't think it was a ring at all."

Candice gave Jada that "Don't go down that road, girlfriend" look.

"He gazed into my eyes, licked his lips, and kissed me ever so softly on mine. Then he said he never wanted the sun to set again without the two of us having a commitment. He said he didn't want to rush into an engagement but he wanted to acknowledge his love for me." Jada quivered. Candice shivered.

"He promised to love, respect, and protect me, always. If I hadn't known better, I would have thought he was rehearsing his wedding vows. He promised me so many things. I thought I was dreaming." Candice's eyes were dazed. Jada placed her hands on top of her chest.

"Then without speaking another word, he opened the box with this ring in it." Jada held her hand in front of Candice so she could get a closer look. Embedded in the surface of the diamond was a specially designed soulmate logo. "He placed it on my right hand. Then he said, 'With this ring I say unto you, Jada Diamond Tanner, you are my soulmate. Today. Tomorrow. Always. We are spiritually bonded. I want you to wear this ring on your right ring finger until we both feel it is time to move it to the left. When the time is right, we will jointly announce our engagement to our parents but I didn't want to wait until then to let you know how much I love you, *my Nubian Queen.*'" Jada remembered every single word.

"Then he licked his lips again and we kissed under the sunset and held each other until the last ray of sunlight was overshadowed by a crescent moon. The rest is history and here we are, my friend."

Candice took a deep breath. Exhaled. Her shoulders rounded from a square position. "Jada, Wellington is so romantic. So, do you believe he's really your soulmate?" Candice stared deep into Jada's eyes. They had been friends so long; Jada knew Candice would decode every message.

"I *know* he is."

Before Candice could respond, Wellington's mother walked up to the table. "So how are you, *darling?*"

"Oh, Mrs. Jones. How are you? This is my best friend, Candice Carol Jordan. Candice, this is Wellington's mother, Mrs. Cynthia Elaine Jones." Jada stood to give Cynthia a hug. Cynthia stepped backward and extended her hand.

"I see, darling," Cynthia commented. "Nice ring. Another gift from your father, I *presume.*"

"It's from Wellington." Jada proudly held out her hand.

"My Wellington?" Cynthia inquired. Her dialect shifted from semiformal to formal. "Well, at least he placed it on the *appropriate* hand."

Jada sat in silence and counted backward from ten. Cynthia had resurrected the hatred she'd harbored for those kids that tortured her.

"Good day," remarked Cynthia as she tucked her Gucci purse under her arm. Cynthia's words sliced like a knife.

"Damn!" Candice whispered. "Why didn't you warn a sister about Broom Hilda? She's a witch and a bitch!"

"Is everything all right?" Jason asked.

"We're okay," Candice replied. Jason walked away.

Candice pushed back her seat. "You want me to go kick her ass? I'll kick her straight up her uppity ass!" Candice paused. Her chest continued to rise and fall. "So what's next?"

"Life." Jada sighed. "I'm not afraid. I plan to take it one day at a time. I love Wellington too much to let his mother come between us."

Chapter 6

Over the next eleven months, Jada and Wellington fell fervently in love. There were no major obstacles—with the exception of Cynthia—in their relationship. Jada grew more comfortable with each passing day. Especially when it came to sex. Wellington had mastered her body from head to toe.

"Wellington, we've got to get up and prepare for our parents. Your parents will be here in a few hours and I have to pick up my mother at one o'clock. And I still haven't started cooking."

"*Sssshhh*, be quiet," Wellington responded. "Relax. Don't move. I'll be right back."

Jada followed his instructions. Unclothed, Wellington went to the bathroom. Jada's eyes followed as far as they could. She heard the familiar sound of fast running water. She smiled. Whenever Wellington rinsed his mouth with hot steamy water—as hot as he could stand it—she was in for a treat. Wellington returned to the bed and pulled back the covers. Jada parted her legs as wide as she could. He placed his warm lips against hers.

Jada moaned, "Oh, Big Daddy, you know I can't resist you when you do this to me." She closed her eyes and totally submitted. She internalized all her senses. Her body embraced the warmth of Wellington's tender lips. To Jada, oral copulation was the best legal drug on the open market. It was her sedative and stimulant, rolled into one.

"Oh, yes. That's the spot. Go nice and slow for Mama," she whispered. Jada positioned Wellington's head exactly where she wanted it. Then she wrapped her chocolate thighs around his ears.

Jada yearned for a taste of Wellington's throbbing caramel delight. She placed her index finger in her mouth and sucked it in and out. Wellington's eyelids rolled back as he watched. Jada became more excited.

His hands moved toward her breasts. He pinched her nipples. Wellington pressed firmly, then just a little harder and a little bit harder still. Jada grunted with delight. Wellington stimulated her clit. Jada concentrated to suppress the orgasm building up inside. It felt like steam about to burst through the hole in a kettle.

She felt the tip of his tongue penetrate her vagina. Then suddenly Wellington sucked the little man right out of the boat. Jada was on the verge of climaxing. Wellington pressed his tongue against her clitoris. He held it there for a few seconds. He captured the little man again and this time held him hostage. The kitty whistled like a kettle. She pleaded with him to let the little man go free. She had exceeded her range of toleration for pleasure. Jada's juices rushed from her pulsating lips to the tip of Wellington's tongue. The liquid inside the kettle overflowed and drenched the burners. He quenched his thirst until she was drained.

Finally, Wellington complied. He set the little man free. Wellington swiftly grabbed *The Ruler* and broke through the gates of chocolate paradise. Deep rhythmic strokes penetrated her soul. Wellington placed Jada's legs over his shoulders and continued his groove. The kettle had stopped whistling but the water inside was still boiling.

Jada grabbed Wellington's ass. She reeled him in close. His head hit rock bottom. She moaned. Wellington pulled back. He straddled Jada's right leg flat against the mattress. He left the other over his shoulder. He balanced himself on his knees. Moved in closer. His penis never left paradise. He restarted penetration. He accelerated from zero to sixty in ten minutes. Jada cupped her breasts and held on for the ride.

Suddenly, he commanded, "Turn over."

Jada rolled the gold comforter underneath her hips. She placed her hands on her cheeks and spread them wide. Wellington rubbed his head up and down her clit. Then he slowly inserted his dick.

"Whose is it?" he asked as he slapped Jada's ass.

Jada screamed, "It's yours, Big Daddy! It's all yours! Bring it on to Mama! Give it to me!"

Wellington struck and moved like a pro. Each time his hand landed, Jada's butt burned with pleasure and pain. She kept pace with Wellington. She squeezed each time he struck. Jada squeezed harder each time he moved.

Wellington grabbed Jada's hips and locked them into his. Jada's muscles rolled up and down his shaft repeatedly. Then quickly he withdrew himself. Jada turned around and watched. Wellington's hands moved so fast she saw doubles. Cum rained everywhere. It landed in her hair. Almost squirted in her eye. Landed on her back. Rolled down the crack of her ass. She massaged all of it into her skin and sucked her finger again.

Wellington stood over Jada. He started beating his chest like King Kong and howled, "Who's the man?"

Jada tossed the pillow in his face. "You're the man. Now let's start preparing for our parents." Jada wanted to remain in bed and let the sedative relax her body. Instead, she switched mental gears and converted it into a stimulant.

Jada lit several scented candles in the bedroom and bathroom to cover their sweet fragrances. Wellington started changing the sheets, so she headed for the shower. Afterward, Jada proceeded to get dressed while Wellington laid out clothes.

"I'll go downstairs and get lunch started," Jada said.

"What are you preparing? My father will eat whatever you cook but I have to warn you my mother's palate is extremely critical." Wellington placed his dress shoes on the stand and started polishing them.

Jada sat at the vanity Wellington bought her and applied her makeup. "How about jerk chicken with penne pasta, vegetables, rolls, and a salad?"

"Chicken is good but duck would have been better."

"Well, it's *chicken* today," Jada responded defensively. "I don't like cooking and I can't prepare duck."

"I'm sure whatever you prepare will be just fine." Wellington kissed Jada on the lips, walked into the bathroom, and closed the door.

Jada prayed he was right. It was the first time she had to cook for his mother. Wellington's mother was so finicky. She noticed how Cynthia pampered Wellington, then turned around and manipulated him.

Wellington opened the door. The black towel was wrapped around his waist. He brushed his chest hairs.

"I hope our parents hit it off well," said Jada as she stood and combed her hair in front of the wall-length mirror.

Wellington walked over to Jada. Put his hands on opposite sides of her cheeks. "What's most important is how we feel about one another. Parents always have their opinions. Most of them didn't choose the right spouses for themselves. So what makes them an expert?" He kissed her lips, returned to the bathroom, and trimmed his goatee.

"Wellington, do you think your mother will ever approve of me?" Jada asked but didn't really want to hear the answer.

"Honestly, I don't care. All that matters to me is what matters to us." Wellington put on his black slacks and collarless short-sleeved tapered black shirt. Jada could see the definition in his abs and the outline of Wellington's chest.

"I'm going to pick up my mother now so she can keep me company while I prepare the meal." Jada glanced at her pale yellow ankle-length dress. One day without splits wouldn't hurt.

"That's a good idea. I need to go to the store. If I'm not here when you return, use your key."

Jada's nerves buckled in her stomach while she drove to her mother's house. Although Wellington said it didn't matter whether his mother liked her, to Jada it did. Thank God her mother wasn't anything like his.

When Jada arrived, her mother was dressed in light blue denim from head to toe. Shirt. Pants. Shoes. Cap? "Mother, is this what you're going to wear?"

"Of course, baby, it's only a dinner. Folk either like you or they don't. It's that simple. People who try to impress you are shallow. They hide behind titles, clothes, sporty cars, or big fancy homes. They brag endlessly about what they have. But if you ask them what have they done to help someone lately, they can't even give you a direct response."

Jada sighed. What was the use? Her mother was right and she wasn't going to change.

"Baby, Wellington loves you and that's enough for me. Before we leave, I need to call Robert across the street. He's going to go with us. He's excellent at analyzing folk. I thought it would be a good idea if he met Wellington's parents."

Jada imagined Mrs. Jones's high-society and Mr. Hamilton's down-to-earth personalities. They would mix like oil and water at two hundred degrees Fahrenheit.

"Hello, Robert, this is Ruby. Are you ready to leave?"

"I'm ready, woman, so let's hit it!" said Robert. "Let's get this show on the road." Jada could hear Mr. Hamilton's voice through the phone.

When they arrived, Wellington wasn't home so Jada pulled out her keys.

"You didn't tell me you had keys to his house," Ruby said. She shook her head from side to side.

"It's okay, Mama. We exchanged keys last month, but we only use them with prior permission. He knew he had to leave for a moment so he told me to let myself in if he wasn't back. Come on in."

"This house is huge!" responded Robert. His head tilted backward. He stared at the black pillars. Glanced around the house. Scurried over to the main patio window and parted the vertical blinds. "He's either selling drugs, laundering money, or doing something illegal."

"Why is it that any wealthy black man has to be a criminal?" Jada asked with her hand on her hip. "While other kids were running around playing, he was managing his mutual fund. His parents didn't allow him to spend money on frivolous toys or expensive name brand clothes until he could afford it. His mother preached that if more black families would do the same, future generations would be wealthy instead of living paycheck to paycheck until they're old and gray."

Robert held a Waterford crystal glass and gently plucked it. "Well, if he *honestly* has that kind of money, he's probably doing drugs." Robert placed the glass on the dining table. "With a house like this and all those fancy cars sitting in his driveway, he must be worth at least several million dollars."

"At least." Jada sighed as she shook her head. "Let's go to the kitchen. I need to finish the salad, and check on the chicken and pasta. We're having Daddy's favorite. I know he's here in spirit. I even baked his favorite guess-what's-in-it-today cake.

And I bought his favorite vanilla ice cream for dessert." Jada placed the covered dishes on the table.

"Oh, that's a pleasant surprise, baby. Do you need help with anything?" asked Mama.

"No. I just want you guys to keep me company." The doorbell rang.

"Oh my goodness. I hope that's Wellington because it's too early for his parents," Jada said nervously as she eyed the kitchen clock.

"Chill out. I'll get the door," said Robert. Jada and Ruby followed. Robert pretended he was the butler. He opened the door and said in a snobbish voice, "*Greetings* and welcome to the mansion of Mr. Wellington Jones. Whom shall I say has arrived?" Then Robert looked at Wellington's father and said, "What's up, cat?" He extended his hand.

"I'm Christopher Jones and this is my beautiful wife, Cynthia Elaine. And you are?" questioned Christopher as he shook Robert's hand.

"Well, Christopher—"

"Please call me Chris."

"Okay, Chris, my man, as I was getting ready to say, I'm Robert Hamilton, Ruby Tanner's neighbor from across the street."

"So, do tell me, Robert. Are you *renting* across the street?" asked Cynthia. She looked at Robert's khaki pants, oxford shirt, and loafers then turned up her nose.

"Oh, please don't answer that, man. She's like this all the time," explained Chris, as he gave Robert a pat on the back.

"Mr. and Mrs. Jones, this is my mother, Ruby."

"Pleased to meet you, Ruby," said Christopher. He kissed Ruby on the hand.

"Where's my Wellington?" asked Cynthia.

Jada was disgusted that Cynthia didn't have the decency to say hello. "Wellington went to the store. He should be back shortly. Everyone can have a seat in the family room until dinner is served."

Wellington's family room had a jazz theme. It was furnished with expensive burgundy leather furniture. A custom-designed rug with a picture of Billie Holiday was centered in front of the fireplace. At the end of each seating area there were brass and copper end tables in the shapes of different instruments. He left the center of the floor spaciously open. Two paintings he'd bought in the French Quarter were displayed on easels. And a huge painting of *The Count* hung over the fireplace.

Jada placed the shrimp appetizers on the table. "This Italian leather set has been in our son's family room for almost three years now," remarked Cynthia. "Christopher, don't you think it is time for him to replace it?"

"No, honey, we didn't teach him how to invest his money so he'd become wealthy and throw it away by replacing perfectly good furniture," responded Chris.

"I guess you're right. It just seems like he's had it for so long. So Ruby, have I seen you somewhere before?" asked Cynthia. "At a sorority meeting or a social meeting. Your face looks very familiar, *darling*."

"I don't believe we've had the pleasure," responded Mama. "I'm not affiliated with any sororities or any social organizations."

"Really, then what on earth do you do with your spare time?" asked Cynthia.

"I spend time with my adopted family. I volunteer time at the church, and I work part-time at the bank."

"Oh, I guess that is enough to keep one busy," Cynthia commented. "Was that the door I heard? Is my Wellington home at last?"

Jada was relieved. Wellington walked into the room and greeted everyone.

"Oh, baby, come and give your mother a hug and a kiss," said Cynthia.

"Hi, Mom. Hi, Dad. Ms. Tanner, you look absolutely wonderful," said Wellington. He kissed his mother, Jada, and Ruby on their cheeks. "I don't believe we've had the pleasure of meeting, sir. I'm Wellington Jones and you are?"

"I'm Mr. Robert Hamilton, Ruby's neighbor from across the street who owns his house free and clear."

Jada noticed the puzzled look on Wellington's face and shook her head.

"Well, it's truly a pleasure you could join us today, Mr. Hamilton," Wellington said.

Jada was ready for this day to end. "Why don't we all relocate to the dining room?" She escorted everyone. Then, she walked into the kitchen. Wellington followed.

"How's my Nubian Queen? What can I do to help?"

"I have everything under control. You can have a seat. I'm right behind you." Jada needed a break so she busied herself in the kitchen. She stood where she could see and hear everything.

"Wellington, your home is lovely," said Mama as he returned to the dining room.

"What's a home without wonderful people like you to share special occasions," said Wellington. He sat at the head of the table.

"My Wellington bought this home immediately after he graduated from Morehouse. He was only twenty-one years old, you know. Wellington has always worked for himself, thanks to his father and me teaching him about investments *early* in life," bragged Cynthia.

"So tell me, Cynthia," said Robert, "where were you born?" Jada watched Robert kick her mom's foot.

Oh, boy. Here we go. Jada leaned closer to the door but stayed out of view.

"Oh, well, I was raised here in California, of course," responded Cynthia.

"So what part of California were you *born* in?" Robert continued. Jada knew Mr. Hamilton wasn't going to let Cynthia bow out gracefully.

"My birthplace? Is that what you are asking, Mr. Hamilton?"

"Yes, that's what I'm asking," said Robert. He kicked Mama's foot again.

Jada noticed that her mother tried not to laugh. Jada was surprised Wellington didn't say a word. He leaned back in his chair. She suspected he was used to it by now.

"I was born in northern Mississippi," said Cynthia. "But my parents moved to California when I was just a *little girl.*"

"You mean you were born in the tri-Delta?" asked Robert.

Cynthia shifted in her seat and looked toward the kitchen. Jada quickly moved back. Jada loved every moment.

"What do you know about the tri-Delta?" Cynthia's voice escalated.

"Not much," Robert said calmly. "Just that most folk—like you—that come from down South want to act like they ain't never been a part of the South. Almost like they 'shamed about where they come from. If you don't understand where you came from, then I reckon it's safe to say you don't know where you been. And you can't possibly know where you're going. That's all I'm saying. I rest my case." Robert flagged open his napkin and laid it across his lap.

Jada perked up to hear Cynthia's response.

"Let me tell you a thing or two, *Robert.*" Cynthia dragged his name out like she was preparing to rake him over the coals. Her slender neck swayed from side to side as her partially gray head moved in the opposite direction. "I'm tired of Niggas like you always trying to put down decent black folk who have worked hard to become wealthy in this society." The room was so quiet you could hear a pin drop. Wellington bowed his head as if he were praying.

"Now that's what I'm talkin' 'bout," responded Robert. "Notice how you automatically reverted to your Southern way of talking without skipping a beat. You do that pretty well." He laughed. "It's nothing to be ashamed of and everything to be proud of, Cynthia. You're no better than anybody else. If I didn't know you better, I'd guess you walk around with gri-gri in your purse."

Jada turned her back and covered her mouth. Everyone else laughed. Except Cynthia.

"What do you know about gri-gri or voodoo?" Cynthia questioned.

"Not much. But I know enough," said Robert.

Wellington must have guessed Jada wasn't coming out anytime soon. So he interrupted, "My Nubian Queen has worked all day. She has prepared jerk chicken with penne pasta and vegetables. And she baked a special cake for dessert." Jada sat next to Wellington and Mrs. Jones.

"Wellington, you know I prefer duck. Why didn't you have her prepare duck instead?" asked Cynthia. Jada viewed Cynthia's fish lips out of the corner of her eyes.

"Jerk chicken with pasta was my husband's favorite. Jada wanted him to be a part of this special occasion, so please let's just appreciate the hard work she has done," said Mama. Jada was surprised to hear her mother speak in such a firm voice.

"I second that motion," said Chris. "Jada, you have done a splendid job."

"Thank you, Mr. Jones."

Mama cleared her throat and said, "Wellington, would you bless the table?"

Everyone joined hands. Mrs. Jones held Jada's hand as if she had some sort of communicable disease. Mrs. Jones's hands were cold. The vibes Jada felt were colder.

"I'd be honored to," responded Wellington. "Heavenly Father, thank You for bringing us together to share in such a joyous occasion as our families unite and become one in Your eyesight. Thank You for the wonderful cook, my Nubian Queen, my fiancée."

Mrs. Jones jerked her hand. That must have been the first time she'd heard Wellington refer to Jada as his fiancée.

Wellington concluded, "Thank You, God, for

Your continued blessings. We ask You to bless those who are less fortunate. In Jesus' name, Amen."

"That was beautiful," Jada said.

"Excuse me, son," Cynthia said. "Did I hear you say fiancée?"

"That's correct." Wellington looked at his mother, then around the table at everyone else. "Today is the day that I'll take Diamond's soulmate ring off her right ring finger and place it on her left ring finger, where it belongs." Wellington gazed into Jada's eyes. "Jada is my soulmate and we've decided we're ready to make a commitment of marriage. The wedding date is set for Saturday, February fourteenth."

"Wellington, son, you have our blessings," said Chris. "Jada, you're a wonderful woman. I know the two of you were meant to be together." Chris walked over and hugged and kissed Jada.

"Now, let's eat," Robert said. "All this love in the air is making me horny. Oops, I mean hungry."

Everyone laughed, except Cynthia.

Wellington's mother ate in complete silence. Then halfway through the meal she said, "Well, dinner was lovely, *my son*. I hate to eat and run but I'm not feeling well so I'm going to go home and rest." Over half of Cynthia's food remained on her plate. Jada looked Cynthia in the eyes. Cynthia immediately looked down, pushed back her seat, and tossed the napkin on the table. "Don't forget about the annual barbecue next month."

"Barbecue?" Robert asked.

"Yes, it's *our* family annual barbecue and social," said Cynthia. "You probably wouldn't be interested in attending. There'll be lots of folk like *me* there."

"Oh, human folk. Those are my favorite kind," Robert replied.

"Everyone is welcome at our home for the barbecue," said Chris.

"Hey, Chris, maybe we can catch a Raiders' game or two this season," said Robert.

"What do you know—I happen to have season tickets for the Raiders *and* the Forty-niners. Call me, whenever you're ready." Cynthia cleared her throat and nodded toward the door.

Chris stood and pushed his chair under the table. "It's been nice meeting all of you." Wellington had gone upstairs for a moment. Cynthia insisted on leaving immediately so Jada happily escorted the Joneses to the door.

As soon as Cynthia was out of the door, she turned to Chris. Jada closed the door, placed her eye against the peephole, and listened. She heard Cynthia say, "Wellington will marry her over my dead body. She is not going to ruin everything I worked so hard to build. Her entire family is a misfit!"

"Yep, that's right, dear, you did it all by yourself," said Chris.

"You know what I mean, Christopher Jones, so don't get cute with me."

"Cynthia, do not interfere with Wellington's life. He's happy with Jada. Leave them alone."

"My Wellington will marry that woman over my dead body, Christopher Jones."

"I'm telling you, Cynthia, you're making the biggest mistake of your life. When Wellington finds out what you're doing, you might lose a future daughter-in-law *and* your son."

"If the truth must be told," responded Cynthia, "that's one daughter-in-law I can live without."

Jada's heart pounded so hard she thought it would leap out of her chest. In a way she felt relieved. She never had to wonder about Cynthia again.

Chapter 7

Melanie cruised along the Golden Gate Bridge in Wellington's silver Jaguar. She reflected on Jada's Monday morning house visit. The sounds Wellington made when he and Jada were making love had turned Melanie on. While they were upstairs getting it on, she was downstairs releasing her pent-up energy. Her orgasms were back to back with the actresses in the video and again with Wellington. The thought of Wellington's hard-on sent chills through her body. She licked her cherry-red lips. She imagined how sweet he tasted.

Melanie crept up the crooked hill five miles per hour and parked behind Cynthia's car. The automobiles were identical, except Cynthia's Jaguar was shimmering silver.

"Hi, Melanie, it's so good to see you. Come in, *darling.*" Cynthia extended her arms and squeezed Melanie as tight as she could.

"I'm really happy you invited me, Godmommy." Melanie returned the same affection. "I needed the break. That's why I insisted on driving. But I will say—the few days I've been here—Wellington has treated me like a queen."

Cynthia stepped back. Her eyes rested upon Melanie's face. Then traveled down to Melanie's feet and back up to her eyes. "You look splendid, darling. I see you're the same size. You're a little fuller, but in the right places. That's great."

"Well, you must tell me your secret because you haven't aged *at all*," Melanie said. "Even the furniture looks the same."

"Plenty of rest and lots of water certainly help. Now the furniture, I simply replace it every three to five years with the same." Cynthia sat on the white Victorian couch and patted the empty space beside her. Melanie sat next to her. "So tell me. How have you been? When I was in D.C., your mother told me she's concerned about you," Cynthia said.

Melanie heaved. She avoided eye contact with Cynthia. "Can we talk openly?" asked Melanie as she stared at the crystal whatnots on the étagère.

"Of course we can, darling," responded Cynthia.

"Well, Godmommy, I've been perturbed lately. I don't think I can take much more. Mother has always compared me to Stephanie. But lately she's been relentless. Stephanie has a house. Stephanie has a husband. Stephanie has three kids. Stephanie started her own business. Stephanie. Stephanie. Stephanie. Stephanie. Stephanie. I'm tired of hearing it. She acts like I'm thirty-two going on fifty-two." The tears rolled down Melanie's cheeks.

Cynthia laid Melanie's head on her shoulder. "I want to get married and have kids more than she can imagine. But she keeps acting like every man I meet is my last opportunity."

"Well, darling, since we're talking, let me tell you something—not to be repeated, mind you."

"Of course not." Melanie lifted Cynthia's hand and held it in her lap. She admired Cynthia's huge diamond ring.

"It's time I let you know. *You* are the *only* child I have ever loved. I've always wanted a daughter just like you. But I couldn't bear any children. My grandfather molested me when I was twelve. I became pregnant. I couldn't afford an abortion, so I did it myself. I thought I was hurting him. But in the end I was the one hurt. My mother took me to the hospital but it was too late. The doctor said because of the improper procedure, I was fortunate to be alive. But I would never bring a life into this world." Cynthia lay back on the couch and rocked Melanie in her arms. The room was quiet.

"When I was twenty-three, I met this woman who was pregnant. She said she couldn't keep the child. We didn't know at the time if it was a girl or a boy, but I agreed to adopt the baby at birth. She said she had gotten pregnant by someone other than her husband, who'd been overseas and his one-year tour of duty would end soon. She said she would have to leave her infant in the trash or somewhere because she was afraid."

Melanie listened. She wondered how this story fitted into hers. The baby photos of Wellington still lined the wall. Melanie scanned them all, one at a time. Wellington was fine from the day he was born.

Cynthia continued, "I promised to take the child. I didn't want a son. I never wanted a male child. I never forgave my grandfather. But I didn't want to see that woman abandon him, so Christopher and I took him. We named him Wellington. I chose the name because it sounded regal, *darling*. She gave us a framed picture of herself. But said she would never tell the real father—"

"I don't mean to interrupt, but how could you live with the pain for so many years. You can't heal if you can't forgive." Melanie decided her personal concerns weren't that great after all. She laid her head back on Cynthia's shoulder.

"Hush, my child, and listen. When Susan gave birth to twins, you and Stephanie, I instantly asked to be *your* godmother. There was something that drew me to you. I practically spoiled you." Cynthia laughed. "So, your mother spoiled Stephanie. My point, dear child, is don't be upset with Susan. You are a beautiful woman, Melanie. You have no need to be jealous of Stephanie."

Melanie sank deeper into Cynthia's arms. It had been a long time since she'd felt truly loved. "But being beautiful is a curse at times. People only see me on the outside. They think I've got it all together. If I could wear my emotional scars, I'd probably look like Medusa. Anyway, I'm glad you invited me." Melanie rubbed her hand along Cynthia's arm.

"What do you think about Wellington?" asked Cynthia.

"Other than the fact that he's handsome, rich, and lots of fun . . ."

"Don't forget *single*, darling."

How could Melanie forget? How could she tell

Cynthia she had already set her eyes on her god-brother? "Godmommy, Wellington is engaged to Jada."

"Yeah, but not for long. You're the perfect woman for my Wellington. That's why I invited you."

Melanie sat up and looked Cynthia in the eyes. Deep down inside she jumped for joy, but she looked at Cynthia with a straight face. "I don't know about that. I may be many things, but I'm no home wrecker." Melanie glimpsed at the color of the couch and wondered if it would be the one she'd wear when she and Wellington married.

"You still have a lot to learn about life, darling. If you truly want happiness, just let me handle this. Men are very basic. Remember that. Plus, Wellington has always had a thing for you. He's too reserved to show it. So you have to make the first move."

Melanie thought this over. No one knew Wellington better than Cynthia. And Cynthia knew her better than her own mother. Melanie's prayers had finally been answered.

"Well, Wellington has promised to take me to Geoffrey's tonight," said Melanie.

"That sounds wonderful. Is Jada joining the two of you?" asked Cynthia.

"No. She's out of town on business. We're going with Walter and Wendy. But she'll be back tomorrow for the barbecue."

"Then it's all set. This is your chance to get Wellington to notice you. You'll have to do it tonight. And speaking of business, I've asked my friend, Terrance Murphy, to hire you at Sensations Communications. You start work Monday, November fourth. Now I've got to get ready. I'm taking your mother on my special tour of the city. You can stay here as long as you like."

Melanie hugged and kissed Cynthia. "I think I'll just head back over to Wellington's. Bye, God-mommy."

Melanie drove down the hill at the same pace as on her way up. Her conscience kicked in. She questioned if she was doing the right thing. Wellington was perfect, but he was engaged. Melanie was becoming confused about what she wanted and what was right. One thought discounted the other. She drove thirty miles per hour along the peninsula. She parked outside Wellington's home. She imagined it could all be hers. If he were deeply in love with Jada, no woman could come between them. If she convinced Wellington to marry her, then his love for Jada wasn't pure. Melanie believed everything happened for a reason. Maybe Wellington was *her* soulmate. She turned the key and entered.

Melanie walked into the kitchen. Wellington was pouring himself a cup of coffee. "Would you like a cup?" he asked.

"Oh, no thanks. What time are we leaving tonight?" asked Melanie.

"We should leave around eight o'clock. That way we can get a table near the dance floor," responded Wellington.

"I'll be ready," said Melanie. "What do you think I should wear?" Melanie put two scoops of sugar and a dash of cream in Wellington's coffee. The little things he liked resurfaced in her mind. She had studied his every move.

"It's definitely not a casual atmosphere. But

don't overdress either. Wear something dressy but comfortable." Wellington sipped his coffee. "Ah, perfect. Well, it's my weekend to help Walter groom his lawn, and since the barbecue is tomorrow, we've decided to do it today. Otherwise it would throw off our schedule of alternating weekends." Wellington licked his cocoa-caramel lips and sat the cup on the counter.

"So that's your secret to keeping your lawn so beautiful," said Melanie. "I thought you paid a professional."

"I enjoy manicuring the lawn. It gives me an opportunity to work with my hands." Wellington wiggled his fingers as if he were playing the piano. "Gardening is another form of art. You shape, mold, trim, cut, and reshape until it's exactly the way *you* want it."

Melanie reached for Wellington's left hand. She turned it over and stroked it softly. It felt so good. "Your hands are soft. Well manicured. And masculine. I would have never guessed you enjoyed gardening." She felt his pulse beat quicken.

"I'd better get going. I'll be back around seven. If my Nubian Queen calls while I'm out, ask her to call me around seven-thirty. I'll see you later," said Wellington.

"Tell Walter and Wendy I said hello," said Melanie as she stood in the doorway and watched Wellington's sexy ass. He had a walk like Denzel Washington.

Melanie sucked her bottom lip and rubbed her temple. She had about six hours before Wellington returned. She took a nap in Wellington's bed. When she awakened, she browsed through Jada's things in Wellington's bedroom.

Melanie sat at Jada's vanity and combed her hair, like Jada's. She sampled Jada's fragrances. Zahra, that was the one she remembered. She was careful to place everything back in its proper place. Then she tried on several of Jada's dresses. She liked the leopard dress best. Melanie's red-hot sexy irresistible dress with the back out was as close as she could get.

Melanie watched a couple of X-rated videos on the big screen. She contemplated her next move for hours. She finally concluded that sex was the common denominator. For strategies, she reached back into her college days—when she was the master, creator, and controller of the best on- and off-campus sexual escapades.

The best scene in the movie had just begun. Melanie removed her G-string. She dropped her hot pink summer dress to the carpet. She lay back on the chaise and spread her legs. She parted her lips and held her clitoris between her fingers. She moistened her index finger and glided it up and down her shaft. Then she rotated it on the head of her clit. The telephone rang. "Damn!" She picked up the cordless, turned down the volume, and continued to watch the video.

"Jones residence, may I help you?"

"Hi, Melanie, this is Jada. Let me speak with Wellington."

"Oh, hi, Jada! I was just thinking about you."

"Really, thinking about what?" asked Jada.

"I was just thinking about how considerate it is of you to go shopping with me before I leave. Wellington isn't here. He went over to Walter's to do the lawn." Melanie braced the phone between her ear and shoulder and stroked her clit.

"That's right. I forgot. Tell him I called."

"Jada," said Melanie.

"Yes."

"How would you like to get together next Saturday night and do something fun?"

"Maybe. Let me think about it. What kind of outings do you enjoy most?"

"Oh, this is your town so you decide." Melanie knew it was best if Jada believed she was in control.

"I'll come up with something. In the meantime, think about what you'd like to do. I've got to go. Tell Wellington to call me on my cell phone. Bye."

"Bye." Melanie hung up the phone, picked up the remote, and turned up the volume. She dozed off on the chaise. The phone startled her.

"Hello," answered Melanie. She glanced at the clock on the VCR. It was six-thirty.

"Hey, are you comfortable over there?" asked Wellington.

"Oh yes, I was just about to take a shower. Do you mind if I use yours?"

"Not at all," replied Wellington. "Make yourself at home.

"Did Jada call?"

"No. No one's called," said Melanie.

"Okay, I should still make it home around seven," said Wellington.

"Sounds good, I'll see you then," said Melanie.

Melanie turned off the video and headed upstairs to Wellington's shower. The scent of strawberries and cream filled the air. Afterward, she covered her body from head to toe in chocolate-flavored cocoa butter lite oil. She dabbed a touch of Zahra behind each ear.

Melanie waited. When Wellington closed the

front door, she tossed the bath towel outside his bathroom. She pinched her teasing tan nipples real hard. Instantly, they popped out. When Wellington walked through his bedroom door, his eyes fell exactly where Melanie had intended. She watched them. They traveled from her perky 38D's, glazed over her six-pack, and landed on her well-trimmed bush.

"I'm so sorry, I thought I would have finished in here before you got home," Melanie said. Wellington was speechless. His vision was restricted to her breasts.

Melanie turned her back toward Wellington. Slowly. She bent over. Paused. Picked up the towel. Paused so Wellington could view both points of entry.

Melanie grabbed her silk robe and placed it across her arm. Wellington remained silent. As she walked out, she saw the bulge in his blue denim overalls. Wellington shook his head and slapped his face.

"Damn, girl. Next time give a brother some advance notice. Put your drawers on or something."

"*Sorry.*"

Melanie waited for Wellington to get in the shower. She tiptoed back into his room for Jada's lipstick. The bathroom door was open. She stood and watched him through the clear shower door. Wellington stroked himself methodically. Nice long strokes. Melanie peeped in closer. She watched. Wellington applied more pressure with each stroke. The base of his thumb revolved on the head of his penis. Then the tip of his index finger moved up and down his shaft. Small circular motions moved in the crevice underneath his head. He combined each movement into each stroke moving up and down. Faster. Faster. Just when he was about to cum, the phone rang.

Melanie quietly rushed out of the bedroom. "Jones residence."

"This is Jada. Let me speak with Wellington."

"Oh, he just called and said he's running a little late, but he should be here by nine. Do you want me to ask him to call you when he gets in?"

"No, that won't be necessary. I'll just come over."

Melanie's heartbeat escalated. "Sure. When will you be here?" Her voice trembled.

"In about five minutes. Bye." Jada hung up the phone.

Melanie dashed into the guest bedroom. Slipped into her fiery red dress. The V dipped right above the crack of her butt. The split revealed her entire left leg. She flawlessly applied her cherry-red lip gloss. She liked it better. She hurried out of the bedroom. All of a sudden she stopped in her tracks. Went back. She reached for the cordless and pressed *69. The last incoming call was received from area code 3-1-0-5-5-5-2-2 . . . Melanie laughed. Clicked the off button and tossed the phone on the bed. "Bitch!"

Wellington was already dressed and watching TV downstairs. "You look stunning," said Wellington. A wide smile crossed his face.

Melanie's cherry-red lips parted. "Thanks. I'm ready. Let's go."

"Why the sudden rush?" Wellington asked.

"I'm so excited. I just want to get there early.

That's all. Shall we?" insisted Melanie as she extended her arm to Wellington for him to escort her.

Wellington opened the doors for Melanie. She liked that a lot. She fastened her seat belt and rested her head back.

"Who called?" asked Wellington.

Melanie never flinched. "Oh, that was my mother calling to tell me what a great time they had on the tour." Jada was an amateur as far as she was concerned.

"Is there something on your mind?" asked Wellington as he drove across the Bay Bridge.

"Actually, I was thinking. You and Jada make such a wonderful couple," Melanie lied. "How *did* the two of you meet?"

As she listened to Wellington talk about the night he met Jada, Melanie's eyes filled with tears of envy. "Oh, that's so romantic."

When they arrived, Walter and Wendy were already seated.

"Hey, man, you clean up pretty good," Wellington said as they walked up to the table.

"You don't do too bad of a job yourself, man," Walter replied.

"Wendy. Walter, let me introduce you to my friend, Melanie Marie Thompson. She's also my houseguest. And pleased to finally get to the hottest nightclub in California."

"Pleased to meet you, Wendy and Walter," said Melanie, extending her hand to greet them.

Melanie engaged Wendy in a conversation about social organizations. Wendy was surprised to learn that they were members of several of the same organizations. Wellington and Walter decided to take a walk over to the bar.

"We'll be back," Walter said. "That'll give you ladies a moment to sort through the various affiliations."

Melanie and Wendy continued their discussion.

"I'm supposed to leave next week," Melanie said, "but Mrs. Jones got me a job in San Francisco. I think I'm going to like life in Cali. Please don't mention this to Wellington. We want it to be a surprise."

"How do you know Wellington?"

"His mother and my mother have been friends practically all their lives. So, how long have you and Walter been married?" asked Melanie.

"Ten years. Walter and I married right after college. I graduated from Spelman and Walter graduated from Morehouse," said Wendy. "We both moved back home to California and the rest is wonderful."

Wellington and Walter returned. "We just ordered a bottle of champagne for the table, ladies," said Wellington.

"If you'd like something else, please let us know," said Walter.

"The two of you seem to have hit it off well," commented Wellington.

"Very well," responded Wendy. "Walter, I didn't come out here to sit down all night. Let's dance."

"Your wish is my command," replied Walter.

"Isn't that sweet. After ten years, they're still happily married and still in love," said Melanie.

"I guess you guys did talk a lot," said Wellington. "Would you like to dance?"

Melanie wondered what took him so long to ask. "Yes. I'd like that."

LTD's "You and I Were Meant to Be" played as soon as Melanie and Wellington stepped on the floor. Melanie placed her hand on Wellington's shoulder. The other he held in his hand. Wellington placed his other hand around Melanie's waist. Melanie inconspicuously pressed her breasts against Wellington's chest. She leaned her face next to his. It felt so right. It couldn't be wrong. They partied the night away. They laughed, talked, and danced all night long.

"Well, I guess we had better call it a night," suggested Wellington. "It's almost two."

"Tell Jada we said hello," said Wendy.

"Oh shit!" responded Wellington. "I forgot to call."

Melanie remained silent.

"Man, you'd forget to call your mama if she wasn't on speed dial." Walter laughed.

On the way to the car Wellington mumbled about forgetting to call Jada. Melanie listened but opted not to comment, to avoid provoking a conversation she didn't want to have.

Wellington pressed a button. The moon roof opened.

"The stars are beautiful tonight. Don't you think so?" asked Melanie.

"Are you connected with them?" asked Wellington.

"I'm connected with *every* living element in the universe," Melanie replied.

"You know, the last time I saw you, you were seriously underdeveloped. Now, look at you," Wellington said as he glanced at Melanie's breasts.

"Well, little girls do grow up," said Melanie. "You always did look good but now your ass is damn near irresistible." She looked from his dick up to his dreamy eyes.

Melanie waited until Wellington opened the door. She walked upstairs and kicked off her shoes. She looked deep into Wellington's eyes. Her lips stood an inch away from his. "Thanks. I had a wonderful time."

Wellington never said a word. He didn't need to. Melanie French-kissed Wellington with all the passion she could muster. She was surprised when he reciprocated. Melanie led Wellington into his bedroom. Undressed him. Massaged his body *all* over. Then she tamed him like a wild horse. She figured Jada was too dainty to have spanked that ass. So she did it for her. Melanie rode Wellington until everything came up, including the sun.

Chapter 8

Wellington tossed and turned. He wanted to believe it was all a dream but the stickiness in his crotch convinced him otherwise. Wellington had just dozed off when his phone rang. The digital clock on the dresser across the room showed 9:45 A.M.

"Hello." He glimpsed over at Melanie. She rolled over and hugged the pillow. He pinched himself. Unfortunately the past several hours were real. Wellington shook his head.

"Good morning," Jada said.

"Oh, hi, ba, I was going to call you, but you beat me to it." Wellington yawned. "How are you doing?" Melanie sat up. He put his finger over her lips.

"I'm getting ready to board my plane. I should make it to my place around eleven. But right now I'd like for you to explain what happened last night?" Whenever Jada was cool, calm, and collected on the outside, Wellington knew her emotions tipped the opposite end of the scale.

"I'd like for someone to explain to *me* what happened last night," Wellington remarked. Melanie gathered her red dress and shoes and strolled out of Wellington's bedroom.

"Well, first let me say, I left several messages with Melanie. Second of all, your first obligation is to me, not her. When did you decide to take her out dancing? And don't worry about how I found out."

"Ba, look, I apologize. I don't want to argue about this. What time should I pick you up for the barbecue?" Wellington knew he'd fucked up. Right now he realized the shortest distance between two pussies was a straight lie. "It was nothing. Really."

"I'm not going," Jada snapped.

"But you have to go." Wellington rubbed his bald head. "This is my first opportunity to introduce *my fiancée* to the extended family."

"They're just a group of pretenders. Just like Mr. Hamilton said. So why should I bother. I'll meet them soon enough, at the wedding."

"Please, do this for me, my Nubian Queen," Wellington begged. "I'll pick you up around noon." He didn't wait for a response. He hung up the phone and walked into the guest bedroom.

"Wake up. I need to talk to you."

"Can't it wait until later?" Melanie asked. "My ass is tired."

"No. So get up," Wellington insisted. Melanie sat in the center of the bed and leaned forward over her pillow.

"Look. What we did last night was wrong. I don't

want you to think I don't love Diamond. I love her more than anything. I just got caught up in the moment."

"It's too early for sentiments. Can you just write it down for me?" said Melanie as she swooped the pillow behind her head and slid under the covers.

"Just promise me you'll forget this happened."

"What happened?" Melanie paused. "See. I've forgotten already."

"Don't be cute." Wellington smiled. "What time are you going over to help Mom?"

"She said she didn't need my help." Wellington watched Melanie turn her back. "I'm riding with you so *don't* leave me. And turn off the light on your way out."

It was a perfect day in the bay. Wellington breezed through the traffic in his black Expedition. He glanced over at Melanie in the passenger seat. His dick got hard every time he thought about last night. He had no idea she had matured so much. The royal blue wraparound top she wore reminded him of his first date with Jada. He noticed she'd changed her hairstyle too. Her cherry-red lips exacerbated his hard-on.

"Melanie?"

"Yes," she replied softly.

"Please don't forget what we discussed this morning."

"Don't worry. I'm not going to get attached. It was all in fun. We both had a great time. And Jada will never know what happened." Melanie smiled.

Wellington redirected his energy as he parked in one of the visitor spaces. "Wait here. I'll be right back. And if you don't mind, please get in the back." Melanie's head moved downward and her eyes flipped up at Wellington. He was relieved when she opened the car door.

"Hello, Mr. Jones," Edward said. "Would you like me to buzz Ms. Tanner?"

"No thanks, Edward. I'll go up," responded Wellington.

When the elevator door closed, Wellington unzipped his blue denim shorts and repositioned himself. He slipped his key into the space marked PENTHOUSE. He stepped into Jada's entrance, grabbed a mint from the lifelike butler statue, and picked up his chilled glass of Moët.

He could always tell what mood Jada was in by what she left at the door. The time she'd left fresh strawberries with chocolate, champagne, a red rose, and explicit instructions on how she wanted him to please her ranked above all.

"Hi, baby," Wellington called out. "You ready?" Wellington sat on the plush couch in the living room.

Jada sashayed out of the bedroom wearing a black strapless crushed-velvet cat suit. "I'm ready," she said. She pecked Wellington on the cheek.

The all-too-familiar fragrance lingered in the air. "So, is that all I get?" he asked as he ran his fingers through her hair.

"For now. Yes." Jada walked toward the elevator.

"Melanie's in the car. She didn't have to help Mom after all, so she decided to ride with us." Wellington watched Jada's eyes cut to the corner as far as they could, and then they rolled front and center. He waited for her to say something. She didn't.

"I know this situation has been uncomfortable for you. It's uncomfortable for me too." Wellington tilted Jada's chin and looked into her eyes. "By this time next week, she'll be packing her things to leave." Jada didn't say a word.

When they stepped off the elevator, Melanie was in the lobby talking with Edward. "Hi, Jada! It's so good to see you."

"Hi, Melanie. You look great!" Jada looked Melanie up and down. Then shifting her gaze toward Wellington, she tightened her eyelids and the corners of her mouth. She immediately turned back to Melanie and smiled.

Wellington's thick eyebrows cringed together. Wrinkles developed along his forehead. He rubbed his temples and opened the door for Jada and then Melanie.

"So, Jada. How was your trip?" Melanie asked. "Who was on the set?"

"Roger Turner and Terrell Morgan," Jada responded. Wellington couldn't see Jada's eyes through her dark sunglasses. But if the corners of her mouth would spread any further, her face would probably crack.

"Oh! Roger *Turner*. Isn't he the biggest flirt?" said Melanie. "I call him Chocolate Thunder. Because when lightning strikes—and he flashes that *Taye Diggs* smile—your pussy rumbles and the rain comes pouring down." Melanie laughed and slapped her thigh. Jada laughed so hard her glasses fell in her lap.

Wellington cleared his throat. "Excuse me. Can we please change the subject, ladies?"

"So, Jada, are Terrell and Candice still an item?" Melanie chuckled.

"They most certainly are—"

"Oh, Jada, before I forget," said Melanie. "This

is the best way to handle the guests. One, always smile and nod agreeably even if you're not paying attention. Two, you can't go wrong asking them questions about themselves. And three, if they ask you a question you don't want to answer, tell them you'll have to do tea with them sometime soon, but right now you have spotted someone you *must* say hello to. Just follow my lead."

Wellington drove behind the shuttle bus that transported the guests up the hill.

"This is going to be great!" exclaimed Melanie. "There are well over a hundred people and folks are still coming." Melanie darted out of the car before Wellington turned off the engine. She opened Jada's door. "Jada, come with me!"

Wellington watched Melanie and Jada disappear into the crowd.

"Oh, Robert. I'm so happy you and Ruby could make it," Wellington heard his mother say as he walked up behind her. He placed his finger over his lip and motioned to Robert and Ruby. "Who are your guests?" asked Cynthia.

"Allow me to introduce you to Jazzmyne and her two children, Brandon and Shelly," Ruby answered.

"Pleased to make your acquaintances," said Cynthia. "Do enjoy your stay. If there's anything you need, ask any of the gentlemen in tuxedos. Now do excuse me. I must greet the rest of my guests."

Wellington grabbed his mother around the waist.

"Boy, I told you to stop that."

Wellington kissed Cynthia on the cheek. "Hi, Mrs. Tanner. Mr. Hamilton. Jazzmyne, Brandon, and Shelly," said Wellington.

"Where's Melanie?" asked Cynthia.

"Oh, she's introducing Jada to the guests."

"Very good," commented Cynthia as she walked away.

"Well, a leopard doesn't change its spots," said Robert. "That woman will live the rest of her life in Cynthialand. But one of these days, you mark my words, her world is going to come tumbling down around her."

Shelly interrupted, "So, Mr. Wellington, we finally meet. I want you to know that I'm *still* averaging a four-point-oh and I love my school. You're the nicest man our family has ever known."

Brandon stood next to Shelly and held his hand out for Wellington to give him five. Wellington slapped Brandon's little hand. Then he held his open for Brandon.

"So you're Mr. Wellington Jones," said Jazzmyne. "Let me give you a great big hug. How can I ever repay you?"

Wellington's forehead wrinkled when he looked into Jazzmyne's eyes. There was a weird familiarity about them. "If Shelly keeps that 4.0 average and Brandon does the same, that's all the return I need on my investment." Wellington scanned the crowd, searching for Jada and Melanie. "I don't mean to be rude but would you please excuse me? I need to find my fiancée."

"Oh, Mr. Wellington," said Shelly, "before you leave. I made a birthday present for you, but I forgot it at home. Mommy said she'd make sure you got it."

"Thanks, Shelly." Wellington swooped Shelly up in the air and spun her around three times. Maybe he would spot Jada.

Brandon jumped up and down. "Do me too, Mr. Wellington!" Wellington whirled Brandon around three times. Brandon sat on the lawn and smiled. Wellington patted his head. There were too many people outside, so he went inside.

"Hey, Dad. How's everything going?" Wellington walked into the living room. His dad was reclining in his favorite beige leather chair. It was out of place amid the Victorian furniture. His dad never liked to mingle for extended periods of time so it was easy for Wellington to find him.

"Where's Jada?" asked Dad.

"Oh, Melanie is introducing her to the guests." Wellington tossed his baseball cap on the coffee table.

"Melanie? Why not you or your mother?"

Wellington wondered why his dad refused to shave his head. It reminded him of a glass of water that was half empty or half full. The salt-and-pepper-colored hair receded so far back you could see the bald spot through the hole in the back of a baseball cap. "Mom's too busy. Besides, Melanie volunteered."

"Sit down for a moment, son. Let me have a talk with you." Wellington sat on the edge of the couch closest to his father.

"Sure, Pops. Is everything okay?"

His dad released the reclining lever. "Your mother likes Melanie because she fits into her circle. Jada doesn't."

"Just be direct," said Wellington.

Wellington's dad glanced toward the door. He lowered his voice. "Son, I want you to be happy. Draw your own circle. And when *you* do, don't let *anyone* erase it. Remember what I'm saying. Soon

there will come a time when you will have to decide what is best for *you.*"

"Pops." Wellington stood and placed his hand
on his father's shoulder. "I've always been my own
man."

Cynthia stepped into the room. "What are you
two doing in here?" She stared at Chris and then
looked at Wellington. "You're supposed to be outside greeting guests. Let's reunite." Cynthia clap-
ped her hands twice. "Shall we?" She smiled. At
fifty-eight, Cynthia didn't look a day over fifty. With
the exception of her shiny gray hair and thin lips,
Cynthia looked a lot like Lena Horne.

"Your wish is our command," said Chris as he
stood and bowed. His reversed one-pack rolled
over his belt and back. Wellington's dad reminded
him of James Avery.

Wellington laughed and headed toward the
backyard. At a distance, he zoomed in on Jada and
Melanie. It appeared they were getting along very
well. The thought of Melanie seducing him flashed
into his mind. As Wellington watched Jada and
Melanie interact, he undressed them. His imagination ran wild. He pictured Melanie's 38D's pressed
nipples-to-nipples against Jada's 36D's. Two nicely
curved waistlines. Two firm, well-rounded butts
cheek to cheek. He bent them over. Jada's beautiful dark chocolate lips and Melanie's tasty tan lips
were in full view. Wellington swiftly shook his head
several times.

"Wellington, I missed you," said Jada as she
planted a wet one square on his lips. He rubbed
his hand over his face.

"Yeah, we missed you," Melanie seconded.

"Hey, I missed you guys too. Thanks, Melanie,

for introducing Jada, but I'll take my bride-to-be off your hands for the rest of the evening."

"Thank you!" Jada kissed Wellington and wrapped her arms around his neck.

"It's been my pleasure," Melanie said. "Jada, don't forget we have *plans* for Saturday."

"I won't."

Wellington watched Melanie walk over to her mother. "What was that all about?"

"Nothing much. I agreed to take Melanie shopping in the city and out to a club before she heads back to D.C. That way I don't have to worry about my fiancé not inviting me. You know what I mean," Jada remarked.

"Count me out." Wellington licked his lips and softly kissed Jada. "I love you, woman. *Mrs.* Wellington Jones."

"I love you too, baby."

Chapter 9

Jada was glad Melanie's visit was approaching its end. In less than forty-eight hours Melanie Marie Thompson would be on the road again. Over the past week, Jada had grown to like Melanie, but what woman wanted another in her man's house? The intercom buzzed. Jada sat the knife on the counter.

"Ms. Tanner. Ms. Jordan is here to see you," Edward informed.

"Thanks, Edward. Send her up, please."

When Candice arrived, Jada greeted her with opened arms. "Come in, girl!"

"I'm not staying long," said Candice. "I just decided to stop by on my way home from aerobics." Candice's hair was pulled back into a short ponytail with a red tie that matched her warm-up suit. Candice looked good even after she had worked out.

"You must be working out to lose your mind, girl, because you couldn't possibly look any better. I was just about to make a wheat grass shake with fresh green apples and ginger root."

"Perfect timing. Make me one, too." Candice sat and stared out the window. The daytime view of Oakland was nice. The sky was clear and no rain was in the forecast.

Jada pressed the mix button on the blender. "What happened to you last Saturday? I thought you were coming to the barbecue."

"I decided to take a last-minute trip to Los Angeles. Terrell and I had a heart-to-heart talk."

"So what happened?" Jada poured the wheat grass into two tall exotic glasses.

"We decided we're ready to take our relationship to a higher level. I really like the fact that Wellington gave you a soulmate ring to signify your spiritual connection. Terrell and I exchanged rings this weekend. See!" Candice flipped her wrist and extended her fingers. The logo was embedded inside the diamond solitaire.

Jada held Candice's hand. "It's beautiful. I really like the marquis cut."

"We know it's not going to be easy," said Candice. "But if the first six months go well, we agreed that I would move to Los Angeles and live on his farm."

"A farm!" Jada's eyebrows drew closer together.

"Gotcha. I'm *kidding*. Terrell's house is exotic. Can you believe he has a man-made waterfall flowing into his pool?"

"Well, the two of you are sure handling your relationship responsibly. Most people just fall in and out of love, lust, or whatever. But they never take time to discuss their expectations."

Candice chimed in, "Some don't even discuss the fact they're in a relationship. After date number one, two, or three, they assume that's a commitment. Especially after they've had sex."

Jada nodded her head. "That's especially true for women. Why is it that people can go on forever about what they don't like? Anyway, I'm so happy for you guys."

"Thanks, but I'm still nervous." Candice sipped her juice.

"Not you, Ms. Thang." Candice could have practically any man she wanted. Her skin was smooth as butter and her ass was big as a butterball. Plus, she earned well over six figures a year.

"Well, don't laugh but I'm still tripping on our age difference."

"Candice, look at me. Spirits are ageless and faceless. Don't nurture the seeds of society. He's too old, too young, too skinny, too fat, too bald, too poor, too ugly, too this, too that, too . . . Nurture the seeds of your spirits. Now tell me. Did you put your get-back booty in that G-string bikini and strut your stuff on Venice beach, girl?" Jada laughed.

"You're going to have to lay off the juice. Oxygen overdose to the brain," Candice laughed. "But you know I tried to get arrested on Santa Monica Beach. The officer was *so* fine. I would have handcuffed myself." Candice finished her drink, rinsed the glass, and placed it in the dishwasher. "So what are you doing today?"

"Melanie and I are going shopping in San Francisco. Then we're going out tonight."

"Melanie? She's *still* here?"

"Yeah, but I'm thrilled this is her last weekend. In fact, I'm so glad she's leaving I might just buy her a going-away present."

"Well, buy two—one from me," said Candice, not cracking a smile. "It's not that I dislike her. I just don't trust her. She seems sneaky and conniving."

"Well, she was pretty nice to me at the barbecue. She introduced me to Mrs. Jones's society friends." Jada remained neutral. "It's the least I can do in return."

"Jada. Mrs. Jones is setting the stage for Melanie to *move in* and for you to *move out*. Please don't continue to ignore the signs. Why did Melanie surface after *twelve* years?" Candice asked, then waited for a response. When Jada didn't reply, she continued, "Why isn't she staying with Mrs. Jones? Why didn't they visit in D.C.?"

"Candice, you know I respect your opinion, but I don't think you're right about this. Besides, Wellington and I are soulmates. We are meant to be together. *No one* can come between *us.*"

"Well, keep in mind that soulmates dissipate for more reasons than one. And the other woman ranks at the *top* of the list."

"Look, Candice, I've got to run. But I promise I'll think about what you've said."

"We can walk out together," said Candice.

"Okay." Jada felt confident that regardless of what Melanie's intentions were, Wellington would never allow anyone to ruin their relationship.

"Let's see, keys, phone, purse, credit cards, make that credit card." Jada tossed the other cards on the kitchen table. "I'm ready."

They took the elevator down, and Candice exited

at the lobby. Jada went down one additional level to the garage. She got in her car, dropped the top, and turned on her radio. She pushed button number five for 102.9.

"We're going to take you way back by special request. Ladies, if you've got a good man you'd better look out for—"The Clean-Up Woman." This is the Mellow Man giving it to you straight. Take those blinders off of your mind. Stop being captivated in time! Because the clean-up woman is busy, and if you get *comfortable*—oh well." Complete silence. Then Jada heard the intro to Betty Wright's song. Jada immediately reached for her cellular and speed-dialed Candice's number.

"Hello."

"Candice. Did you call KBLX and make a special request?"

"No. Why? What's playing?" Candice asked.

"Listen to this." Jada turned up the volume on her radio.

Candice busted out laughing. "No, girl, I did *not* make that request, but you must admit, it is timely."

"Candice, this is not funny."

"Have fun shopping," she said. "And don't forget to buy *my* good-bye gift."

Jada parked in the circular driveway. Her hand traveled to ring the bell.

Melanie opened the door. "Hi, Jada. I'm so excited. I really appreciate you taking me on this shopping spree *in the city,* "Melanie sang. Melanie's hair was pulled back in a ponytail. Her makeup was flawless. Her manicure and pedicure matched her red lips. Her black jean shorts hung loosely over her hips. The black Victoria's Secret top exposed more cleavage than Jada cared to see.

"Well, today is your lucky day," replied Jada. Jada tried to exhibit the same level of enthusiasm.

"And yours!" responded Melanie. She combed her nails through her hair.

"What's that supposed to mean?" Jada questioned.

"Oh, nothing. Stop being so serious. I'm just ready to have fun."

"Where's Wellington?"

"Upstairs, relaxing. He said he was tired after grooming the lawn all morning."

"I'll just be a moment. Let me run upstairs and say hello to my baby." Wellington was stretched across the bed sound asleep. His arms were spread wide. He snored. Jada decided not to wake him. This man looked good even in his sleep. She kissed his lips and pulled the covers up to his chest. When she went downstairs, Melanie was in her car. Jada reflected on some of the things Candice had mentioned.

The drive downtown would take about twenty minutes. "How have you enjoyed your vacation?" Jada asked once they had gotten on the road.

Melanie looked relaxed. Her cherry-red lips curved and parted. "I've had a wonderful time!" Jada expected her to say more.

"What time are you heading out tomorrow?"

"I haven't decided. Have you heard this joke?" Melanie paused. "A woman walks into an antique record shop and asks, 'Do you have Hot Lips on a six-inch?' The owner looks at the woman and responds, 'No, but I've had Hot Lips on a twelve-inch.'" Melanie slapped her leg and laughed. "I love that joke!"

"That's pretty good," Jada agreed, laughing.

"So which stores are your favorite?" asked Melanie.

"I love them all. I have yet to find a store that doesn't have something I like. I love being creative."

"Yeah, I know exactly what you mean. You just can't go wrong shopping in San Francisco. They have all of the major designer stores. Have you decided where we're going to party tonight?" asked Melanie.

"Maybe. Do you like oldies like Parliament?"

"What? There's a place in San Francisco that plays oldies?"

"You can find anything you want in San Francisco," Jada responded. "The question is: Can you afford it?" Jada parked in the Centre's garage. Melanie bounced in her seat then hopped out of the car. It was a typical Saturday afternoon. The mall was packed with people of all nationalities. Almost every shopper had a bag. Saks. Gucci. Victoria's Secret. FUBU.

"Let's go in the lingerie store," Melanie suggested.

"Oh, you'll love this store. It's one of my favorites. Actually, any lingerie store is my favorite as long as the items don't look cheap."

"Check out this black lace bustier with the matching garter." Melanie waved the garments in the air.

"That's sexy. But you haven't checked out this transparent crotchless leopard cat suit. This is so me." Jada held it in front of her and admired herself in the mirror.

"I bet Wellington would love to see you in it," Melanie commented.

"I *know* he would." Jada placed the outfit back

on the rack. "Let's go to the top floor where the really expensive shops are."

"Let me try this outfit on first. I'll be right with you, you go ahead," insisted Melanie.

"Okay. I'll represent the advance team. Meet me in the shoe department of Nordstrom," said Jada. It had been a long time since she'd had this much fun shopping.

They shopped on every single floor from top to bottom. Jada would never forget how Melanie charged over ten thousand dollars on her platinum Visa. She watched the salesperson get excited about the commission. The cashier's eyes blinked faster than the scanner flashed. Then Melanie reversed all the charges and told the woman, "The color of money is green, *black*, and cream— not white. I bet your ass you'll think twice before you show disrespect to another black customer." Melanie tucked her card in her purse, tossed her head back, and walked out. Jada and Melanie laughed out loud as soon as they got outside.

"I almost forgot," Melanie said. "I have to pick up my packages from the lingerie shop." The woman behind the counter remembered Melanie. She handed her two overstuffed bags with wrapped packages.

"What on earth did you buy?"

"Just a few play things for fun. It's starting to get late. Can we go to the exotic shop?" asked Melanie. "I've been looking all over for these special imported fur-lined handcuffs. They must sell them in San Francisco. I couldn't find them anywhere in D.C."

"I know exactly where to take you."

"Oh great! This is so wonderful," Melanie said.

Jada was glad the shopping spree was almost over.

"We're getting ready to close, ladies," said the salesman at the pleasure shop.

"But it's only five o'clock." Melanie tugged on the door.

"I know what time it is." He flipped the OPEN sign to CLOSED.

"But I came all the way from Washington, D.C., just to shop at your store," Melanie pleaded.

He paused. "Do you know what you want?" He turned the key.

"I sure do," said Melanie. She charged into the small store as soon as he cracked the door.

"Okay, I'll let you in but you have five minutes to make a purchase," the man said. Jada walked in.

"Thank you. I'd like two pairs of fur-lined handcuffs and two of the matching blindfolds."

"Why two pairs?" Jada asked.

"Well, one pair is for home and the other is for travel. A true diva is always prepared," responded Melanie. She winked at the man behind the counter.

"Thank you, ladies, and please come again and again and again and again." He smiled and locked the door.

"We'd better head back to Wellington's," suggested Jada.

"I need a nap before we go out," Melanie said.

"You too?" Jada commented.

"Yes. It does wonders for the body and mine needs it."

"I agree. Mine too."

When they arrived at Wellington's, Jada immediately walked over to Wellington and gave him a long, endearing French kiss. He was kicked back in front of the TV. Watching the Forty-niners.

"My goodness, is there anything left to purchase in the city? It looks like you two have bought it all," he said. His body was stretched across the chaise longue. Jada was glad he had on a lounging jacket to cover himself. Her daddy has always said, "Never advertise things that are not for sale."

"Just a few things," Melanie responded.

"A few, yeah right, if you insist," Wellington replied.

"We're going to take a nap before we get dressed to go out," said Jada. As she turned toward the spiral staircase, she heard Wellington clear his throat.

"How about another?" His luscious lips protruded beyond his nose. Jada pranced over, straddled him, and planted a nice long kiss.

Melanie's eyes shifted away from them. "I'll leave you two lovebirds alone," said Melanie. "Wake me at eight."

"I'm going to take a shower first, so all I have to do is freshen up. Wellington, would you please make sure I'm up by eight-thirty, sweetheart." Jada blew him a kiss on her way up the stairs.

"Oh, I'll make sure you are up by seven-thirty," he said. Then he licked his lips again. The phone rang. "I'll get it," shouted Wellington.

Jada listened from the top of the staircase. "Hey, Walter, what's up? You recovered from doing the lawn yet?" Wellington asked.

Jada went into Wellington's bedroom. She heard Wellington's voice escalate but couldn't understand what he was saying. She opened the door and listened.

"You and Wendy are trying to erase my circle and I don't understand why!" Wellington's voice echoed through the house. Jada expected Melanie to step outside her room but she didn't.

"I've never interfered with your marriage! Have I? Good-bye, man. I *will* talk to you later, but for right now, just stay out of my business!"

By the time Wellington clicked the phone, Jada was downstairs. "Baby, is everything all right? What was Walter talking about?"

"Don't worry about it. I'll talk to him later." Wellington leaned back on the chaise. Jada placed her hand inside his jacket and slowly smoothed her hand over the soft hairs on his chest.

Wellington was still disturbed. Jada thought it best if she deferred asking him any more questions. She went into the kitchen and poured two glasses of chilled Dom Perignon. On her way back into the living room, she noticed Melanie coming downstairs in a black lace ankle-length robe.

"Hey, nobody told me the party started already," said Melanie. "I'll get a glass and we'll toast."

Melanie's departure date could not come soon enough. Jada sat on the sofa. Wellington moved next to her and draped his arm over her shoulder.

Melanie pranced out of the kitchen with a full champagne glass in one hand and a newly opened bottle in the other. She plopped down on the opposite side of Wellington, crossed her legs, and said, "A toast to soulmates."

Wellington's mood started to improve, so Jada went with the flow. "A toast to soulmates," Wellington and Jada repeated in unison. Their glasses tipped together.

Melanie went into the kitchen and brought

back another bottle of champagne. "Let's just celebrate a great union of new friendships." She poured Wellington and Jada another glass of champagne. After five empty bottles lined the table, Melanie excused herself. "I'm going to go upstairs and shower. I'll be back."

Jada was happy Melanie had left. She batted her eyelashes at Wellington. "I brought some chocolate for *The Ruler.*" Wellington went from six to nine in five seconds. Clothes trailed from the couch to the shower. Wellington didn't wait for Jada to dry off. He tossed her towel on the floor and kissed her chocolate mounds. In the middle of foreplay, Melanie walked into the room wearing a red sheer robe. Her fingers barely wrapped around the handle of the overstuffed shopping bag she'd brought from the mall.

Wellington froze. The tip of his tongue stiffened. He flicked it back and forth across Jada's nipples. Jada's breasts were sandwiched between his hands. Jada looked at Melanie, then at Wellington, then at Melanie again. She couldn't believe Melanie was bold enough to just walk into Wellington's bedroom without knocking or anything.

"What the hell are you doing?" asked Jada.

"I bought the two of you *going-away* presents," responded Melanie. She handed Jada the neatly gold wrapped package tied with black lace. "You might want to put this on."

Wellington's erection throbbed uncontrollably between Jada's thighs. With his legs straddled on each side of Jada's hips, his dick began to penetrate the opening between her thighs. The head of his penis grazed her clit.

"Wellington, this one is for you." Melanie laid

Wellington's package by the side of the bed. "Carry on." Melanie walked toward the bedroom door.

"Wait!" Wellington paused. "You don't have to leave. *Please,* stay." Wellington looked at Melanie out of the corner of his eyes. His caramel lips swung from nipple to nipple like a pendulum. Then he bit each tip. Jada's nipples hardened. The sensation spread throughout her body and traveled down to her vagina. It pulsated faster than the throbs from Wellington's penis.

Jada felt rather adventurous from all the champagne. And it was obvious Wellington wanted both of them. "You don't have to leave, *if* you don't want to." Jada couldn't believe she said that. She had never been involved in a ménage à trois. But she had fantasized about it on many occasions, especially while she made love. Plus, after tomorrow, Melanie wouldn't be around.

"Are you sure? The two of you don't mind?" Melanie asked.

"Oh, we're sure," Wellington answered.

Jada eased from between Wellington's legs. She went into the bathroom. When she opened the package, she was pleasantly surprised. Melanie had bought the leopard outfit and all of the accessories. When Jada walked into the bedroom, Melanie had already handcuffed and blindfolded Wellington. Melanie's red robe dangled off the foot of the bed. Wellington's two hundred and twenty pounds of tasty caramel candy was spread across the bed six feet and four inches long. His little head stood at Melanie's attention, and sporadically danced back and forth as if it were doing *the jerk.* "Girl, that was quick." Jada posed by the bathroom door.

"You look yummy. Come on over. We're getting ready to play two games. The first one is the guessing game. Wellington has to guess which one of us is doing him."

"Let the games begin!" Wellington said. His dick whipped in the wind like a flag starting the Indy 500.

"Not so fast, trigger." Melanie tightened her fingers around Wellington's shaft. "I haven't finished explaining the rules."

"Women have rules for everything," Wellington responded. His penis budged short distances as if it were grumbling, "Let me go!"

"Wellington, when you guess wrong three times, the first game is over and we take off the blindfold and the handcuffs," explained Melanie. "Then we're going to play the wishing game. Everyone gets to make one wish, and whatever the wish may be, we all must agree to fulfill our obligation."

Melanie seemed so experienced. "I'm game," Jada said. She didn't want to come across like an amateur.

"Wellington, what about you, darling?" Melanie asked.

"Oh, yes indeed!" His dick broke away from Melanie's grip. "Can we play now?"

Melanie gestured for Jada to go first. Jada poured champagne over Wellington's private area. The bubbles flowed over his erection, down his balls, to the tip of Jada's tongue.

Jada paced herself. Wellington knew her so well she was certain the game would go on forever.

While she kissed and fondled his dick, Melanie glided her wet juicy tongue back and forth over Wellington's erect nipples, and then she pinched them real hard. Melanie never allowed her 38D's to come in contact with Wellington's body.

"That's not fair," said Wellington. "How am I supposed to guess who's doing what, if both of you are doing me at the same time?"

Melanie firmly held her hand in front of Jada signaling Jada to stop. Then Melanie pressed her index finger over her lips indicating for Jada to be silent.

"Hey! Why did you guys stop?"

"You have to guess who's doing what, even when we're both doing you," Melanie explained.

"More rules. You can't keep changing the rules in the middle of the game."

"Every game has rules. And if you don't play by them, then we don't play at all," said Melanie in a sweet seductive voice.

Wellington's erection was so hard, if it could have detached from his body, it would have blasted off like a rocket.

"All right," he reluctantly agreed. "Let's play."

Melanie signaled for them to continue. Jada poured a splash of bubbly over Wellington's private area and started to lick it off again. Melanie picked up where she left off. She caressed Wellington's nipples.

"Oh, my gosh," he said, "that's Jada licks." Jada smiled. She was pleased her man had guessed right the first time. "Jada is licking and pinching my nipples." Jada frowned.

"Strike one," Melanie said.

Wellington was wound up. "Who said that?" It

was definitely the champagne talking. Jada felt a little light-headed herself.

Melanie straddled Wellington. She squatted above his penis. Melanie shifted her opening in synch with the movements of Wellington's head until it was in the right spot. Then he disappeared inside her. She worked Wellington out like he was in an advanced aerobics class. Wellington moaned, groaned, and grunted. His body appeared completely relaxed.

Melanie flipped to sixty-nine. Jada watched in disbelief as Melanie's cherry-red lips plunged south nine times. Each time she suctioned a little harder. Each time she went an inch deeper. Ultimately she completely devoured him.

Damn! Jada's focus was redirected when Wellington pressed his thick and luscious lips against Melanie's. Melanie wrapped her hand around the base of Wellington's head. It became enlarged. Melanie licked the drops of fluid and gently sucked his head. Jada was turned on. She didn't interrupt them, but Wellington's ass had better not guess wrong this time. Jada repositioned to the side of the bed for a better view. She watched Wellington probe his tongue into the depths of Melanie's vagina. Jada wanted to cover Wellington's mouth.

It was like watching a live sex video. By the way Melanie's body stiffened, Jada presumed Wellington had captured the little man. His lips sucked softly. Jada stood motionless and watched. Melanie's body vibrated like she was overly accustomed to using the mechanical ones.

Wellington suddenly stopped as if he was trying not to climax. He blurted out, "I know that's my baby." There was a moment of silence. Then Melanie softly said, "Strike two."

"Got damn!" Wellington shouted. "I guessed wrong again?"

Melanie motioned for Jada to join them. "One more strike, and the game will be over." Melanie stroked Wellington's thighs with her cherry-red fingernails. Then she oiled her hands and slowly eased her finger into his rectum a little at a time.

Jada felt she had invested too much to quit at this point. Jada stroked Wellington's erection with rhythmic motions. She twisted with both hands roving in opposite directions while roaming up and down. Jada knew how to make her man's dick expand to its maximum length. Melanie continued to stimulate Wellington with her finger. She closely watched Jada.

Jada couldn't resist any longer. Melanie wasn't the only one who could handle a full-course meal. Jada took all of Wellington into her mouth. Jada showed Melanie how a professional handled business.

Jada gave it to Wellington the way he loved it. Melanie continued to slide her finger in and out of Wellington's rectum. Jada pressed against her G-spot. Her body went into convulsions. Melanie took her other hand and caressed Jada's breasts. First she massaged the left, then the right, and back again. Melanie's nails meandered down Jada's spine and between her cheeks. She slid her fingers in and out of Jada's creamy vagina.

Part of Jada refused to admit she was enjoying the moment, so she diverted her attention toward pleasing Wellington. Suddenly she felt a fast squirt of cum shoot into her mouth. Jada sucked like she was trying to get an oyster through a straw. She experienced back-to-back orgasms. One came from Wellington, the other from her vagina as Melanie continued to penetrate. Melanie's finger was still inside Wellington. His cum seeped from his limp muscle into Jada's mouth.

Finally Melanie said, "It's time to guess again."

"This one is easy. Jada is the only woman who has ever stuck her finger up my ass."

"What! How could you have guessed wrong three times in a row?" Jada sat back on her knees and waited for a response.

"Baby, don't get upset. It's just a game. I knew all along each and every time when it was you. But I also knew if I wanted to live to see thirty-six, I *had* to guess wrong. Well, at least take the blindfold and the handcuffs off." Jada took off the blindfold while Melanie unlocked the handcuffs.

Wellington's eyes popped out of his head. "Okay. Who gets to make the first wish?" he asked anxiously.

"Ladies first," said Melanie. "Jada, would you like to go first?"

"Sure. I like being first," Jada responded. Jada was adamant about not quitting. "I want—"

"You are to say, I wish," Melanie corrected her. This bitch was truly a control freak. "Okay. *I wish,*" said Jada, "Wellington would fuck you while I sit back and watch."

Wellington's eyebrows met at the center of his forehead. "Are you sure?" he questioned.

"Yes. I'm sure," responded Jada as she lounged back on the bedroom chaise with her hands behind her head. She always wondered what it would be like to watch her man fuck another woman.

Wellington began to have intercourse with Melanie. Shortly afterward, Melanie dominated the situation. Jada watched Melanie ride Wellington like it was opening day at the Black Rodeo. Then Melanie changed positions. "Get on top." She gripped his ass in the palms of her hands and yanked him in closer and harder with each stroke. Jada sprang from her semihorizontal position. She considered intervening.

"Give! It! To! Me!" shouted Melanie. She slapped Wellington's ass. "Give it all to me and don't you dare hold back." She spanked him again.

"Damn, girl. What course have you been teaching? Pussy Whipped 101?" Wellington asked.

"Oh, so you want to go to school? Is that it? Well, get up and fuck me in the ass," Melanie demanded.

"It's on," challenged Wellington.

"What in the hell is this? Opening day at the zoo?" Jada frowned and shook her head. Maybe they should be on exhibit in Oakland. At least that would increase the number of animals from two to four.

Smack! "What's my name? Say my name, damn it." *Smack!* Jada had never witnessed this side of Wellington.

"Wake me when you're done." Melanie covered her mouth and yawned.

Wellington pulled Melanie's hair. He slapped her so hard, Melanie's cheeks turned red.

"Big Daddy!" Melanie cried. "Take all of me. Big Daddy."

Wellington showered her with white chocolate cream. Melanie smoothed it on like it was lotion. Jada sat back on the chaise and folded her arms.

Melanie looked at Jada and smiled. "I get to make my wish next."

Jada didn't move. Jada questioned how she had allowed herself to get caught up in the game. She was definitely in too deep. If Melanie's wish had anything to do with Jada pleasing her, the game was definitely over.

Melanie said, "I wish Wellington would perform oral copulation on you, while I kick back and watch."

Jada perked up. She could handle this one. Maybe she could hang in there until Wellington made the last wish.

"Give me a few minutes to freshen up first." Jada smiled. If he hadn't volunteered, she was going to have to recommend it after watching him fuck Melanie in the ass. Jada was surprised. Wellington's penis looked clean when he pulled it out.

"Okay. I'm ready," said Wellington.

"You have great stamina," commented Melanie. Wellington smiled. He began performing oral copulation on Jada. She loved the fact that he knew all of her hot spots. Wellington had gained complete dominance over her when she reached her climatic peak.

One moment Jada moaned with great intensity, and the next thing she knew her ultimate orgasm had arrived.

"Damn, that was quick," Melanie commented. "It's a good thing I didn't pay to watch. Hell, Mike Tyson took longer than that to knock out Bruce Seldon."

"Damn, I'm tired," said Wellington. "But I'm *not too tired to watch*. I *wish* the two of you would make love to one another *and* each make the other have an orgasm."

"Oh hell no! Wellington, have you lost your mind? And besides, that's two wishes," said Jada.

"It's only a game," he explained.

"Well, playtime is over," said Jada. "Just the thought of me having to make her have an orgasm is repulsive."

"It's okay, Jada. I do understand," said Melanie. "But it's only fair that Wellington gets to watch something. So why don't I do you and Wellington can watch."

"In that case, bon appétit!" said Jada. She agreed just to see what Melanie would do. This was her opportunity to learn how one woman could possibly please another. Wellington sat up as if he had a front-row seat on the fifty-yard line at the Super Bowl.

"Lie down and relax," said Melanie. "Take a deep breath. Hold it. Release. Now completely relax your body. You don't want to be tense."

Melanie stroked Jada's breasts with a feather. Soft. Slow. Melanie teased. She glided it over Jada's abdomen. She outlined Jada's hairs and grazed it between her legs. She laid it aside. Melanie kissed and caressed Jada's tasty mounds of chocolate. Deliberately, she alternated from one to the other.

Jada released all of her tension and allowed her body to enjoy the experience. She noticed *The Ruler* had awakened. She watched Wellington masturbate. It turned her on more. She squeezed her breasts.

Melanie's tongue traveled toward Jada's navel and then to the innermost part of her thighs. It stopped at the tip of her clit. The sensation was the same as if it were a man. Jada tried to control her body's reaction, but couldn't. She realized a woman's head was between her legs. In the background, she heard Wellington stroking his penis. Jada reached an ultimate climax—which was her fifth or sixth— since Melanie's tongue had teased her. Wellington had his own sideline entertainment going.

Jada began to shout with delight because she could no longer suppress her fluids. She placed her hands on Melanie's head and pressed it firmly against her lips and continued to cum in her mouth. Melanie started to moan. Jada felt Melanie's body tremble like she was having an orgasm. How could that be? No one was stimulating her.

Wellington walked over to the bed and rained cum all over Jada and Melanie's lips at the same time. Melanie licked Wellington's cum right off his head, and then off Jada's clit. "You could definitely market this. It's lip-smacking good."

Melanie slapped Jada on the ass. She stood up, looked at Wellington, then at Jada. Smiled. "Thanks for the invite. I'm going to retire for the night and leave you two lovebirds alone." Just like that, she was gone.

Jada lay in the bed and stared at what seemed like millions of stars—through the huge skylight directly over Wellington's bed. Wellington was sound asleep. His heads rested against her breast and thigh. Jada's arm wrapped around his shoulders and rested on his chest. She closed her eyes. "What the fuck have I done?" she whispered.

Chapter 10

The morning after came too soon for Jada, but she was grateful it was Sunday. Wellington was still asleep. She kissed his lips and eased out of bed. Jada gathered Melanie's gifts and trashed them. She brushed her teeth, swallowed two Excedrin with a swig of leftover champagne, and headed out. Melanie's door was still closed.

The sunrise was blinding. Jada frantically searched for her sunglasses, put them on, and started the car. Her migraine was intensified by the nausea. She prayed to make it home without having to make a temporary stop.

Her head spun. The elevator ride took an eternity. As soon as the doors opened to her penthouse, Jada ran to the bathroom. She heaved. Only air would come up. She splashed cold water on her face and undressed. Wherever her clothes fell, they remained. She stretched across her bed.

Jada grabbed the towel next to her bed and threw up. The digital clock said eight-thirty. Great. This would give her almost two hours to recuperate before her church service. As soon as her head hit the pillow, the phone rang.

"Hello." Jada's voice was faint.

"Hi. Are you okay?" asked Candice.

"I just walked in. I've got to get some rest before church. What's up?"

"Everything's great," Candice responded happily.

Jada spiced up her voice to conceal her pain. "Sounds like love is in the air."

"I guess you could say that. Terrell and I have set the date. I'm moving to Los Angeles February fourteenth."

"February fourteenth? But Candice, that's my wedding day and you're my maid of honor!"

"Don't go getting all upset. I'll be here to support you through the entire event. You know that. So don't worry your pretty little head. You have enough to be concerned about.

"Look, I called to say my prison pen pal and I have really developed a good relationship." Jada wished her relationship with her pen pal were as strong. "She gets out in nine months. I promised her I'd visit this weekend and bring the things she requested." Jada got a fresh towel and laid it next to her.

"Jazzmyne asked me to speak at the church today about the success in our relationship. So I'm going to read two of our letters. Leslie gave me the green light to read hers." Jada really admired how Candice followed through on her commitments.

"Well, I'm glad you let me know," said Jada.

"Mama is riding with Robert this morning. That reminds me—I need to call Jazzmyne to see if they need a ride."

"You don't have to worry about that," said Candice. "Brother Dupree is picking them up. Jazzmyne told me yesterday." Jada was relieved. She could sleep a little longer. "How was your shopping spree with Melanie?"

Jada's heartbeat felt like it moved to her head. "I'll give you the details after church. Let me get off this phone. I'll see you at church."

"How's your pen pal?" Candice asked.

"Not well. She's fallen back into a deep depression. She keeps blaming herself for not protecting her daughter from being sexually molested by her man. It's unfortunate she trusted her man more than she trusted her own child. I'm going to visit her Wednesday. I've *got* to get off this phone." Jada placed the cordless on the charger. The phone rang again. Damn!

"Hello."

"Good morning, my Nubian Queen. You left without letting me know."

"No, I didn't. You didn't hear me because you were sound asleep. I decided not to wake you."

"Are you going to church this morning?"

"You know I'm not going to miss a Sunday in church if I can help it. I'm lying down trying to recover from last night's activities." Jada sighed.

"Yeah. I can ditto the recuperation part," said Wellington. "I'm beat."

"You going to church?" Jada asked.

"Not this morning," he responded. "But I plan on going to the seven o'clock service. Call me when you get back. I'd better go downstairs and eat breakfast before it gets cold."

"Breakfast sure sounds good. What did you cook?"

"Oh, I didn't. Melanie cooked. I'd better get going. You know I don't eat cold food. Call me when you get home."

"Sure." Jada placed the phone on the charger. She showered. She really needed to get to church on time.

Jada, Candice, and Jazzmyne arrived at church at the same time. They exchanged hugs and greetings. Brandon eagerly awaited his Sunday morning hugs and kisses from Jada and Candice.

Candice squeezed Brandon real tight. "How are you doing, little man?"

"I'm fine," said Brandon.

"Come here and give me a hug, Shelly," said Candice. Candice was in a much better mood than Jada. "Are you still doing wonderful in school?"

"Yes, ma'am! I'm still making straight A's," said Shelly. A proud smile accompanied the sparkle in her eyes.

"You know I'm so proud of you. Remember this, everyone is in your corner when you're doing great but when times get hard, even your best friends may turn their backs on you. I want you to know you can always count on me if you need anything." Shelly gave Candice a great big hug and a smile and ran off to greet one of her church friends.

"Thanks," said Jazzmyne. "She needed to hear that."

"Girl, what have you done to Brother Du-pree?" asked Candice. "He's just beaming and glowing."

"I haven't done anything to him, *yet,*" replied Jazzmyne. "He won't take no for an answer. He's nice to my children and we actually have a lot in common. I don't try to counsel him and he doesn't try to lecture me so we get along quite well." She laughed. "Jada, you look tired. Are you all right?"

"I'll be fine. I overindulged last night. I'm going straight home after church and get some rest."

"Let's go inside and get a seat before it gets too crowded," Jazzmyne suggested.

"Yeah, since Pastor Tellings started the pen pal program, the membership has doubled," said Candice.

"That's because there are so many of our church members and non-church members with relatives and loved ones in prison. Most of society prefers not to acknowledge their existence, including some congregations," said Jazzmyne. "More churches should fulfill the needs of the people and their community instead of the desires of the pastors."

"I hear you," said Candice. "You mean like the pastor *needs* a new car or we *need* a bigger church."

"Exactly," Jazzmyne said.

Jada remained silent. She felt psychologically trapped behind invisible bars. She replayed the prior night's events.

Jazzmyne sat with Brother Dupree. Jada and Candice sat two rows behind Mama and Robert.

Pastor Tellings opened his sermon with a poem entitled, "The Seed You Sow."

The seed you sow
Is the seed I will know
Actions speak louder than words

Not what you say
But what you do
Is what I see in you

The seed you sow
Will continue to grow
You cannot unplant a tree

You can dig it up
But hey, guess what
Your roots are what I see

My reactions to you
Your reactions to me
Are based on what we do

So don't say I'm wrong
When I sing your song
And sing it better than you

"There's an old saying," said Pastor Tellings. "'Put your money where your mouth is.' Well, I want to let you know that this congregation has stepped up to the plate. The male prison facility now has over five hundred *active* pen pals and the women have over four hundred. Many of you are visiting, and let me tell you, you have made a world of difference in their lives. *And* they have made a major difference in yours.

"I can see it in the way you fellowship among

one another," Pastor preached. "I can see it in the faces of the inmates when I visit the facilities and they're shouting, 'Tell Sister Brown I said hello,' or 'Tell Brother Johnson I love him, man.' But I want you to hear from Sister Candice Jordan this morning. She's going to share with you a letter she wrote to Leslie and a letter Leslie wrote to her."

Candice walked up to the front of the church. She stood behind the podium and lowered the microphone. "Good morning. First, I would like to say all glory be unto God. My pen pal, Leslie Washington, and I have been writing one another on a regular basis since Pastor Tellings started the program. After speaking with Sister Jazzmyne yesterday, she asked me to share our letters with you.

"First, I'll read my letter to Leslie and then I'll read Leslie's letter to me. Before I start, I want you to know Leslie gave me her blessings to read each letter.

Dear Leslie,

It's hard sometimes for me to believe you're only twenty-three years old. You are wiser than most who have been on earth seventy-five years. You opened your world to me and explicitly told me how your mother's boyfriend sodomized you at the age of seven. Then you said you ran away from home when you were twelve and lived on the streets for over a year before you went back home to your mother. My heart was saddened and my eyes were filled with tears. As if that weren't enough, you continued to calmly tell me how your mother traded your virginity to the drug dealers in exchange for crack. And how she allowed them to violate your precious temple to fulfill their selfish needs. I just wanted to run to where you were and hold you. I wanted to tell you everything would be all right. You explained how you turned to a life of prostitution because that was basically all you knew how to do to keep from being hungry. The tears poured down my face. But then you wrote me a letter and because of you I'm a stronger person, a better person, and I've learned not to judge others. Because of you I have a better understanding of the saying, Where you stand depends on where you sit. It's so very true. Leslie, I want you to know how much I appreciate you. How much I love you. I will be here for you when you get out in June of next year.

Your sister, your friend,
Candice.

"Now I'm going to read Leslie's letter to me:

Dear Candice,

You're the only person in my life that hasn't judged me. Turned your back on me. Kicked me to the curb and treated me like a slut, a whore, or a prostitute: basically like shit. I've never told anyone this before, but I've always dreamt of becoming a dancer. Most people don't even know I can dance. When I was a child, I danced to keep from hurting. I danced to keep moving. I felt if I could just keep moving, I could make it through another day. I believed if I could make it to another day, it would be better than the day before. Well, here I am twenty-three and still dancing. The inmates say I'm really good at it. There are a few who tell me I'll never be fa-

mous. But I just keep on dancing. When I get out of this awful place, Candice I'm going to dance for you. You are the only person in my life that truly cares about me. Tell Pastor Tellings I said God Bless him and tell him to keep doing positive programs for the community. If it weren't for him, I wouldn't have found you.

Your sister, your friend,
Leslie"

Everyone was in tears by the time Candice finished reading the letters, including Jada, as if her eyes weren't puffy enough.

Pastor Tellings closed the service. "Actions speak louder than words. If you haven't signed up for a pen pal, please do so today. There's someone out there who needs you."

Jada didn't want her mother to see how terrible she looked, so she rushed out of the church. In her haste to get home, Jada hurried past Jazzmyne and Candice. She could hear Jazzmyne thanking Candice. Candice yelled, "I'll stop by on my way home." Jada waved and kept walking toward her car.

On the way home, she called Wellington from her cellular.

"Jones residence," answered Melanie.

Now wasn't that cute. "Hi, Melanie. Let me speak with Wellington."

"You just missed him. He went to his mother's house. I'm not sure when he'll be back."

"Ask him to call me when he gets in." Jada felt her head pound in her throat.

"Anything for you, darling." Melanie hung up

the phone before Jada could get the next word out of her mouth. Jada could have sworn she'd heard Wellington's voice in the background. Maybe it was her imagination.

By the time Jada arrived home, Candice was parked in the visitor's space. Jada wasn't in the mood for company. She parked in the garage and met Candice in the lobby.

"Girl, you have got to get some rest," said Candice. The elevator doors opened. Candice walked straight to the kitchen. She proceeded to pull out a pot, a pan, and a skillet. "Here, drink this glass of cranberry juice and relax. I'll cook us something to eat and you can tell me what happened yesterday. Then you must get some rest."

"Thanks," responded Jada. She didn't know where to begin. She struggled to formulate a response in her head.

"Would you like grits, hash browns, and turkey bacon or hotcakes and sausage?" asked Candice.

"Grits. I'm not in the mood for anything sweet."

"Okay."

While Candice cooked breakfast, Jada busied herself and set the table. She needed to burn off the nervous energy.

After Candice said grace, she looked Jada in the eyes. "Tell me what happened. And I already know whatever it was, it wasn't good, so give it to me straight."

Jada didn't know where to begin, so she started with the shopping spree. Then she told Candice about the champagne. She hesitated and concluded with the games.

"You did *what?*" Candice placed her fork full of

grits on her plate. "Jada, that was stupid and you know how much I dislike using the word. But that didn't make any sense. What were you thinking?"

Jada knew Candice was going to give it to her straight. She had already kicked herself. The interesting part was, she didn't regret what she had done, only with whom she had done it.

"Well, it didn't seem like a bad idea at the time, but now I'm not so sure," Jada cried. Tears rolled down her cheeks and dripped onto the oriental silk print blouse she'd bought in Japan. "When I called Wellington this morning, Melanie was cooking *him* breakfast." A lump formed in Jada's throat. She swallowed hard. She needed Candice to shed some light on the situation.

"I tried to warn you that she couldn't be trusted," said Candice. "That whole thing about introducing you to Mrs. Jones's friends was probably part of her scheme to take advantage of you and your man. I just can't believe you let that happen, girlfriend." Candice shook her head and pushed her plate aside. She was angry. Jada wasn't. She was upset with herself for being oblivious to the big picture. Jada didn't know what to say, so she figured it was best not to say anything.

"Okay, let me calm down," said Candice. "Because I realize I'm not helping you. At least she's leaving today, so we don't have to worry about the aftershocks of Melanie's little games."

The word "aftershock" made Jada's body tremble with the thought of Melanie's head between her legs. "That's true," agreed Jada.

"I know Daddy would have had something to say about all this," said Candice. She looked at Jada and waited for a response.

"Daddy always said, never gamble greed against need. You'll lose every time. In retrospect, I realize there was nothing I needed that I didn't already have."

"Well, look," said Candice, "I want you to get some rest and don't do anything irrational. Go to bed. I'll clean the kitchen and let myself out. Call me when you wake up."

Jada hugged her and said, "Thanks. I really don't know what I'd do without my best friend."

"One last thing," Candice said. "Don't have any contact with Wellington until tomorrow. That'll give you time to compose yourself mentally and spiritually."

Jada removed her clothes and slid under the covers. She thought about what Candice had said about Melanie. Now that she could see the big picture, she concluded that Melanie had staged the sequence of events that led to last night's rendezvous.

Chapter 11

Melanie's investment had finally paid off. After ten home pregnancy tests, she cheered when she saw the pink plus sign. This time she wouldn't hide the results. She tucked it in her purse for safe-keeping. Melanie stood sideways in front of the bedroom mirror. She placed her hand over her belly. It was flat as a pancake but not for long. She stared at the photo she and Wellington had taken at Geoffrey's. Then she envisioned how beautiful their children would look. She'd never told a soul about the fertility drugs she'd taken for the past three months. She ran downstairs and kissed Wellington.

"What was that for?" he asked.

"Would you like to go with us to the airport?" asked Melanie.

"No, thanks. I think I'll stay here, but thanks for

offering. Tell your mother it was a pleasure seeing her."

"I'm sure she'll like hearing that," beamed Melanie. "She's very fond of you. Don't forget, I already prepared dinner, so if I'm not back in time to eat with you, you can warm a plate in the microwave."

"Thanks," said Wellington. "You should use my Jaguar to take your mother to the airport. I'll take your car to my repairman tomorrow so he can tune it up for you before you hit the highway."

"Sure. Thanks." Melanie picked up the keys to Wellington's brand new baby blue Jaguar. As Melanie cruised to pick up her mother, she thought about how naïve Jada was to have allowed anyone to become intimate with her fiancé. But there was no way Jada could have prevented the inevitable. Melanie Marie Thompson had finally found her soulmate. The thought of being pregnant crossed her mind. Her cherry-red lips spread east and west. Now that was truly divine intervention. She parked Wellington's car and ran into Mrs. Jones's house.

"Hi, Mother. Hi, Godmommy," Melanie said.

"Hi, baby. Slow down before you hurt yourself. My flight doesn't leave for another two hours," said Susan.

"Hello, darling," Cynthia responded. She hugged and kissed Melanie.

"Where's Daddy Chris?" Melanie asked.

"Oh, he went to the Raiders game with *Robert* today," Cynthia replied.

"They seem to be hitting it off pretty well," Melanie said.

"Yeah, too well if you ask me," said Cynthia. She walked out the door. Melanie and Susan followed behind her.

Melanie put her mother's bags in the trunk of Wellington's car. Cynthia rode in the front. Her mother sat in the back.

"Susan, you know we're excited. Our Melanie starts working at Sensations Communications in three weeks," Cynthia boasted.

"I am excited," Melanie said.

"So am I," said Susan. "I'm proud of you, Melanie. You're just like a cat, sweetheart. You always land on your feet. Now we just have to find you a husband like your sister Stephanie."

Melanie looked at Cynthia. Her eyes drooped low. She hated when her mother compared them.

"Melanie didn't tell you the good news, Susan. She and Wellington are going to get married."

"Did I miss something in the translation?" asked Susan. "Melanie, when did all of this happen?"

"Well, Wellington doesn't know it yet but—"

Cynthia interrupted. "Let's face it, Susan, Jada is *not* Jones material. I don't want my grandbabies growing up going to public school or thinking it is all right if they don't want to carry on the family tradition."

"I think the two of you are going too far," said Susan. "Jada is a wonderful young lady. What gives you the right, Cynthia, to dictate who Wellington marries?"

"I'll comment on both," replied Cynthia. "Yes, Jada is wonderful. She's just not good enough for my Wellington. Now mind you, if I hadn't taken Wellington in, he'd probably be dead. I don't ask

Wellington for much. This is the *very least* he can do for me."

"Melanie, how do you feel about all of this?" Susan asked.

"Mother, I just want to start work at my new job and let whatever happens between Wellington and Jada happen," Melanie said with a quick wink to Cynthia.

"Well, mother to daughter, I have to warn you, Melanie. This time you may not land on your feet. You might fall flat on your ass. When you play with fire, you will get burned. And speaking of fire, Cynthia, I hope you burn in hell. Wellington doesn't owe you a damn thing," said Susan.

"Well, here we are, San Francisco International Airport," Cynthia said.

"I'll just check in curbside," Susan said. "Melanie, remember what I said. Now, open the trunk so I can get my bags." Susan didn't wait for Melanie to respond.

Melanie's eyes welled with tears. "Don't worry about me, Mama. I'll be fine." Melanie waved good-bye but Susan never turned around.

Cynthia let down her window. "Bye, Susan. Have a safe flight. Call me when you get home, *darling*, to let me know you arrived safely." Susan kept walking.

"Godmommy? Why do you think she hates me so much?"

"Susan loves you, darling. She's just conservative. She'll come around. Give her some time."

"It's almost six o'clock, so I hope you don't mind if I drop you off and head back to the house," Melanie said.

"That's fine, darling. I'm tired from all the weekend activities and need to get my rest," said Cynthia.

"Wellington thinks I'm leaving tomorrow," said Melanie. "Should I tell him about my new job?"

"No. It's best if I tell him," Cynthia replied.

"Do you think I should tell him I'm pregnant?"

"Pregnant! Already! Melanie, you were supposed to wait until *after* the wedding. Oh, my dear. What will my friends think?"

"Well you were the one who said *do it*," cried Melanie.

"I didn't mean have sex. I meant get him to notice you. Oh, my! Look, you're going to have to tell Wellington tonight because he's going to have to marry you before the news gets out that you're expecting. I'll be the laughingstock of the world. I can't believe this is happening," Cynthia said disapprovingly.

"Drive carefully darling. I'll call you tomorrow." Cynthia slammed the car door so hard, Melanie jumped.

Melanie felt abandoned and desperate. She listened to the radio and pondered her dilemma. Booga Bear was advertising his new soulmate rings. A light went off in Melanie's head and she detoured to the jewelry store.

She frantically banged on the door. "I need to buy a ring!"

"Sorry, miss, we're closed. You'll have to come back tomorrow."

Melanie pulled out cash and waved it at the salesman. He opened the door. "You'll have to make it quick. What do you want?" He was cold and callous.

"I need a wedding band for a man. Let me see the one with the diamonds."

"That ring costs twelve thousand dollars, miss."

"I didn't ask how much it cost. I asked to see the ring." Melanie closely examined the ring. It appeared flawless. "I'll take it."

She handed him her American Express card. He completed the transaction and handed it back. He started to wrap the ring. "Oh, that won't be necessary," Melanie said. She snatched the ring box, put it in her purse, and hopped in the Jag.

"Hey, you made it back fast," said Wellington. "What did you do? Fly your mother to the airport?"

"I did not." Melanie laughed. "I drove her to the airport. Thank you very much."

"I was just about to eat dinner. Why don't you join me?" asked Wellington.

"I'd be delighted to," said Melanie. She kept her purse next to her on the seat.

"So, are you excited about returning to D.C. tomorrow?" asked Wellington.

"I've been meaning to talk to you about that. I don't think I'm leaving tomorrow," said Melanie. She tried to feel her way through this awkward predicament.

"Why?" Wellington placed his fork on his plate and waited for a response.

"Wellington. You and I have been friends for a long time. Over the past two weeks, I've fallen in love with you." Melanie paused.

Wellington stood and rubbed his bald head. "Look, Melanie. I'm very fond of you. I care for you—as a friend. But Diamond is my woman and I'm in love with *her,* not you."

"Wellington. Please, sit down." Melanie picked

up her purse and removed the box. She kneeled at Wellington's feet and opened it. "Wellington Jones. Will you marry me?" Melanie's eyes swelled with tears.

Wellington pushed his chair back. "This is way too serious for me. Melanie, I *will not* accept a ring from you. No pussy can come between me and Diamond. She's my soulmate. Melanie. Read my lips. I love Jada, *not you.*"

Melanie felt the lacerations of Wellington's words. She stood and threw the ring on the table. It bounced off and hit the floor, but she couldn't tell where it had landed. She didn't bother to look for it. She had more important concerns. "Well, maybe no pussy can come between you two, but how about a baby! Wellington Jones. I'm pregnant with your child!" Melanie yelled.

Wellington grabbed his head and paced back and forth. "Tell me you're kidding. This is not happening. Aren't you using some form of contraceptive?"

"No. I'm not."

"Why didn't you tell me?"

"You didn't ask. Look, all I'm asking is that you think about the proposal. You don't have to decide right away." Melanie walked over to Wellington and tried to hold his hand. He pulled away.

The doorbell rang. "Are you expecting someone?" asked Wellington.

"No."

Wellington opened the door. "Hi, baby." Jada kissed him on the lips and walked in. "Hi, Melanie. I see you're still here." Jada's eyes shifted from Wellington to Melanie and back to Wellington. Her voice trembled. "What's going on?"

Melanie turned toward the stairs. "Don't you dare take your ass up those stairs until I know what the hell is going on!" Jada screamed with authority.

"Let's go in the family room," suggested Wellington.

Melanie sat in the reclining chair near the fireplace. Wellington sat on the couch. Jada braced herself on the edge of the sofa next to him.

"I have some not-so-good news," said Wellington. "But it's not something we can't work out."

Jada looked at Wellington. Melanie smiled mischievously. "What are you saying?" Jada's voice was faint.

Wellington rubbed his goatee. "Melanie is pregnant."

"Well, obviously it's not yours. Hell, this shit just happened last night!"

Melanie remained silent. Wellington took a deep breath. His hands covered his face. He reached for Jada's hand. She moved it. "I have to be totally honest with you, ba. Last night wasn't the first time."

Jada's eyes rolled to the back of her head. Before she realized what she'd done, her backhand landed on the side of Wellington's face. She jumped up from the couch and headed for Melanie. Melanie scrambled but she couldn't get up fast enough. Neither could Wellington. Jada reached back to 2000 B.C. Melanie saw it coming but couldn't escape. Melanie saw stars as she slid across the Billie Holiday rug like she was sliding into home plate—head first. Well, at least Melanie found the ring. Jada didn't wait for any further explanations. She walked out and slammed the door.

* * *

Candice had warned her not to go over to Wellington's house. But again, Jada hadn't listened. Now, she was flaming mad. She needed a drink. Jada got in her car. Her tires screeched, smoked, and left black tracks in Wellington's driveway.

She pulled into the first dive she saw on the peninsula. Before she could make it to the bar, Jada heard, "Hi, may I buy you a drink? You look like you need one," said the stranger at the table nearest the door.

"Sure. Why not." Jada sat across from him like he had been waiting on her.

"Let me guess, your husband is having an affair."

Jada sighed. "I'm not married."

"Well, you could have fooled me with that rock on your finger."

"It's my engagement ring."

"Well, I don't know what ails you, but you sure look too pretty to have men problems." He chuckled like an old man. It contradicted his youthful exterior. Jada assumed he was about twenty-four.

"I'm not sure it's the man I'm having the problem with."

He leaned back in his chair. His blue-black complexion was stunningly gorgeous. "Well, I'm a great listener if you want a shoulder to cry on." His lips easily separated when he spoke. His teeth were white as snow. "Go right ahead."

Jada rambled on with bits and pieces of her story. She liked the fact that he wasn't judging her. He simply listened. She tiptoed around the ménage à trois. It wasn't her fault, and it wasn't his business.

Three drinks and two hours later, Jada confessed, "Well, I've cried on your shoulder enough. I think I'll just leave now."

"Don't leave without my phone number." He handed Jada a business card and smiled. "If you ever need another shoulder to cry on, I still have a dry one left." He wiped the tears from Jada's eyes and kissed her on the forehead. "Don't worry about the bill. It's on me."

"Thanks." Jada stood and smoothed out her dress. Her hand had started to swell. It felt numb. On her way out, she noticed Wellington's friend Walter was sitting in the sports section watching a game.

Jada didn't want to go home and she definitely wasn't going to call Candice. She drove around aimlessly. She tried to unweave the web of deception. But the sticky threads were too tightly woven. Her emotions vacillated. Anger. Disgust. Hurt. Betrayal. Denial. She grew tired of haphazardly driving up and down Interstate 580. If she never popped the cork on another bottle of champagne, it wouldn't bother her.

Jada stopped at a Safeway and went inside.

She walked past the dairy section. Paused. Walked backward and noticed eggs were on sale. Buy one dozen and get the second free. A light went off in her head. She purchased a bottle of zinfandel and the eggs. She drove to Wellington's house. Twenty-four eggs later Wellington could have named his place the House of Egg Fu Yung. Jada threw eggs on the door, the lawn, the Jaguar, and Melanie's car. She wished he had a dog so she could crack one over its head.

Jada went home. She ignored the little voice inside her. "What in the fuck have you done? That was really dumb. Stupid. Stupid. Stupid." It sounded like Candice's voice. Jada thought she had outgrown her temper tantrums. Maybe this time she should seek professional help. Wellington was going to be pissed when he woke up in the morning and saw dried eggs splattered everywhere. Maybe she would lie and say it wasn't her.

As soon as Jada got home, her phone rang.

"Hello."

"Girl, where in the world have you been? I told you to call me when you woke up," Candice said.

"I know, but I decided to visit Wellington instead. I wished I would have picked up the phone and called you," Jada cried.

"What happened this time?" asked Candice.

Jada told Candice everything.

"Jada, I warned you this would happen. Now do you believe me?"

"I don't know what to believe anymore," Jada responded. "I'm going to bed. Maybe it'll be better in the morning. At least I can go to work early and get a head start." Jada sighed. "I need to prepare for my photo shoot of Justice Price. I'll speak with you tomorrow." Jada really didn't feel like hearing *I told you so* again.

"Good night, egg woman," Candice laughed. "Get some rest. I'll call *you* tomorrow."

Chapter 12

Melanie was ecstatic. Jada's ongoing outrage had become a thorn in Wellington's side. Cynthia had almost convinced Wellington to honor his obligation to the family's name by making Melanie a decent and respectable woman. Susan was wrong. Melanie had landed on her feet, once more.

"Well, how do I look for my first day at work?" asked Melanie. Her hair was pulled back into a bun like a flight attendant. Melanie's neutral-colored lips were lined in a light shade of brown to match her nail color. Her fashionably conservative suit was tailored to a tee. The skirt hem stopped six inches above her knees.

"You look great," said Wellington. "I still can't believe my mother got you a job working at Sensations Communications. Jada's going to have another outburst when she sees you."

"Wish me well." Melanie blew Wellington a kiss. She didn't want to smear her lipstick.

"They are going to love you," Wellington responded.

"I'll call and let you know how it's going," Melanie said. She drove Wellington's Jaguar. She loved it so much she'd stopped driving her own car.

Melanie thought about Jada. The permanent scar on her forehead wouldn't let her forget. She vowed to get even if it was the last thing she'd do.

The Bay area's rush-hour traffic was more than she'd bargained for. She crept bumper-to-bumper almost the entire trip. She refused to cease driving the Jag so she'd either find an alternate route or time. Mr. Murphy had mailed her electronic keycard-parking pass in advance. The buildings in downtown D.C. were midgets in comparison to San Francisco's skyscrapers.

Melanie strolled into the office as if she owned it. "Good morning."

"Good morning. You must be Ms. Thompson."

"Yes. Melanie Marie Thompson. I can see by your nameplate, you are Karen Livingston."

"Let me show you to your office. It's the best office we have; second only to Mr. Murphy's. It has a breathtaking panoramic view of the city, and because it's a corner office, it has more square footage. Mr. Murphy said someone by the name of Cynthia *insisted* you have it. In case you haven't heard, you've already been bumped up to senior vice president in charge of international marketing. That means you'll supervise all employees in the national and international divisions," explained Karen. "Let me introduce you to the best photographer we have on staff in our national marketing division."

"*Had,*" said Melanie, with a sarcastic look plastered on her face.

"Please, be kind. She had to move out of the office that's now yours," Karen whispered. Then she turned and smiled. "Jada, this is Melanie Marie Thompson, our newest staff member in charge of international operations," said Karen. Karen stared back and forth from Jada to Melanie. "Melanie, this is Jada Diamond Tanner. Sensations finest. You won't find a better—"

"This is starting to turn into a nightmare from hell. How in the world did *she* get *this* job?" Jada questioned.

"I'm not so sure you've met *me* before," Melanie said. Then she turned to Karen. "Ms. Livingston, when Mr. Jones calls, put him through to *my* office." Karen stood in Jada's office. Karen hunched her shoulders.

"I'll explain it to you later," said Jada. "Send Wellington's calls directly to my office."

"I'll leave you two *lovebirds* alone." Jada's face turned burnt red. Karen returned to her desk. Melanie went to her office.

"Good morning, Ms. Thompson. I'm really impressed with your résumé," Terrance said. "You didn't need Mrs. Jones to get this job. I would have hired you on the spot based on your credentials."

"I'm not the impressive one, Mr. Murphy, you are," Melanie said. "If I can achieve half of what you've done by the time I'm your age, I'd *retire* at forty-nine."

"Now, how do you know my age?" Terrance

asked with a deep and hearty laugh. He was a short man—about five feet six inches—with broad shoulders. Clean-shaven. His navy blue suit was impeccable.

"Well, you don't look it. You look younger. But let's say, I've done my research and I'm very impressed with the empire you've built," Melanie said.

"Well, I hope you came ready to work," said Terrance, "because I didn't build this empire just sitting around looking good."

"If I didn't know any better, I'd swear that was a compliment."

"It was, Ms. Thompson. I'll let you get situated. Karen will give you a tour of the photo lab, the gallery, and the indoor areas where we shoot. I hope you like Spain because you'll be traveling abroad, real soon."

"I'm starting to like this place already," said Melanie as she clicked open her briefcase. Melanie turned up the volume on her interoffice intercom. It was one of the perks she liked most about being *the boss*.

"Hi, Wellington, I'm so glad you called. I was thinking about you," Melanie said.

"I just wanted to wish you well on your first day. That's all."

"Thank you!"

"How's Jada?" Wellington asked.

"I have to take a tour of the facility right now, but promise me you'll call me later. Kiss. Kiss."

Melanie disconnected Wellington's call and heaved a huge sigh.

"It's time for your tour, Ms. Thompson. Are you ready?" Karen asked.

"I *sure* am," Melanie said. She locked her office door.

"Oh, that's not necessary around here," explained Karen.

"Oh, but it is for me, darling," Melanie responded. "Shall we?"

"You're the boss," replied Karen.

"So, Ms. Livingston, I couldn't help but notice the photo of the handsome young man on your desk," said Melanie. "Is that your son?"

"Yes," Karen said, beaming. "That's the one and only Damien Jamal Livingston Jr."

"He's handsome. How old is he?"

"Fifteen. And in two more years he'll be out of school and hopefully out of the house," said Karen with a smile.

"Where's he going to college?"

"Oh, we haven't thought that far ahead," replied Karen.

"Haven't *thought* that far? When are you planning on getting started, darling?"

"I can't afford to send Damien to college," said Karen defensively, then pointed out more calmly, "This is the main photo lab."

"Who said *you* have to pay for it?" Melanie asked. "There are scholarships and grants galore. Where there's a will, there's a way."

"Well, Damien wants to join the military when he graduates," said Karen. Karen opened and closed the door to the developing room.

"Excuse me for being so blunt, Karen, but the military is no place for a young black male."

"Is there anyplace in this world for a black man? Young or not?" asked Karen. "This is the photo gallery."

Melanie walked around the room slowly. "No, not for one who is afraid to pursue his dreams," said Melanie. "But just the opposite is true if a black man is determined to pursue his greatness. The operative word is *determined*. Look at Mr. Murphy, he's a prime example of what can be accomplished if you're not afraid to live your dreams. Does Damien have a mentor?"

"A mentor. Why does he need a mentor?" Karen asked. "He has a father. This is the most recent wing to the gallery."

Melanie was thoroughly impressed. The photo journalist position she had in D.C. did not compare. "You have got to open your mind. Black male children need as many positive role models as possible in their lives. Here you are working for one of the most *powerful* black men in this country, soon to be in this world when I finish helping him build his empire, and you haven't asked him to mentor your son."

"I can't. He won't," said Karen. "Mr. Murphy is a busy man. He doesn't have time for Damien."

"Ask him, Karen. Ask him today," Melanie insisted.

"I'll ask but I already know the answer."

"Just tell me the answer after you ask the question," Melanie said.

"Well, that completes our tour. Everett Paris is scheduled for an eight o'clock shoot in the morning. If there's anything I can assist you with, please let me know," Karen said.

"Thank you, Ms. Livingston, you're quite the professional." Melanie shook and held Karen's hand. "There is one more thing."

"Yes." Karen loosely held Melanie's hand.

"Ask Mr. Murphy for a raise. You deserve it." Melanie walked into her office, closed the glass door, and turned on her intercom.

"Hello. This is Karen in the photography department. I'd like to schedule an appointment to meet with Mr. Murphy today." Melanie thumbed through the executive manual and smiled.

"He has a ten-minute opening available if you can come right now. Otherwise you'll have to wait until Friday."

"I'll be right there," Karen said.

Melanie heard an unfamiliar voice so she clicked on her viewer. There was a delivery person at Karen's desk with three-dozen yellow roses.

"For me?" Karen said jokingly.

"If your name is Melanie Marie Thompson, they're all yours." He smiled. Melanie zoomed in the camera. His two front teeth were missing. She frowned, and then laughed. The flowers she had delivered to herself had finally arrived.

"Well, that's not my name," said Karen. "But she's in her office. It's the last one on your left. Wait. Do you know who sent them?" Jada walked up to Karen's desk.

"Compliments of a Mr. Wellington Jones." The delivery guy smiled wide and made his eyes bulge.

"Really! I knew he couldn't stay mad at me forever." Jada jumped up and down. Tears rolled down her chocolate cheeks.

"If your name is Melanie Marie Thompson, they're all yours." He nodded once.

Melanie cried out with laughter. Jada ran into her office, picked up the phone, and furiously punched in Wellington's number. "How could you send *her* flowers to *my* job?" she demanded into the receiver.

"Flowers? What flowers?" Wellington paused. "Look, I have a broker on one line and a client on the other. I'll have to call you back." Wellington hung up.

Melanie greeted the deliveryman at her door. "Oh, for me! My goodness. Who sent such lovely roses? *And* so many." Melanie slipped him a fifty for his troubles and winked. He winked back and smiled.

"Thanks, but you're evil. You know that?"

"Thanks for the compliment," Melanie said.

"Karen, can I see you in my office for a moment?" said Jada.

"Sure, I'll be right there."

Melanie meticulously arranged the flowers and listened.

"Karen, I probably shouldn't tell you this but—"

"If you probably shouldn't tell me—"

"Melanie is a friend of the Jones family and very well liked by *Mrs.* Jones."

"She's a very likable person," Karen responded.

"*Anyway,* " Jada continued. "Initially, she was visiting for a couple of weeks. Then returning to D.C."

"I love D.C.," Karen said. "Did she graduate from Howard?"

"Look, Karen, if you don't want to hear the story, let me know."

"I'm sorry, you're right," Karen said.

"I'm not sure how she knew about this job or who helped her get it, but I want you to check her file and let me know."

"This is better than the soap operas. But you're asking me to risk my job *and* compromise my integrity. I can't do that. Not even for a *friend*. Sorry. I thought you were going to tell me something." Karen returned to her desk. Melanie was satisfied with Karen's response so she turned off the recorder.

"Sensations Communications, this is Ms. Livingston."

"Hello, Karen?" Melanie's ears perked up.

"Don't tell me. Let me guess," Karen said. "This is *Mr.* Darryl *NBA* Williams."

"The one and only."

"Where have you been?" Karen asked.

"You know the season has started, so I have very little *free* time on my hands. But I always have time for Jada. Is she in?"

"Yes, she is."

"Hi, baby. How are you? I've missed you so much I just had to call and hear your voice," Darryl said.

"I've been doing great," Jada responded.

"How are the wedding plans?" Darryl asked. Melanie was surprised.

"Everything is going along as planned." Well, she didn't lie, thought Melanie. But she didn't exactly tell the truth either.

"That's cool. So can your number one fan take you out to dinner or is that *still* off-limits?"

"Let me think about that and I'll call you back next week," Jada said.

"Next week?"

"Please, Darryl. I have a lot on my mind right now. I promise I'll call you."

Jada hung up, picked up her purse, and walked out. "Karen, I'm leaving for the day. Send my calls through to my voice mail."

"Will do," said Karen.

*   *   *

Jada arrived at Wellington's by six-thirty that evening and tried her key. "Damn. He was serious about changing the locks." Before she could put the keys back in her purse, Melanie opened the door.

"Hi, Jada. How can I help you?"

Jada brushed past Melanie and entered Wellington's office. "Wellington Jones, I need to speak with you right this minute."

Wellington's eyes narrowed and his lips tightened. His backhand waved in the air like he was sweeping crumbs off his collar. Jada interlocked her arms, extended her left foot, tilted her head, and waited. She looked over her right shoulder. Melanie was nowhere in sight.

"I apologize, Mr. Gray, can I call you back in five minutes? I have an emergency I need to take care of immediately. I *promise*. I'll call you back in five minutes tops." Wellington pressed the disconnect button and slammed the phone. "Are you crazy? *You* are interfering with my livelihood now and I'm not going to accept this! Mr. Gray is one of my largest investors." Wellington stood directly in front of Jada. "Now you have a choice—you can either wait until I finish working with my clients, *or* you can leave."

Teardrops clung to the edges of Jada's eyelids.

She couldn't believe he was the same person she'd met last year. "What has happened to us, Wellington?" She placed her hands on his biceps. His body felt wonderful. Her pussy pulsated once. She shivered. She missed her man.

"Look, just give me a few minutes and we'll talk." Wellington smiled and stroked Jada's cheek.

Jada walked into the living room and sat on the couch. Melanie was lying on the chaise watching the world news.

"I'm about to prepare dinner." Melanie grinned. "Will you be joining us?"

It was a good thing for Melanie she was pregnant because, as angry as Jada was, she would have turned that scene into the WWF championship. "Thanks, but no thanks," Jada said softly. It was strange. Jada used to feel so comfortable at Wellington's. Now she felt like an intruder.

Wellington walked into the living room. "Hi, my Nubian Queen."

Jada looked around the room like an owl. He couldn't have possibly been talking to her. And he had better not have been speaking to Melanie. Was this the same man who'd yelled at her moments ago? "I haven't heard you call me that in a long time."

"Yeah, I know. It's long overdue. Let's go out for dinner so we can talk."

"I'd like that." Jada refused to give Melanie the satisfaction of looking in her direction. Wellington opened the door. "Here's your key." They laughed.

"How does Pier 39 sound?" Wellington suggested as he placed the key in Jada's ignition. She refused to leave her car at his house.

"Excellent choice." Jada reflected on the beautiful moments they had shared at the pier. They would sit for hours and watch the seals. They secretly fed the seagulls. They would have lengthy discussions about what they could see on Alcatraz Island through the telescope. Then they would ride over on the boat and try to find what they saw. A quick laugh escaped her lips. Jada remembered how Wellington gave her a horseback ride and galloped around the carousel. He was her stallion. People stared. They didn't care. Wellington kept trotting until the carousel stopped. Jada could hear the sista with the British accent. "How much to ride that one? He's sexy." Wellington mimicked, "Closed to the public, miss. You'll have to get your own."

"We haven't been here in a long time," Jada said. She held Wellington's hand. They strolled along the pier.

"Yeah, I remember the first time I brought you here," Wellington responded. "You were wearing your blue jeans and that sexy scarf with the African design that you wrapped around your breasts and you wore a matching head wrap. That was sexy."

"I didn't realize you noticed such details." Wellington didn't respond. He didn't have to. Jada tasted the same bittersweet lump in her throat. Wellington walked in complete silence until they entered the restaurant.

"Mr. Jones, we were able to reserve your regular table by the window," said Ralph. "It's good to see our favorite couple."

"Thanks, Ralph," Wellington said as he flipped him a twenty. They were seated at their table overlooking the bay.

"Diamond, I remember almost everything

about you." Wellington picked up the conversation as if it had never ended. "But I don't *ever* remember you acting so irrational." His dreamy eyes drooped.

Jada backstroked in her pool of emotions. "I'm not irrational." Her emotions began to discount her intellect. "Well, maybe you're right. But it's not my fault. It's all because of Melanie. She has manipulated our relationship. I started feeling like I was losing my soulmate," Jada rambled. She desperately needed Wellington's love and understanding.

"Maybe I was *wrong* about us being soulmates," Wellington said. His eyes seemed to look straight through Jada.

Suddenly her emotions took a dip in the pool. She frantically dog-paddled to stay afloat. "What are you talking about? How can you doubt our love?" This wasn't the Wellington Jones that Jada used to know.

"Here's the bottle of Dom you ordered, Mr. Jones," said their waiter, Dominic. "Would you like to sample and give your approval?"

"No need to sample, Dominic," said Wellington. "You can pour the lady a glass and I'll have one too."

"Certainly."

"Wellington. I'm waiting for a response."

"Jada, I thought we were soulmates, but then you changed on me. I saw a side of you I'd never seen before. I didn't realize you had such an awful temper. You always seemed so peaceful. Jada, this was the first authentic challenge to our relationship. And your actions proved you didn't trust me. When I tried to open up to you, you slapped my face and ran out the door. When I called you, you hung up on me. When I went to sleep, you turned my house into the Hunan Garden."

Jada looked out the corner of her eye. Her lips curled.

"I'm serious, damn it! This is *not* a joke," Wellington continued. "You didn't try to meet me halfway. I made a mistake. I was honest enough to share that with you. I'm not perfect and I don't try to be. I told you that the first time we went out. And now that you're ready to talk, am I supposed to be ready too? Look, I still love you. I'll always love you. But I don't think it's a good idea for us to get married."

The wind escaped Jada's lungs. She had been hit below the belt. Jada's heart sank to the bottom of the pool. Every time she gasped for air, she swallowed water. "Wellington, how could you do this to us?" Her salty tears plopped into her glass of champagne. The bubbles fizzled. "It's your mother, isn't it? She's telling you to do this. Cynthia never has liked me. If she tells you to jump, you ask how high."

Wellington remained calm. "Leave my mother out of this, Jada. I'm warning you. When are you going to take a long look in the mirror? You have yet to acknowledge you've played your part." Wellington's dreamy eyes grew stone cold.

"So I guess you *are* going to marry Melanie!" Jada shouted. "Is that what you brought me here to say?"

"Actually, I just wanted to see if we could have a heart-to-heart talk. But I do respect Melanie. At least she's woman enough to admit her mistakes. It's not her fault she got pregnant. I've accepted my responsibility. And I do have an obligation to make her a decent and respectable woman. I don't want to bring children into this world out of wedlock. Jada, I'm hurting. I'm in pain, and I admit, I am confused. Look, I'm sorry all of this has happened, but I want to do what's right."

"Sorry! You're sorry! You've got that right, you really are sorry."

"Should I bring you the check, sir?" Dominic whispered.

Wellington stood. He placed one, two, three one-hundred-dollar bills on the table and handed Dominic a fifty. Then he strolled out like Denzel Washington.

When Jada got outside on the pier, Wellington was nowhere in sight. She heard a familiar voice behind her.

"Ms. Tanner. Mr. Jones asked me to give you your keys. Here is your validation. Do have a good night," said Ralph. Jada's heart felt lifeless.

When Wellington arrived back at his home, he noticed his Jaguar had been wrecked. He shook his head and walked inside. "What happened to my car?" he asked Melanie.

"I reported it. I told the police I didn't recognize the car or the driver, but it was definitely Jada. Poor thing, she should calm down before she suffers a heart attack and dies."

"I'm starving," Wellington said.

"I'll cook you something. What would you like?"

"Well, let's just say it's already cooked." Wellington flicked his eyebrows twice.

Melanie raced upstairs to Wellington's bedroom.

He playfully chased her. She stripped off all their clothes. His lust escalated. Wellington stroked his penis. There was no response. He desperately needed to release his frustrations. He stretched his dick as far as he could. It snapped back like a rubber band.

"Suck it for me?" Wellington asked. Melanie bowed on her knees. There was no response. He pushed back and pulled harder. His penis wouldn't expand.

Finally, Melanie said, "Look, you have a lot on your mind. Relax and let me take control."

Melanie massaged every muscle in Wellington's body. Then she slid his seven-inch dick inside her. She squeezed him from top to bottom. Wellington moaned with relief when he felt the other two inches add on.

"Don't move. That's my spot," Melanie said.

Wellington's head expanded like an overstuffed sausage ready to burst through its skin. Melanie rocked back and forth and rolled her hips in a grinding motion. "Oh, that's my spot. Don't move," she repeated. Wellington felt Melanie hit her G-spot again and again. He licked his finger and rubbed it along the shaft of her clit.

"I'm cumming!" Melanie yelled.

Wellington stroked her clit faster. His fluids shot off in her like Fourth of July fireworks. His body went limp with gratification.

Melanie continued to grind as she licked and sucked her own nipples. Wellington reached for the little black box on his headboard and opened it. Melanie was so excited she didn't wait. "Yes! Yes! I *will* marry you."

Chapter 13

Jada spent the next month wondering: Was it her fault? Was Wellington to blame? Melanie? What could she have done differently? She slouched on her sofa. Her eyes wandered aimlessly.

Jada's heart ached. She didn't deny she was still in love with Wellington. But at what point would she get over him and at what cost? She had already lost twelve pounds. With each passing day neither her migraines nor her nausea would subside. Jada faintly heard the phone rang. She had turned the volume down to its lowest.

"Hi, baby, this is Mama. Are you keeping your appointment with Dr. Bates today? I'm really concerned about the migraine headaches you've been having lately."

"Yes, Mama, I'm going to keep my appointment and Candice is going with me. How's Mr. Hamilton?"

"Oh, Robert is fine. We went to the movies yesterday," Mama laughed. "I really do enjoy his company. If he gets any funnier, we're going to have to put him on Comicview."

"I'm happy for you, Mama." Robert made Mama feel young again.

"You know I spoke with Jazzmyne last night. She said she's willing to talk with you and Wellington."

"Wellington would never agree to talk with Jazzmyne." Jada wasn't sure if she wanted to talk with Jazzmyne or Wellington. Jada selected a gold sarong and tied it about her waist.

"Well, she has a way of getting information and people don't even realize it," Mama said. "She said if you preferred, she could go to Wellington's house. Talk with him. Then come to your house. Just think about it. If you decide you want her help, let her know."

Jada checked her hair and her makeup. Just because she didn't feel good didn't mean she had to look bad. "Sure, Mama, I'll keep that in mind. I have to go. Candice is here. I love you. Bye."

"Bye, baby. I love you too."

"Hey, girl. How are you feeling today?"

"You know how it is. You are constantly in pain until you go to the doctor. At the moment, my head hurts a little. But I bet you any amount of money, as soon as I step out of Dr. Bates's office, it'll feel like someone's pounding on it with a hammer."

"It's only temporary and self-imposed, mind you. You know the minute you get what you want—or get over Wellington—you'll be fine. I'll drive," Candice said. "You ready?"

"Yeah, let's go." Jada gave her a hug.

"Perhaps a vacation will help clear your mind." Candice reached for the button to turn on the radio.

"I've been thinking about taking some time off," Jada replied. "Permanently. But for right now a short trip to Mexico or Hawaii would be nice. You should go with me." Jada pressed her hands against her temples.

"That sounds like a plan. Make reservations for two. Let's go to Oahu. It's great to take a break from reality and live in a fantasy world every once in a while. Besides, I need some place to wear my *new* G-string bikinis."

"Get-back boo-tay." Jada laughed and pressed harder.

"Here we are," Candice said. "I'll let you out and meet you inside."

"Thanks." Jada got out of the car slowly. She tried not to agitate her headache. She checked in with the receptionist. Jada sat on the couch and thumbed through an old copy of *Essence.* Dr. Bates's office always smelled woodsy like the fresh outdoors.

"Jada, hi. How are you doing?" Dr. Bates asked as she stood in the doorway. "Come in. Bring the magazine with you if you like." Dr. Bates was fifty-five, but no one would ever guess. She dyed her hair black to cover the few strands of gray. She slicked her hair back and behind her ears. The waves bounced on and off her white lab coat when she walked.

"So you've been suffering from frequent migraine headaches lately?"

"Yes."

"How often do the headaches occur and how long do they last?"

"They started about four weeks ago. They start early in the morning, as soon as I lift my head off my pillow, and continue until I go to bed at night."

"Are you able to sleep at night?"

"No. The headaches usually wake me up at least once. I've been taking extra-strength medicine but it only reduces the level of pain."

"What do you think is the cause of your headaches?" she asked.

"Melanie."

"You've been concerned about Melanie?"

"It's a long story, but basically she's stolen my fiancé away from me *and* turned him against me."

"What role does your fiancé play in all of this?"

"I'm not sure I understand what you're asking."

"If he is or was your fiancé, then what made him turn to another woman?"

"This is becoming too much," Jada protested. "My head is starting to pound again."

"Okay, I won't ask you any more questions," said Dr. Bates. "I'll write you a prescription, recommend you see a counselor, and consider taking some time off from work. Perhaps you should take a vacation. I can recommend a great counselor. If you'd like to see her, ask my receptionist for the number," said Dr. Bates as she opened the door.

"I already have someone I can talk with. Someone I trust."

"That's great. Always remember to love yourself, Jada. Self-love and faith are the best medicines on the market and they're still free. So stock up."

"Thanks. I'll see you next week." Jada walked out and bypassed the receptionist.

"So, what did the doctor tell you?" Candice asked as she gave Jada a hug.

"The same thing Mama told me this morning. I need to see a counselor. The same thing you told me earlier. I need a vacation. She prescribed medication for the headaches.

"I wish I could take the rest of the week off, but I have *two* shoots scheduled for tomorrow and one all-day shoot on Friday. At least Karen will be in the office," Jada said. Candice maneuvered through the traffic. "Let me call Jazzmyne and see if she can come over this evening."

"Hello. This is Jazzmyne. May I help you?"

"Hi, Jazzmyne. This is Jada. I really need to talk with you about *my* problems. If you're too busy, I can schedule with someone else."

"I'm never too busy to help a friend, and Jada, you've been like a sister to me. When would you like to get together?"

"How about seven?" Jada suggested.

"Seven is good. That gives me time to cook dinner. Calvin will drop me off, but I need a ride home."

"No problem." Jada turned off her cellular.

"Well, I'm glad she can make it," Candice said. "Time heals all wounds. You'll be fine and I'll be here by your side. What are you going to do until seven o'clock?"

"Nothing really," Jada responded. "I'll probably lie down and rest. Maybe prepare something to eat later. Candice, I don't know what to do with myself, I feel so lost without Wellington. I wanted to have his children, share his dreams, *and* grow old with him. I wanted so many things with Wellington. I don't know if I'll ever love anyone the way I love him." Jada didn't want to start crying again but she couldn't help herself. Her heart ached and her head pounded.

"You have to calm down," said Candice. "I'll draw you a nice warm bath and stay with you until Jazzmyne comes."

"Thanks, but I really want to be alone," Jada insisted. "I'll be fine. Really, I don't want you to stay." Jada waved good-bye to Candice and walked into the lobby. When she got upstairs, Jada took Candice's advice. She drew herself a nice hot bath. She lit her favorite scented candles, put on some smooth jazz music, and swallowed two extra-strength Excedrin tablets with lots of water.

Jada's Jacuzzi felt heavenly. The last time she'd been in it, Wellington was with her. The intercom startled her. Jada realized she must have dozed off. She grabbed the soft oversized red towel from the rack and wrapped it around her dripping wet body. A light trail of water followed. Jada greeted Jazzmyne at the elevator door. "Hi, thanks for coming. Excuse me for a moment. I fell asleep in the Jacuzzi. Make yourself comfortable. I'll be right back."

Jada dashed into her bathroom, rubbed coconut oil over her body, and toweled off. She slipped into a casual, ankle-length, sleeveless black cotton dress and returned to the living room.

"Hi, Jada. How are you?"

Jada hunched her shoulders, shook her head, and sighed. "I'm trying not to fall apart again."

She figured it was best to speak her mind. She took two large throw pillows from the couch and placed them on the floor.

"It's better if you sit while we talk," said Jazzmyne. "When you lie down, your emotions move to the foreground and your ability to rationalize moves to the background. Now, I want you to start wherever you feel comfortable. I'll just listen until you are finished, and then we'll have a discussion."

Jada took a deep breath and paused for a moment. Jazzmyne patiently sat in silence. "In the beginning, it all seemed like a fairy tale. Sometimes I had to pinch myself to make sure I wasn't dreaming." Jada stared into the unlit fireplace. "I mean Wellington was the perfect gentleman. We'd talk for hours about any and everything. We laughed, and a few times we even cried. When he gave me this ring, he told me it was my soulmate ring. And when the time was right, he moved it from my right ring finger to the left one. No one ever gave me a diamond soulmate ring." She drifted for a moment, but Jazzmyne continued to sit in silence.

"He announced our engagement at his house," Jada continued. "In front of his parents, my mother, and Mr. Hamilton. It was beautiful. Wellington reassured me our feelings were the only ones that mattered. But his mother was virtually outraged.

"That's when Melanie came to visit. Mrs. Jones asked Wellington if Melanie could stay with him. Of course, he agreed. She was supposed to visit for two weeks. Next thing I knew she had a top position with my company. So now *I work for her* and I hate it.

"I pleaded with Wellington. I tried to get him to see she was tearing our relationship apart. That's when he told me he was going to marry her, and my life has been going downhill ever since."

Jada paused again. "I guess that brings us to this point." She didn't want to ramble on or sound like an owl so she stopped talking.

Jazzmyne paused for a moment. Jada looked at her face, which resembled a computer processing information. Jada could almost hear the programming unit churning.

"So, do you still take time to meditate and pray daily?" asked Jazzmyne.

That's not what Jada expected her to say at all, but she answered, "I still pray, but I must admit I haven't taken time out of my schedule to meditate and pray daily like I used to."

"After I leave tonight," she said in a quiet voice, "I want you to spend at least thirty minutes praying and at least thirty minutes meditating." Jazzmyne's voice had a calming effect on Jada. Her body began to relax.

"Now I have to be honest with you, Jada. I've been a counselor for almost ten years. Except for the few months when I was homeless. I had *faith* that if I sat on the same corner *every day*, someone would eventually help us. I'm blessed that person was you. At certain times in my life I was the client. You know that. So, *I can tell*, you've intentionally left out some very important information. Jada, you have to trust me. I'm only here to help you. Not to hurt you. But I can't if you won't tell me the real reason why your relationship with Wellington has failed."

Damn, was Jada talking with a psychic or a counselor? But at this point, the tables had turned. Jada decided to tell Jazzmyne everything.

"I'm embarrassed and ashamed that I would allow such a thing to have happened." Jada's eyes began to swell with tears. A lump was lodged in her throat. "Melanie, Wellington, and I had a ménage à trois. At the time it seemed like fun, but immediately afterward Melanie started acting like *she* was Wellington's woman.

"I became threatened by her acts and over-reacted out of fear, I suppose. I was afraid of losing Wellington to her. Then Wellington said she was pregnant. He confessed they had been intimate before the three of us were involved. My emotions raced out of control. I slapped Wellington *and* Melanie. I acted like I was the starting pitcher at the World Series and threw eggs on everything I could at Wellington's house, except the dog. And that was only because he didn't have one.

Jazzmyne's eyes never widened. Her eyebrows didn't move. "I see," she said. She sat on the floor and faced Jada. She held her hand and said, "You must learn to forgive yourself. You've got to stop carrying around the guilt of your sins. We all sin, Jada. You're *not* infallible. And there's no measuring scale in heaven that says your sins will be weighed heavier than the sins of others. You're a Christian woman. Therefore, you already know that God has forgiven you." Tears silently streamed down Jada's face one behind the other as if they were taking turns.

"You also have to accept responsibility for your actions," she said. "You must stop blaming Melanie for what she has done as a means to justify what you have done. You must forgive yourself and as difficult as it may be—as a Christian—you must forgive Melanie.

"As far as Wellington is concerned, he seems confused. I would bet money on the fact that he still loves you, except I don't bet. But you get my point. His mother has put her desires and needs before that of her son. She acts like she loves her son. Only God can judge her. As long as Wellington and Chris do what she wants, Cynthia's happy.

"Wellington will only be free to love you when he realizes that he does not have to live up to his mother's expectations. You can't open his eyes so stop trying. But one day he will see his mother for what she truly is. If it is meant for the two of you to reunite, it will happen. But don't live your life waiting for it."

Jazzmyne was so wise and so rational. "Let me share a poem with you entitled 'Soulmates Dissipate,'" said Jazzmyne. "Maybe it will help you to understand what you're feeling:

> *Soulmates Never Dissipate*
> *And they never part*
> *The spiritual bond that connects the two*
> *Is connected heart to heart*
>
> *It matters not—dead or alive*
> *The bond cannot be broken*
> *And you feel the pain of the other*
> *Even when words are not being spoken*
>
> *You can deny in your head*
> *But never in your heart*
> *What God puts together*
> *No man can tear apart*

Soulmates Never Dissipate
And they never part
The spiritual bond that connects the two
Is connected heart to heart

Sure you may have another lover
Or a husband or maybe a wife
But the eternal bond of your Soulmate
Gels the existence of your life

Flesh will perish
We all must die
But the spirit of a Soulmate continues
Because your Soulmate lives within you

For man was not meant to live alone
So your Soulmate you must embrace
To ignore the existence of your Soulmate
Is to doubt your very own faith

Soulmates Never Dissipate
And they never part
The spiritual bond that connects the two
Is connected heart to heart

"Wellington will always be a part of your life. Whether you accept that or not, is up to you.

"Now let's talk about Jada," Jazzmyne said. "It is time for you to move on with your life. You may want to consider changing jobs. It's not running away from your pain. It's detaching yourself from that which is causing you pain. You'll never be happy working at Sensations as long as you have to work with the constant reminder of *all* you have lost."

Jada began crying and laughing and gave Jazzmyne a big hug. "I love you."

"And I love you too," said Jazzmyne. "Every once in a while we lose our lease on life, but it's up to us to determine if we want to renew it or let it expire." Jada finally understood what Jazzmyne had written on that sign the day they met.

"I'll talk with Wellington, but I won't tell him what we've talked about and I won't discuss our conversation with you. So don't ask."

"How are you going to convince Wellington to talk with you?"

"I have my ways. Don't forget, Shelly is his biggest fan," Jazzmyne said and smiled. "He's so proud of her. Wellington has a big heart, Jada. But he's still *a man*. And he was honest enough to tell you the truth. Maybe it wasn't what you wanted to hear. But it was the truth. The problem is you refused to meet him halfway. It wasn't his entire fault. Jada, you must learn to break the cycle that kills. Be true to yourself, and the others will heal."

"Speaking of healing, I know I didn't mention this, but Wellington told me he was adopted and someday he would like to find his real parents." Jada hoped it would give Jazzmyne some insight.

"Now *that* is interesting," Jazzmyne said as she shook her head. "Actually that helps to shed light on why his mother is so selfish. She's probably never embraced him as her child. He may just be another token of all the great deeds she has accomplished in her life. I'm so glad you told me."

Jada could hear the CPU turning again. "I'd love to stay longer, but I'd better get home to my kids before it gets too late. I'll call Wellington tonight."

"Thanks, you don't know how much you have helped me." Jada stood and stretched her legs. "I'm going to pray and meditate as soon as I get back home."

Chapter 14

Jada high stepped in her beige three-inch heels and brand new pantsuit. "Good morning, Jada," Karen said. "My, don't we look refreshed."

"Karen, I've renewed my lease on life." Jada strutted in front of Karen's desk like she was modeling.

"How much did it cost you?" Karen asked. "First month, last month, and a deposit?" Karen laughed.

"The wonderful thing about renewing your lease on life is . . ." Jada paused. She struck a pose and said, "It never costs you more than you can afford."

"Melanie has you scheduled to shoot Terrell Morgan again this morning and Reginald Washington this afternoon," Karen said. "Guess what?" Karen didn't wait for a response. "I have some great news!"

"Well, out with it. Tell me," said Jada as she backed up to Karen's desk.

"Mr. Murphy gave me a *five percent* raise and said if I really worked hard he'd consider paying for me to take photography classes," said Karen. Jada didn't remember ever seeing Karen so excited.

"Great news! How did you convince him to do all that?"

"Melanie told me to ask for a raise. So I did and Mr. Murphy told me to tell him how much of a raise I wanted and why," Karen explained. "Melanie helped me to present my offer and he accepted it. Melanie also convinced me to talk to Mr. Murphy about mentoring Damien and he agreed to that too."

Jada felt guilty because she should have done more to help Karen. "Well, it certainly looks like you're on a roll. Congratulations! I'm happy for you and Damien." Jada walked into her office and immediately took two prescribed tablets for her migraine.

Jada picked up the phone and dialed three digits. Terrell peeped into her office. "Hi. I was just about to call Candice."

"Hey, beautiful lady. Are you ready to photo shoot a brother or what?" Terrell asked.

"Come here and give me a hug. I sure need it." Jada grinned from ear to ear.

Terrell stretched open his arms. "You've got it."

"Let's go into the studio. They should be finished setting up by now. Candice is so excited about moving to Los Angeles."

"I know how close the two of you are. You should consider moving too."

"We're shooting you in swimwear today so you need to slip into these right quick." Jada handed Terrell a pair of form-fitting boxed-cut black swim trunks.

"Be back in a flash." Terrell flashed a dazzling smile.

Before Jada had finished checking her camera equipment, Terrell was back.

"Was that fast enough for you?" he asked as he posed.

"Damn!" The zoom lens bounced in and out of Jada's hand twice. "I mean damn that was quick." The third time she quickly snatched the lens and replaced it. She really did love her work. It was the boss she couldn't live with.

"So, did you give some thought to what I said about moving to Los Angeles?" he asked. "I know Visual Revelations is hiring experienced photographers. Plus, I know the president and vice president. Just say the word and I can make it happen. Just don't wait too long to make up your mind."

"I'll give it some serious thought and let Candice know," Jada responded. "You know everything happens for a reason and sometimes we just have to step out on faith. Even though we don't totally understand. Everything will be all right. Hey, where'd you learn how to strike that pose?" Jada laughed as she watched Terrell bend over backward like a crab. His chest, abs, and crotch were in a perfect arch. Well, almost perfect. "Awesome." Jada admired the view through her lens.

"You haven't seen anything yet," he said. "Watch this and this and this. Keep up with me now. I don't want you to miss my good side. Oh yeah, that's right, all of my sides are good." Terrell bragged and then smiled.

"You already have an eight-pack, and from the looks of it, you've been working out more."

"In this business, you gotta stay ahead of the game," Terrell explained. "Have you seen the black male models from Jamaica? They make the competition tougher every year."

Jada nodded and raised her eyebrows. "Yes, I've seen the layouts. They're hot! Well, that raps up our session for today." Jada prepared her equipment for her next shoot. "Meet me back in my office. That is, if you don't have to rush off."

"Be there in a flash."

As Jada passed Karen's desk, she could hear Melanie over the intercom. "Ms. Livingston, I need mailing addresses for all the top-level executives in the company, including the ones we don't see around here. I'm preparing my wedding invitation list. I've been meaning to ask you, would you like to be in my wedding?" Jada slowed her pace. "I'd be honored to be in your wedding," Karen replied.

"Great, Wellington and I will take care of all your expenses," said Melanie. So, Melanie still controlled the decision making. "My identical twin sister Stephanie is going to be my maid of honor." There are two of them? Jada walked into her office. She left her door open so she could hear the remains of their conversation.

"That's all for now," said Melanie. "If I'm not here when you get the list, leave it in the center of my desk. Oh, one last thing I forgot to mention,"

Melanie said. "I've moved the wedding up. Wellington and I are getting married in two weeks."

"Two weeks!" Karen said.

"Two weeks." Jada couldn't believe her ears.

"It can only enhance your social life, darling," Melanie told Karen. "You know all the national and international models will be there."

Jada was just about to slam her door when Terrell stepped in, smiling. "So what are you doing for lunch?"

"I'm going to get some fresh air. I need to clear my mind before my next shoot. Thanks for the offer." Jada waved good-bye to Terrell.

"Don't mention it." Terrell moonwalked out the door backward.

Jada laughed, picked up her purse, and headed out.

"Jada, Candice is on line one," Karen said.

"Thanks, Karen. I'll take the call." Jada went back into her office. "Hey, girl, you just missed your man. He did a great shoot this morning. You would have been proud."

"I *am,*" Candice said.

"I'm glad you called. I need to book our reservations for Hawaii two weeks from today. I'm going to stay for seven days. If that doesn't fit your schedule, let me know, but I've *got* to get the hell away from this place," Jada said as she thought about Wellington's new wedding date.

"What's the rush?" Candice asked.

"Ms. Thang is broadcasting she's moved the wedding up. They're getting married in two weeks."

"Why don't they just elope?" Candice said and laughed. Candice always had a great sense of humor. "She's *really* working fast."

"That's not all. She has an identical twin sister named Stephanie. I wonder why she never mentioned her."

"This is beginning to sound like straight drama."

"Well, all this drama is making me consider Terrell's suggestion to move to Los Angeles."

"That would be perfect. Go for it!"

"Why not? I have nothing to lose, that's for sure. But I am concerned about my mother."

"Your mother has more of a social life than you," Candice said. "Mr. Hamilton has been coming to church regularly and they're always on the road going someplace when they don't have Jazzmyne's kids. You've got to start thinking about Jada for once."

"You're right, I'll do it." Just like that, Jada had decided to move out of Oakland. "But I won't leave until you do. And I'm going to start my own business."

"What kind?"

"The best business, of course, is what you love to do most. And you know photography is my passion. I'll give Ms. Melanie and Mr. Murphy some real competition. I've already selected a name, *Black Diamonds.*" Jada thought about the list Karen was going to leave on Melanie's desk and made a mental note to make a copy of her own.

"I like it," Candice said. "Sorry, but I've got to run. We'll celebrate later. I love you, girl. Bye," said Candice.

"I love you too." Jada hung up the phone, danced, and smiled like the Grinch. She knew she had made the right decision. She could feel it. She walked out of her office and pranced by Melanie and Karen. Karen was whispering to Melanie.

"Hello, ladies," Jada said.

"What's she so happy about?" Jada heard Melanie ask Karen.

"I have no idea," Karen responded. "She mentioned something earlier about renewing her lease on life."

Chapter 15

Saturday morning brought the regular routine for Wellington and Walter. It was their weekend to manicure Wellington's lawn. Wellington distanced himself from Walter. He questioned if marrying Melanie was the sensible thing to do, since his heart wasn't in it. Walter had cast his vote in favor of Melanie. "Overall, she's a better match. She's well known throughout the organizations. And *she's pregnant.*" There was no point in discussing the matter with him again.

Wellington didn't care about any of those things, except the pregnancy. He didn't want to disgrace his family or hers. He watchfully trimmed each hedge to ensure they were perfectly even. Why couldn't Jada have heard his side? Didn't she understand his confusion? His pain? It wasn't too late to say no to Melanie. But it seemed impossible to regain Jada's trust. He sighed. The phone call was a welcome distraction. Wellington sat the clippers on the lawn and ran over to the patio table to answer the call.

"Hello."

"Hi, Mr. Jones, this is Jazzmyne, Shelly's mother."

"Oh, yes. Hi," Wellington said. "Everything all right?"

"Everything's fine," said Jazzmyne. "Shelly's still eager for you to get the birthday present she made. She wants me to deliver it to you today. She said if you didn't get it soon, it would be a Christmas present."

Wellington smiled. "You don't have to come over here. I'll be happy to pick it up."

"You know how children are. Shelly insisted I deliver it to you," Jazzmyne said in a friendly voice.

"Well, if you insist."

"Is ten o'clock too early?" Jazzmyne asked.

"Ten is fine." Wellington gave Jazzmyne directions. "Thank you so much, Mr. Jones. This means a lot to Shelly."

"I'll see you shortly." Wellington finished the hedges so he wouldn't have to resume the task after Jazzmyne left. There was something about her eyes. Where had he seen them before?

As Jazzmyne pulled into the circular driveway, Wellington motioned for her to park behind his Expedition.

"It's a pleasure to meet you again, Mr. Jones."

Wellington opened Jazzmyne's car door. "Please call me Wellington. Let me introduce you to my friend, Walter W. Wright *the Third.*"

"Wow. You have a wonderful name," said Jazzmyne.

"Pleased to meet you, Jazzmyne." Walter looked at his soiled fingers. "Forgive me for not shaking your hand."

"It's quite all right." Jazzmyne's brown lips curved.

"Let's go inside, shall we?" said Wellington. "Walter, I'll be right back."

"Take your time, man," said Walter. "I can handle the yard."

Wellington escorted Jazzmyne into his family room. "Have a seat. Can I get you something to drink?"

"That would be nice," Jazzmyne said. "Do you have lemonade?"

"As a matter of fact, I do," Wellington said. "Melanie made a fresh pitcher this morning." Wellington went upstairs and removed his overalls. He slipped into a black T-shirt and a pair of black sweats. He washed his hands and face, went downstairs to the kitchen, and poured two tall glasses of fresh lemonade. "Here you go." Wellington sat on the sofa next to Jazzmyne.

"Congratulations are in order." Jazzmyne smiled. She extended her hand to Wellington.

"Thanks." Wellington thought the handshake was odd. He felt slightly uncomfortable. He wanted to ask about Jada, but he didn't think it was appropriate.

"So, when is the wedding?"

Wellington was in a daze. "Oh. We're getting married next week. Fortunately, I don't have to worry about the details. I've decided to leave that up to Melanie and my mother. But I'll make certain your family is on the guest list." Wellington sat back on the burgundy leather sofa and moved a few inches away from Jazzmyne.

"Thank you." Wellington watched her eyes peruse the room. "Where's Melanie? I'd like to congratulate her."

"She's out with my mother finalizing last-minute arrangements."

"You have a beautiful home. It's filled with love and happiness. I can feel it in the air."

"Thanks."

"This is the first time we've had an opportunity to talk. I must tell you that I've sincerely appreciated all you've done for my family," Jazzmyne said. "Specially Shelly and Brandon. They just go on and on about their Uncle Wellington all the time. That's what they call you. It's always, Uncle Wellington this and Aunt Jada that and Grandma Ruby and Grandpa Robert." Jazzmyne giggled.

"So, did Mr. Hamilton and Ms. Tanner tie the knot? They seemed so happy together when they were here for dinner."

"Not yet, but we expect them to announce it any day." Jazzmyne smiled. Her full cheeks rounded nicely and complemented her eyes. "Let me ask your opinion on something personal," said Jazzmyne. "I need a man's point of view. That is, *if* you have time. I don't want to keep you from doing your yard work."

"I have time," Wellington said. Thoughts of Jada weighed heavily on his mind. He hoped Jazzmyne would say Jada had asked about him.

"My ex-husband, Franklin, wants the children and me to move into his new house with him. He claims he's miserable without us. But I've moved on with my life. Franklin had numerous opportunities to do the right thing, but he never would. He couldn't make up his mind. He was confused." Jazzmyne sighed. Wellington noticed the familiarity in Jazzmyne's eyes again. It bugged him. "The kids and I are happy. I've met a wonderful Christian man who loves my children and me. I'm thinking about accepting his marriage proposal. Now, how do you think I should handle my relationship with Franklin? He uses the children to get next to me."

Wellington's mind was cluttered by the words coming from Jazzmyne's mouth. He frowned. He tried to give her his undivided attention, but thoughts of Jada were on his mind. Finally, Wellington said, "What does your father think about all of this? Have you asked him?"

"He died when I was ten years old."

"Oh, I'm so sorry." Wellington looked into Jazzmyne's half-opened eyes. "Well, I think you should follow your heart. Keep the relationship that makes *you* happy. Shelly and Brandon can always visit their father."

"Thanks for listening and thanks for the advice. I won't take any more of your time." Jazzmyne pulled out a framed portrait of Wellington that Shelly had drawn from a picture Jada had given her. The photo was professionally framed in black with gold trim. "Shelly wanted me to give this to you." Jazzmyne uncovered the drawing.

"I love it! I had no idea Shelly was so talented. We should consider enrolling her in fine arts. Please, ask her if she is interested. If she says yes,

I'll take care of the rest. I know exactly where I'm going to hang it—between the pictures of my mothers. Let me show you."

"Mothers?" Jazzmyne repeated.

"Yes, I was adopted at birth. I'm blessed to have a picture of my real mother. So, when I moved into this house, I decided to hang both pictures side by side. And there's exactly enough space between the two to hang Shelly's drawing. They were hanging in the living room, but I moved them to my office. I often wonder if my real parents are alive."

"If you'd like, I could put you in touch with someone who can help you find out," Jazzmyne said. "But I have to forewarn you, the results can be rewarding, but they may also be devastating. Think about it and let me know."

Wellington escorted Jazzmyne to his office. She had already met Cynthia so he didn't acknowledge her. "This is a picture of my biological mother." Wellington pointed at the photo. Before Wellington could speak her name, Jazzmyne dropped the crystal glass—half full of lemonade—onto Wellington's hardwood floor.

"Are you all right?" Wellington grabbed Jazzmyne's shoulder.

"I'm fine," Jazzmyne stuttered. She stooped down to pick up the glass.

Wellington gently pulled her back up. "Don't worry about the glass. It is only crystal. It can be replaced."

"I'm so sorry," Jazzmyne said as she held her hand over her mouth. She stared at the picture on the wall. "I've got to leave."

"Wait!" Before Wellington could speak another

word, Jazzmyne was out the door and had taken off in the car.

Wellington cleaned up the broken glass. He stared at the picture of his mother. "That's it! Those eyes!" He went outside to help Walter.

"Man, what was wrong with her? She ripped out of here like she had seen a ghost," Walter said.

"What's scarier than that is, I saw it too," Wellington said.

Chapter 16

Dear Wellington,

You will always be my love, but I'm not going to continue to compete for your heart. The curtain is drawn. I've played my part. I lost the round, but I won the fight. I'm granting you your wish, letting you go, and I'm moving on with my life. The crazy things I did to prove my love, only I proved I had a foolish heart.

You, like so many other men, will eventually learn that soulmates never dissipate and they never part. I hope you're happy with your new life. I hope you're happy with your new wife. I lost the round, but I didn't lose the fight, because I—unlike your wife—will always be a part of your life. Now that I have opened my eyes, I can clearly see. You didn't truly want a wife. You needed another mother in your life.

Don't worry about me. I am free and eventually I'll be happy again. I'll find another lover. I'll find another friend. Time heals all wounds, and if I never see you again, it'll be too soon. But I'll always be with you in spirit and I will always care. I lost the round, but I won the fight. See you around, in your second life.

Remember . . .

Diamond is Forever

"Let's get this party started quickly," Candice sang. She snapped her fingers to the beat. "Are you ready?" Candice stood in front of Jada's closet door mirror and danced to the radio music.

"I'm ready." Jada had two suitcases on wheels ready to go. "I just need to seal this envelope. Do we have time to stop at the post office on our way to the airport?"

"If you hurry," Candice said. "Jada, girl, you are looking better than ever. Now let's go. We can't keep the limousine driver waiting all morning."

"No, you didn't hire a limo driver to take us to the airport."

"Girl, we're on vacation!" Candice partied all the way to the limo. "We need to stop at the post office first," Candice instructed the driver while he put their bags in the trunk.

"Certainly, madame," he replied, staring at Candice's breasts. "We can do anything you'd like."

The driver parked in front of the post office. People peeped through the tinted windows to see who was inside. When he opened the door, Jada stepped out like Diana Ross in *The Boss*. One woman said, "She's so beautiful. Who is she?" Jada felt as sexy as she looked. She proceeded to strut into the post office to overnight express her letter to Wellington.

"The package will be specifically delivered to Mr. Wellington Jones by noon tomorrow morning," said the postal woman.

"Thank you." Jada smiled, pressed her sunglasses against her nose with her index finger, and placed a twenty-dollar tip at her window. Before the woman could refuse it, Jada walked away.

"What was so important that you had to mail it on the way to the airport?" Candice asked. She handed Jada a chilled glass of Dom.

"Let's toast to new beginnings," Jada said.

"I'll definitely toast to that," Candice said. They elegantly tipped their glasses.

"What's the first thing you want to do when we get to Honolulu?" Candice asked.

"Put on my bikini and lie out on Waikiki beach all day. Then I want to go to the best luau on the island and party until my feet start a boycott."

"Girl, you're trying to do it all in one day. Save something to do tomorrow," Candice said. She sipped on the coconut rum with fruit juice the flight attendant had given her.

"Tomorrow is not promised to any of us. So I'm living each day of the rest of my life to the fullest," Jada proclaimed. "I have done my research and there's a lot to do the rest of the week. In fact, we probably won't have time to do it all. We're going to the Polynesian Culture Center, the Kodak Show, Pearl Harbor, the Dole Factory, the Bishop Museum, and you can't go to Hawaii and not go deep-sea diving, scuba diving, and snorkeling. The only thing I won't do is ride in one of those helicopters. I'm not feeling that adventurous."

"Well, now that you've planned everything, I'll just hang on for the ride." Candice held on to the arms of her seat.

"Hold on tight, girl!" Jada rocked from side to side. "I never could understand how anyone could take a vacation and not take time to appreciate the sites." Jada reclined her seat, put on her headphones, and turned on her CD player. The CD Wellington made with the songs from the concert was her favorite. But she'd stopped listening to it months ago. Whenever she heard any of those songs, it brought back painful memories.

On the day of the wedding, Wellington was still confused and unsure. At least Melanie had left the night before and had stayed with his mother. Wellington started to call his best man, Walter. Then he changed his mind. Why bother, he wouldn't understand. No one—especially Walter—would understand that he still loved Diamond.

Wellington walked upstairs to his bedroom and picked up the envelope the postman had delivered earlier. He stood in front of his full-length mirror and talked to himself.

"Should I open it or *not*?" Wellington stared at the letter. "If she still wants to marry me, then what would I say to Melanie *and* my mother? I couldn't possibly disappoint them." Wellington rubbed his head. "If she's found someone else, I'll be hurt. What if she needs me and I ignore her plea?"

Wellington sat on the side of the bed and opened the letter. Jada's fragrances were immediately released. He deeply inhaled her once more. Then he removed the letter from the envelope and read it.

"Dear Wellington . . . " He could hear Jada's voice and smell her perfumes. A tear rolled down his face but he refused to outwardly break down and cry. Wellington took a deep breath and continued. He read the letter three times, went downstairs, and placed it in his briefcase.

Wellington sat at his desk and gazed into the darkness of his life. The past year flashed before his eyes. Somehow the day that was supposed to be the happiest of his life had turned into a nightmare from which he could not seem to awaken.

Chapter 17

Monday morning came too soon for Jada. Along with it, her migraine headaches returned. They reminded her of the man she was trying so hard to forget. Would Wellington read the letter? She concluded that it didn't really matter. He was a married man now. She was determined not to let it get her down again. Jada swallowed two prescribed tablets, held her head as high as she could, and waltzed into the office.

"Good morning, Karen," Jada said.

"My, don't we look refreshed," Karen said.

"Thanks. That's what a vacation in Hawaii can do for you too," Jada said, as if she were auditioning for a commercial. "How's everything around here?"

"It's been quiet, since you and Melanie were out at the same time."

"Good morning, all," Melanie said. "Ms. Livingston, you looked wonderful at the wedding, darling." Melanie strutted by Jada as if she weren't there.

Karen avoided eye contact with Jada and fumbled through her in-basket. Jada walked into her office and closed the door. Jada turned on her computer and typed her resignation letter within ten minutes. She knew she had to leave Sensations before *she* ended up needing a pen pal to write letters to from prison.

Jada handed the letter to Karen. "Karen, would you please give this letter to Mr. Murphy."

"Are you feeling all right?" Karen asked.

"No, but I will be as soon as I get the hell away from this place. I quit."

"But you can't just quit," said Karen.

"I'll send for my things." Jada looked at the clock on Karen's desk. Not even seven o'clock yet.

Once outside, Jada's headache disappeared. She called her mother. "Hi, Mama. I've got great news!"

"Oh, baby. What's your great news?"

"I just quit my job at Sensations Communications and I'm moving to Los Angeles to start my own business."

"Well, baby, I know you haven't been happy lately. But do you think quitting your job and moving so far away is the right decision?"

"Mama, you could get to Los Angeles in less than an hour," explained Jada. "And yes, I'm sure I made the right decision. I know I don't have to worry about you because Mr. Hamilton is taking great care of you. I have to do this, Mama. I just have to get away from here." Jada crossed her fingers that her mother would understand.

"I always want you to be happy, and right now I

know you're not, so I think you *should* move to L.A. Robert and I can take Shelly and Brandon to Disneyland this summer. Before I forget, Jazzmyne wants you to call her. I've got to go now. Robert is waiting to take me to breakfast."

"Okay, Mama. I'll talk with you later. I love you."

"I love you too, baby. And don't forget to call Jazzmyne."

Jada didn't delay. She speed-dialed Jazzmyne's work number from her cellular.

"Hello, this is Jazzmyne."

"Hi, Jazzmyne, this is Jada. Mama said you wanted me to call."

"Yes, I really needed to talk to you about my visit at Wellington's, but I decided to wait until you returned from vacation," said Jazzmyne. There was discomfort in Jazzmyne's voice. "How was your vacation?"

"Candice and I had enough fun for ten people!" Jada said and laughed. She reflected on how they had teased all the military men with their G-string swimwear.

"It's so good to hear you laugh again," said Jazzmyne. "I mean really laugh."

"It *feels* good," said Jada. "Now what about your visit?"

"You've seen the photos of Wellington's mothers?" Jazzmyne asked.

"Yes."

Jazzmyne inhaled deeply. "Well, his biological mother is also my mother."

Jada's chin hit the flap on her phone. "Are you serious? Are you sure?"

"Of course I'm sure."

"Did you tell Wellington?"

"No, and please don't mention it to him."

"Other than the fact that we're not speaking anyway, I promise I won't tell."

"I even asked him if he wanted me to assist him with finding *his* biological parents. Of course that was before I saw the picture."

"So you have the same father too?" Jazzmyne had her really curious about Wellington's background.

"No. Are you sitting down?" Jazzmyne asked.

"No. Why?" Jada was standing outside her car.

"You may want to."

"Okay, I'm sitting." Jada opened the car door and sat behind the wheel.

"Wellington said he doesn't know his father, but I do. My father's last name is Jones. His dad's last name is Thompson."

"Oh, shit!" Jada accidentally pressed against her horn. She jumped.

"It gets worse," Jazzmyne said. "Our mother, Katherine, told me the story before she died. She said she wanted to clear her conscience although she had promised not to tell a soul. I'm just piecing it all together because she always referred to Cynthia as Cyn Baby. Cynthia and Katherine are sisters. Their grandfather raped Cynthia when she was twelve. She became pregnant so Cynthia performed her own abortion. That's why she can't have children." Jada gasped and covered her mouth. "Wellington's father, Keith, is still somewhat of a player. He slept with Cynthia, Katherine, and Melanie's mom. It's pretty scary when you think about it. They all grew up in a small town in Mississippi."

"Stop right there. This is getting too freaky.

What if Wellington and Melanie are brother and sister?"

"I'll get to that part. When my mother got pregnant, she couldn't tell my father because it wasn't his child. He was due to return from his two-year tour of duty in Japan. So, Cyn Baby agreed to take her child at birth as long as she could name him. My mother gave Cyn Baby an old photo of when she turned sweet sixteen. She wanted Wellington to have it. She looked very different by the time Wellington was born, so they figured Cynthia's husband, Chris, would *never* figure it out. Men seldom pay attention to details like women do."

Jada's ear was stuck to the phone from perspiration. She hurried to dry it off. "So what about Melanie's mom?"

"Well, let's hope for the kid's sake that Wellington and Melanie are not related. My mom said Susan swore she didn't marry her husband because he had the *same* last name. Each of the women desperately wanted Wellington's dad. So he played them to his advantage. Eventually, Katherine and Keith moved to Oakland. Cyn Baby followed them. Susan moved to D.C. because she wanted to get as far away from them as she could. Wellington's father lives right here in Oakland. Just think, Uncle Wellington is truly Uncle Wellington," said Jazzmyne.

"Are you going to tell the kids?"

"I don't know. I just needed to tell somebody."

Jada empathized with Jazzmyne before she told her the news. "I want to tell you *before* you hear it from Mama. I quit my job today, and I'm moving to Los Angeles with Candice."

"Oh, no! How am I going to sort through this mess? Even though Mother told me, I never planned to search for my brother. Now, that I've found him—"

"I'm just not happy here." After she'd listened to Jazzmyne, Jada was convinced relocating was in her best interest. "And since I'm responsible for my own happiness, I'm taking control of my life and moving on. But I'll *always* be there for you."

Jazzmyne heaved. "I'm happy if you're happy. Is Candice still sending for Leslie when she gets out?"

"Definitely."

"Well, tell her if she needs me to pick up Leslie or let her stay with me for a while, just let me know."

"What are you going to do about Wellington?" Jada asked for her own selfish reasons. "Will you tell him?"

"I'm not sure. I'll have to pray on this one."

"I'm sure you'll make the right decision. I'll see you at church Sunday?"

"Yes, you will," Jazzmyne said.

"If you need someone to listen, call me. We can get together. I have *lots* of time."

"Can you afford to take two months off?"

"I can afford to take two years off," Jada responded. "My daddy took excellent care of us before and after he passed away. Two weeks after the funeral, we met with our financial advisor and diversified our financial resources. Daddy would say a girl named Diamond and a woman named Ruby should never be broke. But he would have done the same if our names were Stella and Ella," Jada said and laughed.

"Does Wellington know you're investment literate?" asked Jazzmyne.

"No. I didn't ask him about his money and he never questioned me about mine. Daddy said a woman should always have enough money to leave a relationship that's not working. There's enough miserable people living together because they cannot afford to live apart and he never wanted me to live in a situation where I was unhappy."

"Your father was a wise man. I could have benefited from his advice. Maybe it would have saved me from years of Franklin's abuse. I'm going to let you go and we'll *definitely* get together and talk soon. Jada, do *not* mention a single word of this to Wellington."

Chapter 18

Melanie was excited about the wedding and the honeymoon. She had a captivated audience of employees in her office during lunchtime soaking up the intimate details. "I really wish I could have invited all of you to the wedding, but there were so many people I had to limit our number of guests," Melanie explained. "I did bring each of you a personalized gift bag with party favors and a CD with our wedding photo on the cover. The CD has all of our wedding songs and a special intro of Wellington and me exchanging our wedding vows."

As the women opened their gift bags, Melanie continued. "I brought the wedding pictures and some of the photos from our honeymoon in Paris. Everything was so perfect. I really don't know where to begin . . ."

* * *

Wellington was at home engaged in a telephone conversation with his fraternity brother, Deon.

"Man, I apologize for not being able to make it to the wedding but Gina *and* the baby both had the flu. That's why we had to cancel at the last minute. I hope you received our gift before the wedding. I shipped it overnight."

"Man, we had presents everywhere," Wellington said as he stretched across his chaise longue. "I'm sure we received it. Melanie's already planned a gift opening celebration over the Christmas holiday, so we can show everyone the pictures from the wedding and the honeymoon. She's going to show the wedding video on the big screen TV and play the special CD she had made. The exchange of our wedding vows is the intro and we've selected songs from the reception like the one played during the bride and groom dance. To tell the truth, I can't remember any of the songs. Our wedding photo is on the front and a photo of the bridal party with our parents is on the back cover." Wellington paused. His hand grazed over his chest hairs. "Melanie reminds me too much of my mother. She plans everything we do down to the smallest detail and I just do the same thing my father does with my mom. I just show up present and accounted for."

"Man, I've listened to you ramble, but you haven't mentioned how *it feels* to be a married man," Deon said.

"That's because I'm not sure." Wellington clicked channels constantly, but didn't pay much attention to what was on. "Everything is like a blur to me. It seems like one day I was engaged to Jada and the next day I was married to Melanie."

"Yeah. What happened between you and Jada? You always had excitement in your voice when you spoke about her. What's up?"

Wellington rubbed his head. "It's hard to explain and even harder for me to understand when I reflect back. It seems like it all started with the ménage à trois. Actually, it started before that. It was one of those situations where the little head dominated. Sex with Melanie was better than I had expected. So we did it a few times." Wellington walked to the kitchen and grabbed a beer out of the refrigerator and returned to his chaise.

"Wait a minute. You mean to tell me that the three of you did the wild thang?" Deon's voice escalated so high, Wellington moved the phone away from his ear.

"Yeah, but everything seemed all right. No one was uptight about it afterwards," said Wellington. "Next thing I knew Melanie was pregnant. Then Jada started acting different and I saw a side of her that I'd *never* seen before. Then our boy Walter called and said he saw Jada at the bar with this man. That made me question whether or not *she* was being faithful. I didn't say anything to her, but I'm not stupid. I know Jada still talks with Mr. NBA. Melanie said they went out a few weeks ago. At the same time, I had Melanie here cooking breakfast, lunch, and dinner. We started bonding, and before I knew it, everyone was encouraging me to marry her. Man, does any of this shit make sense to you?"

"Man, hell no! That shit doesn't make any sense. What kind of question is that?" Deon asked.

Wellington hoped someone would understand his position. "How do you feel about Gina?"

"Gina is the only woman for me, man. I love that woman so much. When I think about straying, I think about life without Gina. The choice is simple. She's my lover, my wife, and my best friend rolled into one. Gina is my soulmate. I can't imagine what life would be like without her."

"I knew Wellington was the man for me the first time I laid eyes on him," Melanie said. "I just had to show him how to consider his options. Look at this picture." Melanie pointed. "This is my maid of honor, who also happens to be my twin sister Stephanie. This is my mother and these are Wellington's parents, Mr. and Mrs. Jones. These are the snapshots of our suite in Paris where our first child was conceived." Melanie posed and smiled.

"You're pregnant already?" Karen asked. Everyone looked at Melanie and waited for a response.

"Sure. I didn't see any point in waiting."

"So how do you know you conceived in Paris?" asked Karen.

"It really doesn't matter *where* it happened," said Melanie. She gave Karen a sharp look. "It makes for a more interesting story to say *I conceived* my firstborn child on my honeymoon in the City of Love. Actually, I hope we have twins."

"Doesn't it skip a generation?" Karen questioned.

Melanie closed the album. "Usually, but I've also

been taking a fertility drug so we'll be fortunate if it is only two. I don't plan to be pregnant again so I thought I'd get it all over with the first time around. Wellington has lots of money so we can afford to pay someone to stay home with the children. I have no intentions on being a full-time mother. I have too many other obligations. My career and organizational involvements alone keep me busy enough. I just want to love and mother my children. Someone else can change diapers, feed them, and take them to the park during the day. I could actually be the poster mom for the new millennium." Melanie laughed and ran her fingers through her hair.

"It's great to see someone happy and in love," said Wellington. "I have to go, man. Someone is ringing my doorbell."

"I wish you the best always, man. Bye," said Deon.

"Yeah, thanks," said Wellington. "Tell Gina I said hello." Wellington placed the cordless on the charger and headed toward the door.

"What took you so long to open the door?" Chris asked.

"Oh, I was talking on the phone with Deon," Wellington responded.

"The dynamic Deon! How's he doing?"

"He's doing great, still in love with Gina. Gina *and* the baby had the flu. That's why they couldn't make it to the wedding."

"The flu is going around. I hope you got your flu shot," said Chris.

"You know I don't get flu shots, Pop," said Wellington.

"You will when you get older," said Chris. "It's wonderful that Deon is still in love with Gina. What about you, son?" Chris followed Wellington to the living room. "Are you in love with Melanie?"

Instead of sitting, Wellington went to the kitchen and grabbed two beers. He handed one to his dad. "What if I were to tell you no? What would you think?" Chris sat on the couch so Wellington decided to sit on the chaise.

"I'd think you were telling me the truth," responded Chris. "That's one of the reasons I came by to see you, son. I know you're confused. This whole marriage arrangement was never what *you* wanted. You and I both know that Jada is your soulmate. But Melanie is the one who fits into the picture. Not to mention the pregnancy."

"Wait a minute, Pops. What do you mean *arrangement?*" Wellington moved over to the couch.

"Your mother will kill me for this but I guess it's time you knew. After you announced your engagement, your mother arranged to have Melanie live with you. You know everyone is indebted to Cynthia. So, she insisted Terrance give Melanie a position over Jada. And I guess you've heard the news. Jada quit the company and she's moving to Los Angeles to start her own business. Terrance called and told Cynthia that Jada turned in her resignation unexpectedly."

"What? I can't believe this!" Wellington paced back and forth. "Why now? Why are you telling me this now?" Wellington stared down at his dad. "Why didn't you tell me this before I married Melanie?" He paced again.

"I'm telling you now, son, because I, too, made the same mistake. I lost my soulmate to your mother. There's not a day in my life that goes by when I don't think about Sarah. She's the one that got away. And if I could do it all over again, I'd beg Sarah to take me back. I wouldn't care about my pride. Pride doesn't love anybody, son," said Chris as he braced his hands on the sides of his partially bald head.

"I can't believe this. This was planned?" Wellington's eyebrows met. Then he threw his hands in the air and laughed. "I guess she planned for the three of us to have sex together too."

Chris stuck out his chest. "I knew you were a chip off the old block, but I didn't know you had it in you. You always act so conservative."

"Yeah, I'm just like you, Pops. A real chip." Wellington walked over to the patio door and opened the blinds. "Well, *I'm* not going to make the same mistake you made. Melanie and I are getting an annulment first thing tomorrow morning. I'm not going to stay married to some conniving tramp."

"You can't divorce her. She's pregnant. Your mother and I worked hard to become successful and we made sure you were successful too. You're obligated to honor the family name and do right by your wife." Wellington's dad walked over to him.

Wellington looked his father in the eyes. "Let me ask *you* a question, Dad. Are you happy with Mother?"

"Son, you can learn to love anybody. I love your mother and I've learned to adjust." Chris's eyes frantically roamed the room. "I still wonder about Sarah, but I know for a fact that I'll never divorce your mother. Jones men don't divorce their women."

"Well, maybe I'm not really a Jones man anyway. So that doesn't apply to me!" Wellington sat on the couch.

"You know what I'm saying," Chris said calmly. He followed Wellington and sat beside him. "Don't go down the road of asking about your real parents again. I told you we don't know who they are. We decided to give you the picture of your mother because she mailed it to us. We're not sure how she got our address. She mailed the picture along with a letter saying she would keep her promise. *We* don't know your father. I've explained this to you before, son."

Wellington started to tell Chris he had an idea where he could find out. "Well, right now, I don't know who I am. I need to be alone. I think you and Mom have done more than enough for me. I love you guys but I can't understand why you're ruining my life!" Wellington decided he would invite Jazzmyne back to the house.

Chris walked toward the door. "I'll let myself out. I'll come back after you've calmed down. I do understand. I love you, son."

Wellington went into his office, pulled out the letter Jada sent him, and read it aloud. "How could I have been so blind?"

"Well, ladies, this reflection on my wedding has me missing my man, so I'm going to call it a day," Melanie said. "It's been my pleasure and thanks so much for sharing. Ms. Livingston, if I get any calls this afternoon, put them through to my voice mail. Don't tell anyone I've left for the day."

"Sensations Communications, this is Karen.

How may I help you?" Karen looked at Melanie and mouthed, *Wellington*. Melanie shook her head.

"She's away from her desk. Would you like me to put you through to her voice mail?" Karen asked. Melanie tiptoed out the door.

Melanie drove along Highway 1 and took in the scenery. Pleasant thoughts of the wedding danced before her eyes. She heard her cell phone humming a tune, but she couldn't find it.

"Where is it?" She quickly fumbled through her purse. She turned her head for a split second and flipped open the phone. She heard Wellington's voice echo.

"Hello."

She looked up. *"Oh, my God!"* Melanie dropped the phone and slammed on the brakes. The recreational vehicle collided head-on. The baby blue Jaguar dangled over the edge of the cliff. Melanie prayed. The car squeaked. She saw her wedding CD slide off the passenger seat. She heard a loud crunch. Her life flashed before her eyes. The airbag pressed painfully against her body. She felt for the door handle. It was stuck. Melanie took a deep breath and screamed as the car gave way and plunged toward the ocean.

Chapter 19

Wellington and his parents waited in a private room at the hospital for the doctor to deliver Melanie's status. The temperature and the tension in the room were bone chilling. Wellington sat in the corner and scanned his *Fortune* magazine.

"Has anyone called Susan?" Cynthia asked.

Wellington knew anyone meant him. "No, Mother, I haven't had time to think about calling Melanie's mother. Since you're so great at arranging things, why don't you send her a ticket? She can stay at my house, and who knows, maybe I'll even marry her," said Wellington. He peeped over his magazine at Cynthia.

"Wellington, that's no way to speak to your mother," Chris said.

"She's not my mother!" said Wellington. "A real mother wouldn't deceive her son. I sincerely pray

Melanie has a successful recovery, but as soon as she's well, I'm filing for a divorce."

"Son, I know you're upset," said Chris. "But you have to stop and think about what you're saying. Don't make a mistake."

Wellington folded his magazine and twisted it like a piece of licorice. "*You* made the mistake when you didn't tell me what was going on." His voice escalated. "Mom made a mistake when she lured Melanie here. So what you should be telling me is not to make the same mistakes the two of you made!" Wellington threw his magazine in the trash.

"I've heard enough of this nonsense," Cynthia said. "I'm going to call Susan."

"Don't forget to send her a ticket!"

"Son, you have to calm down. The first thing we have to do is make sure Melanie is doing well. You never walk out on someone when they're down. You have to stand by your wife's side."

"I said, as *soon* as she is well, I'm going to file for a divorce. And if it's not too late, I'm going to marry Diamond."

Cynthia rolled her eyes at Wellington. "Hello, Susan, this is Cynthia. I have some bad news. Melanie has been involved in a *terrible* automobile accident."

"Not my Melanie!" Wellington could hear Susan through the phone. "How is she doing?"

"We're waiting for the status of her condition. She's a fighter, Susan, so we're confident she'll make it."

"I'm going to call my travel agent. I'll be on the next plane out of D.C.," Susan said.

"I'll have Chris pick you up at the airport. Call

me with your arrival information. Bye." Cynthia flipped up the mouthpiece on her phone.

A man wearing a white lab coat entered the room. "Who is Wellington Jones?"

Wellington stood and met him halfway. "I am."

"Hello, Mr. Jones, I'm Dr. Robinson. We are fighting to stabilize your wife's condition. The good news is, she'll *probably* recover. The bad news is, we may not be able to save the triplets."

"Triplets?" Wellington's mouth opened. He looked directly at his mother and shook his head.

"Your wife is almost three months pregnant, Mr. Jones." Wellington's head snapped back and faced the doctor. "I promise we'll do all we can to save your wife and your children, but I have to warn you: We may lose all of them."

Wellington gnawed on his fingernail and frowned. He couldn't believe what he'd heard. Triplets? Melanie. Life. Death.

"I have to go check on your wife. She'll be in the Intensive Care Unit for a while," said Dr. Robinson. "There's really no reason for any of you to sit around here and wait. Mr. Jones, if you'd like to see your wife, I can let you see her for five minutes. She's very weak and heavily sedated."

Wellington stopped. His eyes squinted.

"Of course he wants to see his wife. Don't be ridiculous," Cynthia responded.

Wellington walked out of the waiting room.

"Where are you going?" Cynthia demanded. "You can't walk out on her. I raised you better than this. Wellington Jones, you get back here this instant!"

Wellington stared at Cynthia. His eyes were fixed on hers.

"Christopher, don't let him walk out on her like this. Go and talk some sense into that boy."

Christopher looked at Cynthia. "He's not the one who needs sense, you are. Haven't you ruined the boy's life enough? Leave him alone, and I'm not asking you, I'm telling you. You push him any further and we'll lose him for sure."

"He won't leave because I'll cut him out of the will if he does."

"Over my dead body," Christopher responded.

"Don't tempt me, Christopher Jones."

Wellington shook his head and slowly walked down the corridor in the opposite direction from ICU.

Chapter 20

As soon as Jada walked through her mother's door, everyone shouted, "Surprise!" Jada's mother had planned a going-away dinner and had invited Candice, Jazzmyne, Brother Dupree, Darryl, Terrell, Shelly, and Brandon.

"I don't believe you guys did all this for me!" Jada was astounded. No one had let the cat out of the bag. Jada froze in the doorway. "Thank you so much, Mother. I love you."

"Give me a hug, baby. There's someone special that wanted to say good-bye to you," Mama said.

"Who?" Jada hoped it was and wasn't Wellington.

Darryl walked out of the kitchen holding a gift box wrapped in purple African print cloth and tied with a gold silk scarf.

"For me!" Jada jiggled with excitement. As Darryl handed her the gift, Jada noticed his long masculine manicured hands. His strong Indian features. His beautiful gray eyes. Damn! He still looked good and smelled scrumptious. For a moment, she lost herself in the memories. Jada kissed his lips. "Thank you so much."

"I'm going to miss you, Jada. I guess I'll start racking up lots of frequent-flyer miles because I still plan to visit you in Los Angeles," Darryl said.

In the dining room Mama asked, "Robert, would you please say grace for us?"

"I most certainly will," said Robert. "Dear God, thank You for blessing each person at this table. We pray that You bless those who are less fortunate and may not know where their next meal is coming from. Please bless the beautiful cook and the food she has prepared before us today. In Jesus' name, Amen."

"Amen! Pass me some peas," said Brandon. He was so cute everyone laughed.

"Robert and I have an announcement to make," Mama said. Everybody looked at her, except Brandon.

"I want peas!" Brandon yelled. Jada picked up the peas and started putting some on Brandon's plate.

"I can do it *myself*. I'm a big boy. Mommy said so."

"Of course you are, Brandon. I'll just hold the bowl for you," said Jada. He helped himself to two heaping spoonfuls.

"What's the good news?" asked Jazzmyne.

"Robert and I got married yesterday."

"Mama! Why didn't you tell me?" Jada whispered between her teeth.

"We decided that we didn't want to make a big

fuss about it. If we had told *anyone*, then everyone would have made plans for us."

"I'd like to propose a toast to eternal happiness," Darryl said.

Everyone held their glasses high in the air and said, "To eternal happiness." Brandon and Shelly toasted with their champagne glasses filled with apple cider. Terrell looked at Candice and gave her a smile. Jada gave Darryl a seductive look. Love was definitely in the air.

"So, Mother, are you moving in with Mr. Hamilton or is Mr. Hamilton moving in with you?" asked Jada.

"Well, baby, we decided to keep our houses. Sometimes I'll sleep across the street and sometimes Robert will sleep over here. If we tire of the situation, we can always change our minds later. By living apart, it adds spice to our lives. I can put on something sexy and call Robert and tell him to come over. Then I'll hide until he finds me."

Jada's mouth sprang open. "Mama! Not in front of the children."

"It's healthy for children to see positive relationships," said Robert. "That's the problem with this world. They've become so obsessed with sheltering kids from the natural things in life and showering them with negativity. It's okay if they listen to rap, watch violent cartoons and movies, and play violent video games. Then when they put soap in the teacher's drinking water, the courts want to send them to jail. The children are confused by a society that sends them mixed messages," Robert continued. "My grandchildren are going to be raised in a constructive environment."

"Speaking of grandchildren, Jada, Mama isn't getting any younger."

"Mama, not now." Jada knew she was going to bring up the subject sooner or later. Especially since Darryl was there. Mama and Darryl had developed their own relationship over the past sixteen years. Jada hardly believed she and Darryl had been an item off and on for over a decade.

"I'd love to marry Jada," said Darryl.

"Uncle Darryl, I wanna computer," Brandon said. "Shelly too." Everyone laughed again. Then Brandon leaned over and whispered to Jada, "You ask him."

"Brandon, that's not nice," Jada said. "Apologize to Mr. Williams."

"Sorry. Uncle Darryl," Brandon said. "Please." The room was filled with laughter.

"I'll have to see what I can do for you, little man," Darryl responded. "I might just do that."

"Who wants apple pie and ice cream for dessert?" Jada wanted to escape before Mama revisited the subject of having grandchildren.

"I'll get it," Candice said. "This is your going-away celebration."

"I'll help you," insisted Jada.

When they walked into the kitchen, Jada bent over and grabbed her stomach.

"Are you all right?" Candice asked.

"I'm all right but there's something wrong with Wellington. I can sense it." Jada inhaled long and deep.

"Girl, don't go down that road *again*. You're just missing him because it is almost time for us to leave *and* it's getting close to February fourteenth—the day you and Wellington were supposed to get married."

"I'm not going to call him. But I know something's not right with him." When Jada considered all that Jazzmyne had told her, maybe she had learned too much. "I'll serve the pie if you serve the ice cream," Jada said.

"Okay, pie and ice cream for everyone," said Candice.

"I'll just have a little piece of pie," said Robert. "I have to monitor my intake of sweets. If I don't, the next thing you know I'll have eaten the whole thing." Robert's belly jiggled. Although he was overweight, he was an attractive man. "So Jada, tell us more about Black Diamonds."

Jada perked up. "Black Diamonds' mission is to promote beauty and culture. No race of people is truly a minority and it's up to us to realize that. This country is based upon economics, power, deception, and illusions. The bottom line is, those who have dictate to those who don't. The so-called minorities—the everyday consumers—are the real economic powerhouses of America. Black Diamonds is going to enrich cultures by producing what *they* want, educating them on what *they* need, and investing in *their* dreams. Not the American Dream. Well, I can't tell you guys everything. Just consider this the calm before the storm," Jada said. She finished her ice cream and pushed her plate aside.

Shelly yawned. "Grandma."

"Yes, Shelly. I'll help you clean up the kitchen." Mama said.

"Ms. Tanner, Shelly and I will do the dishes. You

newlyweds have done enough." Jazzmyne stood and gathered a few plates.

"It's all right, Jazzmyne. Shelly and I will do it," said Mama. "That's how I knew what she was getting ready to ask. It's part of our *special* bonding time."

Jazzmyne handed the plates to Shelly. "I can respect that."

"Mother, I'm getting ready to go home," Jada said. "Candice, I'll talk with you tomorrow."

"Sounds good," said Candice. "Be strong, girl. You want to go out Friday night? We only have two more Fridays to party."

"Sure. Where?" Jada asked.

"Jimmy's."

"What! Girl, you're so crazy." Darryl pushed Jada's chair under the table and waited. "You know that's the party until you drop or until you run out of ginseng, whichever one comes first." Jada laughed.

"Jazzmyne, would you like to go?" Candice asked.

"I'll think about it and let you know," said Jazzmyne. "It's been so long since I've been out."

"Well, you don't have to worry about feeling out of place," said Candice. "You'll have a great time."

Jada looked at Darryl. "I'll walk out with you," he said. "Would you like some company tonight?" Darryl whispered softly in Jada's ear.

Jada winked. "Sure. I'd like that." Jada gave her good-bye hugs and kisses to everyone. "Good night everybody."

Darryl followed Jada to her condo and parked in his usual space as if it were reserved just for him.

"Are you feeling all right?" Darryl asked as they stepped off the elevator into Jada's place.

"I'll be all right. I just need to relax and un-wind." Jada knew Darryl was not the one to discuss Wellington with.

"I can help you do that," he said. Darryl walked into the kitchen, poured two glasses of chilled champagne, and joined Jada in front of the fire-place. He handed her a glass. Jada sat on the couch. Darryl ran to Jada's bedroom and returned with her chocolate-flavored cocoa butter lite oil. He sat on the floor and massaged Jada's feet. Dar-ryl gave the best foot massages in the world.

"That feels so good." Jada rested against the fluffy throw pillows.

"I could make you feel better," Darryl said. "Jada, I've been in love with you for almost sixteen years." His thumbs rotated on the ball of her foot. "I've taken for granted you would always be there for me." He paused and slid his fingers between her toes. "But when you said you were getting mar-ried, I *tripped out*. That's why I stopped calling." Jada remained silent. Darryl's thumbs stroked the top of her foot. "For the first time in my life I felt like I had lost my best friend and my best lover." Darryl braced himself on one knee and reached into his pocket. "Jada, will you marry me?"

Jada's lips parted. Darryl was quiet. "My head says yes because we've been together for what seems like forever. But my heart is still cloudy. I can't make a rational decision about marriage at this point. But I promise you I'll consider it." Jada had already moved Wellington's ring back to her right ring finger.

"Well, at least wear the ring until you make up your mind." Darryl kissed Jada's hand.

After Jada lost Wellington, she'd promised to

always be true to herself. "I love you, Darryl. There's a part of me that will always love you. I'm not saying no. I'm saying, not now. If it's meant to be, we'll be together." Jada enclosed the box inside Darryl's hand and wrapped her hands around his. She kissed his lips softly. "I'm going to take a shower."

"Mind if I join you?"

"You know where the towels are." Jada picked up the champagne glasses, put them in the kitchen, and went into her bedroom. She slowly unbuttoned her ankle-length dress and dropped it to the floor.

Darryl watched Jada undress. The matching towels escaped his grip. His erection expanded. Jada watched it grow. She was always fascinated by the extreme contrast. When Darryl was limp, it didn't appear he had much. But by the time he stopped, it was longer than *The Ruler.* She often teased him and said, "Tell another lie." Then she'd watch him make it grow another inch. Darryl had incredible control over his dick.

"It's been a long time. You know I still love you, Jada."

Jada snapped her red thong. She turned and slowly walked into the bathroom and turned the shower on pulsating hot until it steamed. Then she turned it down a notch and stepped in. Darryl was right behind her. He massaged her neck and shoulders.

"That feels so good," Jada moaned. She relaxed at the touch of Darryl's strong hands stroking her tense body. He brushed her hair to one side and ran his tongue along the nape of her neck. Then he gently caressed Jada's chocolate mounds of pleasure. Her nipples protruded. Darryl was a patient lover.

Jada faced Darryl. She sandwiched his perfect size ten between her breasts. Each time his head came up for air, she sucked it in and circled it with her tongue.

Jada rubbed chocolate cocoa butter lite oil all over Darryl's penis. She positioned the pulsating water over his erection. She squatted like she was doing a bench press. Froze. Then she alternated. Deep throat. Lemon twist. She kept going. He motioned for her to stop, but it felt so good to her she couldn't. Jada inserted her finger in and out of her vagina several times. She slid her moistened finger into Darryl's mouth.

"Umm. Do that again," he pleaded.

When Jada's head came up, Darryl pushed it down. Up. Down. Up. Down. She covered her teeth with her lips. She became more aggressive each time he pressed.

Darryl's toes curled and his eyes rolled to the back of his head as she worked him over. "I've missed you so much. Let's go to the bedroom," he whispered. Darryl turned off the shower. "I want to taste your dark sweet chocolate flesh."

Jada grabbed her towel. Handed Darryl his. She sprawled across the blue satin comforter and spread her legs parallel. "Welcome to Jada Diamond's all-you-can-eat dessert buffet." Jada spread her lips so Darryl could get a good view. "We have chocolate mousse, chocolate cream, chocolate delight, and chocolate supreme. And for the special, we have chocolate-flavored whipped cream delight supreme. Eat up, it's all yours, Big Daddy."

Darryl dove in and started feasting. Jada purred

as he stroked her clit with his tongue. She felt the tip dart in and out of her vagina repeatedly. Then he resumed stroking her shaft. She felt his long fingers penetrate her at the same time. "Yes!" she screamed. Jada closed her eyes and concentrated on the orgasmic flow. She was on the edge. She fought to hold on to the big one. Jada slapped the bed and rubbed it. Once. Twice. Again. The third time Darryl stopped. Jada liked their one-on-one tag matches. Darryl jumped up and stood with opened arms. Since she signaled for the switch, he got to choose the next position.

Jada firmly hugged her arms around Darryl's neck and wrapped her legs around his back. He inserted his head. She squeezed it. Slowly she lowered herself until he was completely inside. He lowered his face and bit her nipples. Jada's pussy snatched Darryl's dick like a kung fu grip.

"Damn! Jada. This shit is illegal. You know this."

She galloped like she was horseback riding. She climaxed again and again. Darryl pressed his head as deep as it would go. Suddenly he pulled out. Darryl pumped cum shots on the wall, the nightstand, and the comforter. Darryl was definitely back on her active list. Jada freshened the linen. They dozed off in each other's arms.

The phone startled her. Jada rolled over and looked at the digital clock. Who could be calling her at six-thirty in the morning?

"Hello," Jada whispered.

"Hi. I didn't mean to wake you, but I really need to talk." Jada turned over to see if Darryl was awake. He was sound asleep.

"Is everything all right?" Jada asked.

"Not really," Wellington said. Jada detected the sadness in his voice. She tried not to awaken Darryl. Jada slipped from under his arm. She tiptoed into the kitchen and poured a tall glass of cold water.

"I sensed something wasn't quite right with you." Jada tried to sound concerned but detached.

"How could you tell?"

"Yesterday while at my mother's house a strange feeling came over me and I began to feel weak. I sensed something was terribly wrong. I wanted to call, but then again, I didn't."

"Well, you're right," Wellington said. "It's not good news, but I'd prefer to tell you in person. Can you stop by my house later today, around noon?"

Jada hesitated for a moment. "It's not a good idea for me to come to your house. Can we meet at the New Orleans Grill downtown Embarcadero?"

"Trust me Jada, you can come over to my house. It's safe."

"No. I won't come to your house." Jada's voice began to escalate. She lowered it. "We either meet downtown or we don't meet at all."

"Fine. I'll see you there at twelve."

"I'm going to go back to bed." Jada yawned.

"Thanks. Bye," Wellington said.

Jada slipped under the covers and cuddled underneath Darryl. She began to wonder what could possibly be wrong in the World of Wellington the Great. Maybe Jazzmyne had broke the news to him about their mother.

* * *

Jada got out of the bed. She looked for Darryl but he was nowhere to be found. She looked in the bathroom, the kitchen, and the living room. She looked out the window. The space where he'd parked was empty. When the doorman buzzed, she thought it was Darryl.

"Yes."

"Ms. Tanner. Candice is here to see you."

"It's okay. She can come up."

"Hey, girl. What are you doing out so early?"

"Girl. It's almost three. You must have had a *long* night," Candice said.

"Are you sure?" Jada rushed to the nearest clock.

"*Yes,* I'm sure. Why? What's wrong with you?"

"I was supposed to meet Wellington at noon. He really needed to talk. He sounded like he had a lot on his mind. I have to call the restaurant."

"It was meant to be, Jada," said Candice. "He probably wants to have his cake and eat it too and personally I think he has eaten you enough. Don't bother to call him. He'll be just fine with his wife."

"I have to at least call the restaurant." Jada pressed 911 and hung up. Then she dialed 411.

"Fine. Do whatever you like. How many times are you going to let him use you? I'm going home. Call me later."

"Thank you for calling the New Orleans Grille."

"Yes, is there a gentleman by the name of Wellington Jones in your restaurant?" Jada crossed her fingers.

"Sorry, but we don't page our guests. If you'd like to leave a message, we'll do our best to deliver it."

"This is an emergency," Jada insisted. "Let me speak with your manager."

"Hold, please."

Jada tapped her nails on the kitchen table.

"Are you still there?"

"The question is are *you* all there?" Jada snapped.

"They really don't pay me enough to provide telephone entertainment. Are you Jada?"

"Yes. Yes I am. Is he still there?"

"No. He's not. But he did leave a message for you. He said, '*Thanks.*'"

"Is that it? Hello! Hello!" Jada pressed the off button on her cordless and sighed. Maybe Candice was right. It simply wasn't meant for her to see Wellington.

Chapter 21

Wellington nervously paced the floor in his office. He wondered what could be so important that Jazzmyne had to come over immediately. He looked intensely at the photo of his mother. Jazzmyne undoubtedly had the same eyes. He heard a car door shut. Wellington opened his front door. Walter walked in as if Wellington were expecting him.

"Wellington, man, you cannot continue to bury yourself in your work and never leave the house. You've got to get out," Walter said. He followed Wellington into the kitchen.

Wellington grabbed the pitcher of orange juice. "Want some?"

"Sure."

"Have you ever heard of solitude?" Wellington asked.

"Solitude has nothing to do with it. You're becoming depressed. You've stayed in your house day after day. When was the last time you went out?"

"Monday."

"Today is Friday, man! You haven't been outside in *four* days. Look, I'm going to chill here with you for a while then I'm coming back to pick you up at nine. We're going out tonight. And I'm not taking no for an answer."

"Suit yourself. You're overreacting."

"Well, I'm not overreacting about Melanie. I wish I could convince you to visit her. Wendy says Melanie asks for you all the time. It's not right that you don't visit your wife. She's suffered enough from the accident *and* the miscarriage."

Wellington sipped on his juice and stared at the big screen.

"You've already made one mistake," Walter continued. "With all her faults, man, she's *still* human. *And* she still loves you. Jada clearly doesn't want any part of you. She stood you up. She doesn't return your calls. *Forget* about her. Move on with your life. She's moved on with hers."

"Walter, I've already told you. You don't understand. So, I'm not going to explain it to you *again*. Jada will always be a part of my life. I've accepted that. Now, if you don't mind, I have work to do before the stock market closes," Wellington said.

"I'll be back at nine." Walter rinsed his glass, set it on the counter, and walked out.

As Walter drove off, Jazzmyne pulled up in the driveway. Wellington's mind raced at the speed of lightning. "Hi. Come on in."

"I apologize for such short notice," Jazzmyne said.

"Don't mention it. Would you like something to drink?"

"Only if you have plastic cups." Jazzmyne laughed.

"No such luck," Wellington teased. "What would you like?"

"Your orange juice looks good."

"Okay, have a seat in the family room. I'll be right there." Wellington poured Jazzmyne's juice into an eight-ounce glass.

"I hooked you up with a smaller glass. How's that?"

"Perfect." Jazzmyne's eyes roamed the room. Wellington waited for her to say something, but she didn't. She shook her leg.

"So. What was so important?" Wellington asked.

"I'm just sorting where to begin and end," Jazzmyne said.

"That's easy. Start at the beginning and don't stop until you get to the end. How's that?"

Jazzmyne took a deep breath. "Wellington, I'm your sister." Wellington didn't respond. "What I'm about to tell you may make you angry. But you have a right to know."

Wellington stared into Billie Holiday's face and listened. Jazzmyne started at day one, all right. She went back to Katherine, Cynthia, and Susan's history in Mississippi. Wellington felt anger. Hatred. Disgust. Jazzmyne continued. Wellington's knee moved up and down.

"So, the fact that Cynthia's last name is Jones is coincidental?" Wellington questioned.

"Perhaps," Jazzmyne answered. "But I'd bet it was by design. Like Susan's."

"So, it's a possibility I've just married my *half-sister?*"

"Sometimes small towns are too small. Let's hope not. Our mother said Susan swore Keith wasn't the father."

"Did you tell Jada?" Wellington rubbed his head.

"I had to tell someone. And she was the one I could trust. But this is not about Jada. Wellington, your father, Keith Thompson, lives in Oakland. Here's his address and phone number."

Wellington stood and covered his ears as if he didn't want to hear another word.

"I'll let you sort through all of this. Let's talk again tomorrow," Jazzmyne said.

Wellington gave Jazzmyne a brotherly hug. He rocked her in his arms. "As frustrated as I am, I'm glad to have you in my life. You have no idea how painful it was for me. Not knowing my parents. My sister. My niece and nephew." Tears streamed down Wellington's face. *"I'll call you,* tomorrow."

Wellington walked Jazzmyne to the door. He went into his office and removed Cynthia's picture from the wall. He forwarded his business calls to the voice mail paging operator and drove off in his car.

Cynthia had stooped to an all-time low. He'd never forgive her for this. Wellington busted through the door. He finally found Cynthia and Chris on the third floor in the sunroom.

"Cynthia *Elaine* Jones." The words crawled out like a snake on its belly. Cynthia sat up and stared at Wellington. Chris jumped up and stood in front of Wellington.

"Son! What's the matter with you? Back up off of your mother."

The word "mother" hit Wellington below the belt. "She's not *my* mother. But her sister is."

Chris stared at Wellington. Cynthia was quiet. "Cynthia. What is Wellington talking about?"

"Yeah, *Cynthia*. What is Wellington talking about?"

"Stop calling your mother Cynthia!"

"I'll *never* call her mother again as long as I live. You could have told me Jazzmyne was my sister! I've missed over thirty years of her life because of your games. Why didn't you tell me?" Wellington paced the hardwood floor. "Answer me! Answer me, damn it!"

Chris stared at Cynthia. Cynthia remained silent. "Cynthia. I think you owe Wellington *and me* an explanation."

Cynthia stood and stepped up to Wellington. She stopped two inches from Wellington and stared up into his eyes. "That *bitch!* Katherine vowed *never* to tell *anyone*. If she hadn't been such a slut—and stole my man—you would have never been born a *bastard."* Cynthia's spit splattered across Wellington s face. *"All my life* I've sacrificed for *you,* for *her.* And this is the thanks I get? I should have let our grandfather rape her like he raped me! I hate you! And I hate your father!"

Wellington dropped to his knees, pressed his hands together, and prayed in silence. He heard something fall. He opened his eyes. Cynthia was on the floor holding her chest. She gasped for air.

"Call 911," she said faintly. "Call . . ."

Wellington looked at Cynthia. Her mouth turned into her cheek and stayed. Wellington stood. Cynthia reached toward him. Her arms collapsed to the floor. Wellington walked out. He stopped. Looked back at Chris's face. Tears streamed from Chris's eyes. Wellington flipped his cell phone open and dialed 911.

Chapter 22

Jada partially listened to Candice and Jazzmyne as they all shopped for dresses at Macy's in San Francisco. Her body was there, but her mind wasn't. Maybe she was experiencing separation anxiety. The Bay area had been home all her life.

"I'm so glad you decided to go out with us tonight," Candice said.

"Between work, the kids, and Calvin, I barely have time for myself," Jazzmyne said. "I wasn't coming at first, but Calvin insisted I needed to have some fun with the girls. After I thought about it for a moment, I said to myself, he's right. I do need to get out and have some fun with two of my closest friends, before they head to L.A."

"I'm going to pick out the diva dress of the century for you, girl," Candice said. "I might even buy a little something for myself while I'm at it."

"Now you know I'm somewhat conservative. And don't forget I have two children who will both be wide awake when I leave. I don't want to give them the wrong impression."

"Don't worry, I've got it all under control," Candice said. "We'll just get you an outfit that instantly converts into the diva dress. We'll find something with two pieces. When you have on both pieces, you'll be Jazzmyne, but when you take off that top layer, girl, you'll be so hot we'll have to change your name."

"How does Simone sound?" asked Jazzmyne.

"Too conservative. Leave it to me. I'll think of something. Just leave everything up to me."

"Jada, you've been awfully quiet. Are you all right?" asked Jazzmyne.

"Yeah, you have been too quiet, girl," said Candice.

"I'm fine. I was thinking about how much I miss the Golden Bay Bar. I used to go there almost every Friday before I met Wellington."

"We can remedy that real quick," said Candice. "We can all leave two hours early, go to the Golden Bay for a couple of hours, and then we can head over to Jimmy's."

"I really can't leave two hours earlier," Jazzmyne said. "Pick me up on your way to Jimmy's."

"I'll wait until next Friday," Jada said. She wanted to go alone.

"What do you think about this dress?" Jazzmyne asked.

"It's nice, but put it back. Just put it back right now," said Candice, "and go to the fitting room.

Take *this* dress with you. Try it on, and I'll bring you the outfits until we find something we like."

"Have it your way," Jazzmyne said. "Just make sure whatever you bring is a size fourteen." Jazzmyne took the black dress to the fitting room. She posed in front of the three-way mirror. "Don't you think this dress shows too much cleavage? And it's a little too short."

"Ask any man and he'll tell you there's no such thing as too much cleavage," Candice said as she jiggled her breasts and danced in front of the three-way mirror.

"I like the dress, girl. It's sexy," Jada complimented Jazzmyne.

"It's perfect!" Candice said. "Am I great or what? Now, all we have to do is work on your 'I know I'm a diva' walk."

Jazzmyne looked at Candice and batted her eyes. "You mean I should walk like *this?*" Jazzmyne strutted back and forth, struck a pose, and glided her hands from her tapered hairstyle down to her shapely hips.

"Go on, Ms. Jones! You've truly got it going on." Jada tossed back her head with laughter. "I didn't know you had it in you."

Candice looked at Jazzmyne and said, "You've got skills, Ms. Diva."

"We've *all* got skills," Jazzmyne said. "Some of us just don't feel the need to exhibit them all the time. You see, just when Calvin thinks he knows me well, I show him something new."

"Well, I'm glad you use your powers for good," Jada said.

"Let's go, diva woman," said Candice.

"I'll pick you guys up tonight. Bye." Jada stopped by her mother's house, since it wasn't far from the mall. Jada popped in a cassette with love songs. Wellington had made it especially for her. She listened to "When I'm With You" and reflected on the good times they'd shared, beginning with the night they met. No one could have told her she wouldn't be Mrs. Wellington Jones. Daddy always said *never say never*. Jada was glad she was finally getting Wellington out of her system. Daddy would have agreed it was *time* for her to move on.

Jada noticed her mother's car parked in the driveway. At least that was an indication she was nearby. Either at home or at her husband's house. Jada had stopped using her key after her mother remarried. She knocked on the door three times. Her mother opened it. Jada walked in.

"Baby, I didn't know it was you. I thought you were Robert. I told him to come over at six," Mama said.

Jada's eyes traveled down and back up. She couldn't believe her mother was dressed in a black lace bustier with a matching garter. Her G-string had silver stars on the front. She tried to conceal the can of whipped cream.

"Just give Mama a minute so I can put on my robe."

"That's all right, Mama. I don't want to ruin Robert's surprise. But please, take it easy on him." Jada kissed her mother on the cheek. Robert was on his way over. He smiled and waved good-bye to Jada.

Jada couldn't believe what she had seen. Was that *her* mother? Was that the future grandmother of her children? Jada admitted her mama looked damn good for sixty-three. Now she understood why women lived longer.

Jada drove home and parked her car in the garage. She had already set aside time to pray and meditate before going out. She picked up her phone and got a broken dial tone. She checked her voice mail. There were two new messages.

"Hello, Jada, this is Darryl. I'm calling to see if you'd like to have dinner with me next Saturday. Call me."

Unless Darryl was flying to L.A., that wouldn't be happening. Jada erased the message.

"Hi, Diamond, this is Wellington."

"That's it? That's not a message. This is his way of trying to get me to call him and I'm not going to do it." Jada erased the message.

Jada masturbated in the shower, took a nap, meditated, and prayed so her mind, body, and spirit would be free and her hormones wouldn't be racing out of control.

"Candice, let's go. We have to pick up Jazzmyne," said Jada. Jada waited for Candice in her car. If she went inside, Candice would start a mini-fashion show and she would have to judge.

"I'll be right out," Candice said. Jada hung up her cell phone and turned up the volume on her stereo.

"I apologize. Girl, I was on the phone talking with Terrell. He's in Paris this week." Candice said as she got in the car.

"Yeah, Paris. The City of Love." Jada sighed.

"Girl, don't you start thinking about Wellington again. Be strong."

"He called me today and left a *strange* message." Jada looked in her rearview mirror to see if traffic was clear to merge onto I-580.

"What did he say?" Candice's voice was flat.

"He said, *this is Wellington.*"

"And?" The pitch in Candice's voice was slightly escalated.

"Nothing. That was it. Strange. Don't you think?"

"He's just trying to get you to call him, and when you do, he'll make it seem like you're the one trying to get in touch with him. Forget it, Jada. We'll be gone in less than eight days."

Jada pulled up in front of Jazzmyne's house and called her from the cell phone.

"Hello," Jazzmyne answered.

"Hi, Jazzmyne, we're outside waiting," Jada said.

"I'll be right out. Give me three minutes."

Jazzmyne stepped out of her front door looking like a new woman. "Hi, ladies. I'm ready to have a good time tonight," Jazzmyne said.

"Girl, you look like a new woman. Hair. Nails. Makeup." Candice popped her fingers to the beat. "Let's get this party started."

Traffic was light on the freeway and on the streets so they made it to Jimmy's in about fifteen minutes. "Let's sit upstairs," Jada suggested. "I want to see the *entire* dance floor."

They walked single file. The narrow staircase dictated two lines—one went up and the other came down. Before Jazzmyne could make it to the top, a handsome athletic man with broad shoulders and bulging muscles stopped her.

"You sure are looking lovely tonight. Do you mind if I have this dance?" he asked.

"I'll savor it for you," Jazzmyne said and smiled.

"Are you sitting upstairs?" he asked.

"I will be."

"Then I'll be back shortly," he said. Then he handed the waitress in front of Jada a fifty-dollar bill and gestured toward Jazzmyne. "Serve the beautiful woman whatever her heart desires and make sure her glass is always at least half full."

"Now that's what I call a real man," said the waitress as she tucked the fifty in her bra.

As soon as they were seated, Julio, the flower man, walked over to the table and placed a dozen red roses in front of Jada.

"Compliments of the gentleman at the bar with the black blazer on." Then he rushed off.

Jada and Candice looked in disbelief.

"Julio definitely gets around. Candice, do you see Wellington at the bar?"

"No."

"Well, what does the guy in the black blazer look like?" Jada refused to turn around.

"Oh my goodness, he's the running back for the Oakland Raiders," Jazzmyne said.

"Are you sure?" Jada still would not look.

"No. I'm not sure. I'm *positive*," Jazzmyne said. "I'm a sports fanatic and that's him, all right."

"Somebody give these roses to him," Jada pleaded. That many roses from any man would only remind her of the night she'd met Wellington.

"This is a bad sign," Candice said.

"I'll take them back," Jazzmyne said. Jazzmyne picked up the flowers. Jada watched Jazzmyne. She walked over to the running back and politely placed the flowers on the bar. "Please, don't ask." Jazzmyne turned and walked away.

"I hate to ruin everyone's night, but I have to leave. I'll take a taxi. Candice, you can keep my car and drive Jazzmyne home."

"No way. We came together. We're leaving together," Jazzmyne said. "Besides. I've had enough already."

Chapter 23

Wellington thought long and hard about everything Jada had told him. His real father didn't make any excuses for what happened in Mississippi. He didn't deny he was his father, but he wasn't aware he had a son. He doubted Melanie and Stephanie were his, but he could not guarantee they weren't.

"Mrs. Jones, you have a visitor," the nurse said. Wellington stood at the doorway.

Melanie's back faced the door. "Who is it?"

"It's your husband."

Melanie rolled over. "So he finally decided to show up the day before I'm scheduled to be released from the hospital. That's wonderful," Melanie said. "Send him in."

"Hi. How are you?" Wellington asked. He handed Melanie a bouquet of long-stem red roses.

"Does it really matter how I'm doing?" Melanie

handed the roses to the nurse. "Could you please find something to put these in?"

"Certainly, Mrs. Jones. I'll be right back."

Melanie looked at Wellington. "I've been in the hospital almost three months and you make two appearances, one on the day I'm admitted and another the day before I'm released. At least you could have come when our children *died.*"

"I apologize. I really didn't want to upset you. I had to sort out a lot of things in my life. I thought it was best if I stayed away," Wellington said.

"You didn't want to make me upset!" Melanie shouted. "You didn't want to make me upset! Wellington, we exchanged vows, to have and to hold, for better or worse, through sickness and in health. But I see now that those words just rolled off of your lips without any *true* meaning." Melanie buried her face in the pillow and cried. "I love you, Wellington. I married you because I love you." She looked up at Wellington. "But it's obvious you don't feel the same."

Wellington pulled a tissue out of the floral print box and dried Melanie's tears. "Melanie, please calm down. I told you in the beginning. I wasn't in love with you." Wellington remained composed. "Isn't there something *you* want to tell *me?*"

"Like what?" Melanie responded. Her eyes shifted away from Wellington.

"Exactly why did you come to San Francisco?" Wellington asked. "How did you find a top-level management position at Sensations Communications? Why did we have to *rush* and get married? Why, Melanie? Why? Answer me!"

"I don't know!" Melanie cried louder and harder. "I don't know!" Melanie turned her back.

The nurse stepped into the room. "Is everything in here all right?"

"It's okay." Melanie sniffled.

"I need to check your vital signs, Mrs. Jones," said the nurse. Silence filled the room. "Mr. Jones, I have to ask you to leave. Mrs. Jones needs to rest."

"Please wait, Wellington. Don't leave. I need you," Melanie begged. Her eyes drooped. "Nurse, please give us a few more minutes. Please."

"You have ten minutes, Mr. Jones."

"Wellington, please sit down," Melanie said. "Not over there. Sit here, next to me." Wellington sat on the bed. Melanie picked up Wellington's hand and softly stroked it.

Wellington studied Melanie's facial features. There was no resemblance.

"Forgive me?" Melanie asked. "I know I haven't been completely honest with you, but you haven't been completely honest with me either. You're still in love with Jada. I thought I could compete for you and win. And I did. When I saw how much you loved Jada, I was convinced I could get you to love me more."

"I *do* love you," Wellington said. "Like a friend, not a wife. I'm just sorry I couldn't see through your lies and deceit. Not to mention Cynthia's. The doctors approved her release for tomorrow, but she has to do rehab for twelve months. Her deception rolled up into a major heart attack. It almost killed her. She stopped breathing. I performed CPR on her until the paramedics arrived."

"So, where do *we* go from here?" Melanie asked.

"Judge Judy," Wellington said. "I just want out." Melanie shoved Wellington's hand away. "You're not thinking about divorcing me, are you? I'll never grant you a divorce, Wellington Jones. I'll take you for all you have! Every single dime!"

"You already have, Melanie." Wellington slowly stood and looked down into Melanie's piercing eyes. *You already have.*

"That's why I wrecked *both* of your Jaguars." Melanie smiled and leaned back on her pillow.

The nurse stepped into the room. "Mr. Jones, I'm going to have to ask you to leave."

Wellington looked at the nurse and softly responded. "I was never here." Then he turned to Melanie. "Your mother will be here tomorrow to pick you up. You're staying with Cynthia. The two of you can recover together."

Melanie picked up a plastic cup of water and threw it in Wellington's direction. He never looked back.

Wellington decided to drive to the Golden Bay Bar in the hopes that Jada might be there. It was crowded. If Jada was there, he'd find her. All he had to do was observe which direction the men's heads turned and he would find his Diamond.

Wellington sat in the corner in order to stay out of view. Slow jams filled the air along with the cheerful voices of professionally dressed men and women who were thankful it was Friday. A short and sassy woman walked in and went straight to the bar. She looked at the bartender. He handed her a drink. She proceeded to join a group of ladies and men sitting at a table in the rear. She was definitely a regular. Jada used to be one too. He remembered she'd brought him there a couple of times before they'd established their own favorite places.

"Excuse me. What would you like to drink?" asked the waitress.

"I'll have a Hennessey," responded Wellington. "Make that a double." Wellington was willing to sit all night just for a chance to see Jada. She had stopped returning his phone calls. She'd stood him up. He laughed. He must have been crazy.

Wellington reminisced about the good times. Bad times. Several hours had passed. Most of the faces in the crowd had changed.

"Would you like another Hennessey?" asked the waitress.

"No, thanks. I think I'll call it a night. You can give me the check. Wellington pulled out his wallet. As he stood up to pay his tab, he noticed how the men's heads turned. He watched them greet his Diamond. Jada flirted and kept walking. She seemed happy. The group at the table next to Wellington's could have been Jada's welcoming committee. They were elated to see her. Wellington pushed his chair back as far as he could so she wouldn't notice him.

"Where in the world have you been, Ms. Thang?" asked Raymond as he snapped his fingers and gave Jada a warm embrace. Wellington remembered Raymond too well. He was so busy looking for Jada all night he hadn't noticed that was her group of friends. He was relieved they hadn't noticed him.

"Raymond, you haven't changed a bit," Jada said.

"You're not privileged to fall out of sight and then fall back in fashion looking new and improved. I'm the only card-carrying privileged diva around here and don't you forget it," said Raymond.

"Save some love for the rest of us, Raymond," said Sheila. Sheila stepped between them and gave Jada a hug. All of Jada's friends gathered around and showered her with hugs and kisses.

"Jada, here is your favorite, a glass of chilled champagne," said Donna. Donna had a memory like an elephant when it came to alcohol. She was the best waitress Wellington had met. She could remember what everyone in the bar was drinking without writing down a single order.

Jada's spirit was so beautiful. He noticed she wore his favorite leopard dress. The one she'd had on when they met. When the bartender announced last call, Wellington walked over to Jada's table. Everyone stopped laughing and stared. He felt like he was on display or trial.

"Excuse me, may I have a moment of your time?" Wellington asked Jada.

"I thought you would never ask," said Raymond. Everyone started laughing. Wellington figured if you can't beat them, join them. Since the odds were not in his favor, he laughed too.

"I'm so glad I had a chance to see you guys before leaving," Jada said. She hugged each of her friends.

"We'll be in L.A. to visit you," Raymond said. "Jada?"

"Yes, Raymond."

"You can have your diva card back, girl, but if you need some help"—Raymond nodded in Wellington's direction—"I'm only a diva wink away." Raymond snapped his finger.

"I love you too, Raymond," Jada said.

Wellington knew Raymond was dead serious.

"How did you know I was here?" asked Jada as they walked outside.

"I didn't. I hoped I would see you one last time before you left. Do you mind if we go to my place? I need to talk with you," asked Wellington. So much had changed between them over the past four months, but his feelings for Jada hadn't changed at all.

"Actually, I do mind," Jada responded. "Wellington, I've moved on with my life."

"Are you seeing someone?" Wellington asked.

"Not yet."

Wellington was relieved. "Please, Diamond, I really need to talk with you. There are so many things I need to say."

"All right. We can talk, but not at your place. You can come over to mine."

When Wellington walked into Jada's penthouse, he noticed everything was packed in boxes. "Damn, you really are moving?" Reality hit him below the belt once more.

"I leave tomorrow." Jada walked around the boxes and sat in the living room. "The movers will be here at noon."

Wellington looked around the room. "Are you selling your penthouse?"

"No. I have a renter moving in next weekend. So, what did you want to talk about?"

"I really don't know where to start, but let me say I was foolish to let you go." Wellington paused and took a deep breath. "You know I believe everything happens for a reason," he continued.

"Yes. I remember," Jada said. Her face was beautiful, but expressionless. Her hazel eyes stared at him.

"I realize the reason we're not together is because I allowed my decisions to be influenced by others. I'm wiser for the experience, but it cost me a price I couldn't afford to pay. It cost me you." Wellington stroked the side of Jada's face. Softly. Gently.

"You were right in your letter." Wellington paused. "But you didn't mean if you never saw me again it would be too soon. Did you?"

Jada held Wellington's hand next to her heart. "Those were my feelings at the time. Wellington, I lost a part of me trying to hold on to you. You hurt me. But the biggest lesson I learned was that I hurt myself."

"I thought about you every single day." The feel of Jada's breasts was distracting. Wellington moved Jada's hands next to his heart. "And each day you weren't there, I was in pain. I was so confused then, but I'm not anymore. Jazzmyne told me she had talked with you about my past." Wellington desperately sought Jada's affection.

Jada went into her bedroom and returned with a small black box. "This is for you." She handed it to Wellington.

Wellington held it. His eyebrows locked together.

"It's your soulmate ring. I was going to give it to you on our honeymoon." Jada placed the ring on Wellington's right ring finger.

"I want you to know I'll always cherish it." Then he French-kissed Jada's hand the way he did the night they met. Jada closed her eyes.

"I need you, Diamond. Please let me hold you just one more night."

"Do you have any protection?"

"No. Do I need it?" Wellington asked. He rubbed his head and frowned.

"For more reasons than one," Jada responded. "I stopped taking my contraceptives, and you have a wife, remember."

Wellington licked his lips and kissed Jada. He was thrilled she returned the passion. He knew she wanted him as much as he wanted her.

Jada stopped. "Wait. That's not fair."

"Life isn't fair," Wellington responded and smiled. He tossed the pillows on the floor. Leaned Jada against them. She welcomed him into her world once more.

Wellington stood. His pants fell to the floor. Jada tasted his rich caramel cream that oozed to the tip of his head. She braced herself on her knees and devoured him. Tears streamed down her face. Wellington couldn't tell which was harder, the lump in his throat or the one in Jada's. Wellington carried Jada to the bedroom. He laid her on the bed. "I'm thirsty."

Jada's chocolate thighs parted like a blooming flower. Wellington couldn't seem to quench his thirst. He drank for hours. Jada never dried out.

"I want you to penetrate me."

Wellington moved methodically. He entered Jada's welcoming walls of wonder. She pulled him in like a strong pulsating current on the ocean shore. Damn!

He stroked as deep as he could. Just the way she liked it.

Jada whispered in Wellington's ear, "I'm cumming. I'm cumming." Her nails began to dig deep into his flesh.

"I'm cumming with you, baby."

Wellington held Jada's firm chocolate ass in the palms of his hands and continued to rock deeper. Her pulsating walls pulled him in closer.

Their orgasms created a wave of love. Emotions. Unspoken devotion. It traveled until it slammed against the ocean shore. They froze. They were locked into one another at the peak of their climax. Wellington held Jada close to his sweaty caramel chest. He inhaled her favorite fragrance.

"Diamond is Forever." Wellington paused. He felt Jada's spiritual energy. "Where do we go from here?"

Jada kissed Wellington's lips. She wrapped her arms around him. He felt their souls gel. "I'm still in love with you, Wellington. You will *always* have a place in my heart. I don't know where we go from here." She spoke softly. Jada looked Wellington in his eyes. "But I do know I've renewed my lease on life. I have a business to start and a plane to catch to Los Angeles. Maybe I'll call you. Maybe I won't."

Deception

It's funny how deception
Will mask
Its own perception
And justification
Begins manifestation

So you hold and mold
Someone else's soul

It dominates the conscious
'Til you can no longer see

The pain killer
Is now the thriller
I use to kill you
You used to kill me

Our Spirits—they die
Our subconscious multiplies

Because I've contaminated your soul
So now you hold—a grudge
Against the world
Faceless strangers
You will meet
Their spirits will trample
Under your feet

Because deception
Was the perception
And now justification

Is the contagious—subconscious
Manifestation

Break the cycle that kills
Be true to yourself
And the others will heal

The Art of Finding
Your Soulmate

Introduction

Finding your soulmate is an *art*. Understand that art is created through the mind, body, soul, and spirit of the artist. And once you have read *The Art of Finding Your Soulmate*, you will be equipped with the necessary tools to assist you with identifying your soulmate(s) based upon your awareness. Because soulmates are spiritually connected, you may discover that you have more than one. Also, realize that sacred connections are neither gender nor race oriented.

FIVE KEY ELEMENTS

Take time to learn the five key elements:

1. Understand Your Spirit—Be true to yourself
2. Spiritually Connect with the Universe—Take time to smell the roses

3. Stop Suppressing Your Spiritual Energy—Let go of the negative energy
4. See What You Hear, Hear What You See—Eliminate the psychological noise
5. Think With Your Head, Feel with Your Heart—Release your inner spirit

The underlying concepts are a challenge because you must first comprehend *your* inner spirit.

When you find your soulmate (if you haven't done so already), your souls will gel together as one. Only *you* will truly know. While you may question and/or doubt your spiritual bond, don't deny it. Accept it. Also understand external influences may have physically separated you from your soulmate, but the spiritual link cannot be broken. Denied. Yes. Ignored. Absolutely. Broken. Never.

At the end of each element you will find a *reflective moment* that relates to my novel *Soulmates Dissipate*. The main characters in *Soulmates Dissipate*, Jada Diamond Tanner, Wellington Jones, and Melanie Marie Thompson, exemplify real life situations in an unexpected twisted taste of fiction and faith that may help you to better understand why *The Art of Finding Your Soulmate* is intangible. Your soulmate holds the ultimate key to your highest level of spiritual relationship awareness. Remember, love is never what you want. *Love,* is what *you* make it.

One
Understand Your Spirit

Be true to yourself

In this world, we are surrounded by deception. The words *I love you*, often rolls off the tongue for inappropriate reasons. Lust. Greed. Security. Fear. Sometimes the deceit is so deeply rooted you begin to believe what's wrong, is right. Whenever you find yourself justifying your actions based upon those of another, stop. Be true to yourself.

Don't tell your mate what you think he/she wants to hear. Remember, the first person you lie to is yourself. You sacrifice *your* spirit. If you are in love, accept it. If you're not, acknowledge your feelings. That doesn't suggest you need to dissolve your union. People fall in *and* out of love all the time. However, it does mean you can grow with honesty as a basis for a lifelong friendship whether the two of you stay together, or part. If you haven't found your soulmate, you won't if you're preoccupied exhausting your spiritual energy in an unfulfilling relationship.

If you're not in a relationship, take a moment and ask yourself why. Whatever the basis, do not say there's a shortage of men. What really exists are too many women with excessive limitations and a profusion of men who are reluctant to make a commitment. So what's the real deal? Are you too busy for love? Perhaps you're waiting for Mr. or Mrs. Right? Or have you lost faith in finding your soulmate? Think about your reasons as you continue to read. Now let's look at some of the reasons why soulmates dissipate. It's equally important to learn how to maintain a relationship with your soulmate.

One of the most common examples of treachery is when you think, say, or feel *two can play that game.* When you discover your lover, husband, wife, or soulmate has been unfaithful, you feel betrayed. Used. Abused. Hurt. Angry. Vindictive. Here's a word of advice. Get off of the roller coaster. It will immediately kill your spirit and eventually you'll become resentful. Your misdirected anger can unconsciously manifest into revenge. You engage in emotional warfare with your mate and a physical affair with an innocent party as a desperate attempt to gain attention and inflict pain. You'll probably succeed, but the blameless victim becomes bitter and the vicious cycle never ends. Give up the dreadful thrills. Don't keep taking the same ride. You've already seen the view. Search your soul and do what's healthiest for *you.*

If you want to date outside your relationship, say so. You'll be consciously free to live your life and the other person can make an informed decision to do the same or call it quits. This doesn't mean your life has to be an open book and you must divulge every single thought. You must learn to be true to yourself. Your spirit must be free before you can find your soulmate. In reality, you may already be with your soulmate and not know it. If you're not in tune with your spirit, you won't be receptive to his/her spiritual energy.

Here is a simple test on how you can feel your spirit die when you lie to yourself.

STEP 1: Take a deep breath. Think about your soulmate or someone you're in love with.

STEP 2: Allow yourself to remember all the good times you've shared together.

STEP 3: Now, take another deep breath. *Silently* tell yourself . . . *I truly love* . . . <u>use the person's name</u>. Feel the love?

STEP 4: Keep thinking about that person.

STEP 5: Inhale. Exhale. Silently tell yourself . . . *I do not love* . . . <u>use the same person's name</u>. Do you feel the difference?

You kill a piece of your spirit each time you lie to yourself. Positive energy lifts your spirit up and you actually feel the movement inside your body. Negative energy does the exact opposite. If you didn't notice it the first time, it may help if you close your eyes and focus from within. It is important that you understand your spirit.

REFLECTIVE MOMENT
Soulmates Dissipate

Chapter 4

"**A**re you the type of man who will commit to one woman? And before you answer, let me say fidelity is extremely important to me."

At least this was an easy question. "Well, I had a wife once but her husband came and got her." Wellington slapped his leg and nudged Jada's shoulder. She laughed too. "I'm happy you have a sense of humor. You just passed your first test."

"What do you mean?" Jada inquired.

"If you had taken me serious, I would have known you weren't comfortable with the subject even though you asked the question. Therefore, I wouldn't have discussed any of my personal relationships with you. It's a major turnoff when women get defensive about my past experiences. I'm not perfect, and I don't try to be." Wellington glanced down at Jada's thighs. The front flap of her skirt had formed into a V at her crotch.

Two
Spiritually *Connect* with the Universe

Take time to smell the roses

Where is your universal energy source? God? Ocean? Moon? Stars? Flowers? Sun? Birds? Trees? Air? Rain? There is no limit on the number of connections you may have. You should not ostracize other forms of spiritual existence. Take time to discover where your connections are. Then embrace them. They are powerful energizers when you need or want spiritual uplifting and they're essential if you strive to reach *cosmic ecstasy*. Some people love water. It can be the ocean, the sea, a stream, or a river. It doesn't matter. The connectedness fuels their spiritual energy.

Just as humans cannot exist without oxygen and trees cannot survive without carbon dioxide; if you are not in tune with your spiritual synergy, you are not complete. It's like being alive on life support.

You should start seeking your natural companions today.

As you journey to smell the roses, remember everyone does not connect everywhere. For example, you may discover that you enjoy still water, but you do not like the rain. You may bond with both, but fear thunder and lightning. That's okay. Allow yourself to feel what you feel. It's like love and hate. Both are very real and both have varying degrees. Positive and negative energy balances us within the universe.

Understand that everyone creates and hold good and bad spiritual energy—sometimes called vibes. You cannot avoid being affected by a person sending you despondent messages if you're listening to him/her. Fortunately, you can detach yourself from most of it by telling the person you're not interested in hearing their redundant complaints . . . especially if they haven't sought a solution to *their* problem. It's okay to let others lean on your shoulder. Just don't allow them to leech.

Habits are difficult to break. Know that the human brain is a conditioning tool. You can do whatever you want! If you are a pessimistic person, try being optimistic. Improve your way of thinking about others and yourself and you will open doors that will allow you to tap into your universal sources. Take time and notice all of the external energy forces surrounding you.

REFLECTIVE MOMENT
Soulmates Dissipate

Chapter 4

Wellington unwrapped the back of Jada's scarf. "What are you—?"

"Sssssshhh. Don't speak. Just listen and bond spiritually with the sounds of the ocean, and the setting of the sun. Soon will come the full moon and the twinkling of the stars." Wellington turned the volume low and popped in a CD with all the songs played from the night they met. "This is the ideal time to be on the beach. Within a few hours, we'll experience it all."

Jada turned her head to the side and closed her eyes. Wellington pulled out the oil and began to massage her back. Deep, strong strokes glided along her soft skin. . . .

Three

Stop Suppressing *Your* Spiritual Energy

Let go of the negative energy

Do you suppress your spiritual energy? Before you answer, think for a moment. Do you hold in your feelings? Do you say yes, when you really want to say no? Do you try not to hurt people's feelings? Do you pretend to like or love someone when you actually don't? Do you find yourself taking relationship advice from your friends who haven't had a relationship in so long even they can't remember?

The list of questions goes on, but these are just a few examples of how you suppress your divine energy. Remember, each time you prevaricate you are restricting your spiritual growth.

A relationship is an investment of your time, energy, and money. You'll spend hours, days, weeks, or even months bargaining for the automobile of your dream. You'll shop online, test drive the car over and over, even haggle over the price repeatedly. But when it comes to your relationship, you have no time, very little patience, and seldom will you spend your money. It's still true. The best things in life are free. Unfortunately, even those items seem to cost you too much time.

Sure you used to go out to dinner, in the beginning. And perhaps you now buy a gift or two throughout the year. But how often do you give or get a massage from your significant one? How often do you spontaneously exert effort into doing something nice? When was the last time you sent flowers? Ladies, that applies to you as well. Most men do like roses.

Now, the moment something goes wrong, you have all day and night to nitpick. When you're not complaining to the other person, you're driving yourself insane thinking about the situation continuously.

When your girlfriend or guy friend calls, you have all the time in the world to listen. You even change the tone in your voice. Smile. Laugh. Whatever the emotional bond calls for, you are ready, willing, and able to support the cause. But as soon as you hang up the phone, the negative thoughts about your spouse resurface.

Most people don't marry, many more may never meet, and some don't even realize they're with their soulmate. Unconstructive energy can ultimately destroy a relationship. Stop suppressing your spiritual energy. Learn to let go of the things that destroy your positive energy. Only then will you be free.

One last comment, all men are not dogs. In fact,

most of them aren't. And, all women do not grow up and become sugar and spice and everything nice. Excessive pessimism is mental conditioning. It's one of the worst forms of abuse. Enhance your outlook on life. If you don't, at some point your relationship will explode. Remember, negative energy drains your spirit.

REFLECTIVE MOMENT
Soulmates Dissipate

Chapter 13

"**A**fter I leave tonight," she said in a quiet voice, "I want you to spend at least thirty minutes praying and thirty minutes meditating." Jazzmyne's voice had a calming effect on Jada. Her body began to relax.

"Now I have to be honest with you, Jada. I've been a counselor for almost ten years. . . . So I can tell, you've intentionally left out some very important information. Jada, you have to trust me. I'm only here to help you. Not to hurt you. But I can't if you won't tell me the real reason why your relationship with Wellington failed."

Damn, was Jada talking with a psychic or a counselor? But at this point, the table had turned. Jada decided to tell Jazzmyne everything.

"We all sin, Jada. You're not infallible. And there's no measuring scale in heaven that says your sins will be weighed heavier than the sins of others.

You're a Christian woman. Therefore, you already know that God has forgiven you. . . .

"You also have to accept responsibility for your actions," she said. "You must stop blaming Melanie for what she has done as a means to justify what you have done. You must forgive yourself and as difficult as it may be—as a Christian—you must forgive Melanie. . . ."

Four
See What *You* Hear
Hear What *You* See

Eliminate the psychological noise

Have you ever met someone who has a nice personality? They're attractive. You engage in conversation. You're peripheral vision scans the person from head to toe. Nice body. Your mind wanders. They are talking, but you are thinking . . . *Damn! He/she sure looks good.* You use your body language to disguise your thoughts and pretend to be interested in what is being said. Or the exact opposite could have been the case, so you say to yourself . . . *this person has bad breath. Where are my friends? It's definitely time to go.* Did you stop and think perhaps the individual had food with garlic for lunch or dinner? He/she had every intention of eating a mint, but didn't have one and did not have time to get it before he/she met you.

Irrespective of the reason(s), far too often you

do not *listen* to the other person. Likewise, they too fail to receive your message(s). Society has already dictated what type of man or woman you should marry. Basically, one who can fulfill *your* needs. Your family and friends have imposed their opinions, as well. So now you're looking for love in all the wrong places and wondering why you haven't met your soulmate. Work on enhancing your self-sufficiency and self-actualization. That's what builds self-esteem and healthy relationships because you no longer depend on society to validate your relationship choices. Look at the other person and see what you hear. Observe their body language. Then, search within yourself and hear what you are seeing. Don't judge. Listen to your spirit.

Another important factor is, don't choose your mate or leave them based upon someone else's opinion. Make your own decision. You're the one who has to live with it. If you need time away from an unhealthy environment, take it. Heal from within and you'll be free to love again. If you're already in a relationship with your soulmate, paying attention to what the other person is saying may help the two of you grow together instead of drift apart. If you haven't found your soulmate, you won't find him/her as long as you continue to focus on the physical.

Remember, people are not perfect. Far too often we hold others to a higher level of expectation than ourselves. If you stop and think, you can probably recall at least one occasion when you promised to call someone or do something for your significant one, and you either forgot or simply didn't have the time. Even worse, you may have not been true to yourself when you made the commitment. You may have hung up that phone and immediately said . . . *I am not going to call him back and I hope he doesn't call me.* A good rule of measure is . . . always judge yourself harder than you evaluate others.

Additionally, if you have to revisit the same argument or disagreement for days on end, someone isn't listening. Resolve your relationship issues as quickly as possible so your spirit can be at peace. You can't live and lie and then question why your relationship failed. The *truth* of the matter is, you already know. Just as if you don't check your financial statement, you cannot balance your bank account. If you never check yourself, you can't possibly balance your relationship. Remember; listen with your eyes, ears, and spirit.

REFLECTIVE MOMENT
Soulmates Dissipate

Chapter 12

"Jada, I thought we were soulmates, but then you changed on me. I saw a side of you I'd never seen before. I didn't realize you had such an awful temper. You always seemed so peaceful. Jada, this was the first authentic challenge of our relationship. And your actions proved you didn't trust me. When I tried to open up to you, you slapped my face and ran out the door. When I called you, you hung up on me. When I went to sleep, you turned my house into the Hunan Garden."

Jada looked out of the corners of her eyes. Her lips curled.

"I'm serious damn it! This is *not* a joke," Wellington continued. "You didn't try to meet me halfway. I made a mistake. I was honest enough to share that with you. I'm not perfect and I don't try to be.

I told you that the first time we went out. And now that you're ready to talk, am I supposed to be ready too? Look, I still love you. I'll always love you. But I don't think it's a good idea for us to get married."

Find out these few things, we'll think whether
else you're ready to ...... and I say ...... I am be-
ward to you? Give ...... you. The bottom line
with hard data think it's ...... you're no longer
insure...

Five
Think with *Your* Head
Feel with *Your* Heart

Release Your Inner Spirit

Generally women are too quick to point the finger and men are too fast to bail out. At some
point we all have to just own up to our responsibility. People are human beings, not perfect beings.

For men, sex is a recreational sport and love is
totally separate. For women, sex is sacred and syn-
onymous with love. So how on earth do we ever hit
a home run when we're constantly playing the
field in different parks? One wants to play the out-
field while the other insists on being the short
stop. It really doesn't matter because no one is covering the home plate. And even if someone were
playing catcher, they'd never catch the ball because the pitcher is at a totally different ball game.

This explains why a woman can say *I love you* to a
man after dating for only a few months. This is

perplexing to a man who may not honestly be able to say those same three words after being in a relationship for a year. Just like sports, a man can throw his heart and soul into the here and now, but after the sex is over he's ready for a greater challenge.

Some may think this is cold and callous when in fact it's conditioning. Men are reared differently from women. When a man cries, he's perceived to be weak. However, when a woman cries, she's understood to be hurting. Pain is painful irrespective of gender. A failed relationship with a loved one can silently scar a man for life; thereby, making it difficult for him to make a commitment to the next woman. Men do think with their heads and not as often with the little one as women believe. Very seldom does a man treat his woman the way he *expects* another man to treat his daughter. On the other hand, a woman seldom expects another woman to treat her son as well as she does. So what does this say about how men and women think and feel? This is mental conditioning at its worst.

As a result women become wounded. But men already think . . . she'll get over it. It's expected. More often than not, she will and she does and she moves on to the next man. Eventually women begin to believe all men are alike. Well, let me tell you . . . they're not. The problem is neither the woman nor the man changes her/his expectations. Three months after the next relationship she's right back where she failed the first time and a year later, guess what, he still hasn't said those three words she's longing to hear.

This repetition often keeps one from connecting with his/her soulmate. Women need to think more with their heads and men need to think more with their hearts. Only then will both play the same game in the same park. You can start today by dismissing societal expectations and *release your inner spirit.*

REFLECTIVE MOMENT
Soulmates Dissipate

Chapter 5

"**S**o how is Mr. Terrell Morgan doing these days?" Jada asked as she looked over the San Francisco Bay.

"Well, let's see. We still talk at least once a week and I am so tempted to have a serious relationship with him but long-distance never works out. Someone eventually ends up having to move and I don't envision moving to Los Angeles and he's in the peak of his career. *Every* modeling agency wants him."

Jada nodded. "We get at least three inquiries per day." Terrell was labeled the new Tyson on the block.

"I just don't know."

"You don't know what?"

Candice sighed. "I know girl, it is so unlike me. My heart says yes but my head says no. So until one or the other gives in, I'll just be in limbo."

"As long as you realize he may not be in limbo as long as you. It's cool." Jada recognized this was the first time Candice was concerned about dating a younger man.

Food for thought when you are searching for your soulmate

DO: Love yourself more than anyone else.
DON'T: Allow others to convince you shit smells like roses.

DO: Make your own decisions.
DON'T: Take advice from the lonely.

DO: Question the actions of others.
DON'T: Fault them for yours.

DO: Look inward first.
DON'T: Blame others if you get caught up in the game.

DO: Compromise.
DON'T: Settle.

The following is reserved for you to write down—right now—a message to your lost, found, or future soulmate. As you write, remember the five key elements. Regardless of your decision, verbally communicate your feelings to your soulmate. Understand that the true meaning of your soulmate is not in words: it's inside of you. So, let your spirit flow from your heart to your pen. Remember, art is created through the mind, body, soul, and spirit of the artist. You are now, *the artist.*

Dedicated to My Soulmate:

_____

_____

_____

_____

_____

_____

_____

_____

_____

_____

_____

_____

_____

_____

_____

_____

_____

_____

Love always,

Turn the page for a look at Mary B. Morrison's
Never Again Once More

Chapter 1

"**L**ord give me strength," Jada whispered as she dropped her cell phone into her purse. Inhaling through her nose, she removed her electronic notebook from the overhead compartment and sighed heavily. Never mentioning Wellington Jones by name, she had posed multiple relationship questions to the stranger seated next to her in row one, since he had been happily married to the same woman for over fifty years.

"Sir, thank you for lending an ear." Jada took one step back, allowing him to retrieve his belongings. His brown scuffed briefcase was torn at every corner, and the gold-plated latches had turned mostly silver. The black rubber beneath his walking cane was worn to the slanted wood.

The elderly man licked his dentures, scratched his receding hairline, and replied in his raspy voice, "That's why God gave us two. One so we can listen to how selfish we sound and the other for us to hear. Seems as though you've been listening, but you're so busy hearing yourself, you haven't heard what he's trying to tell you. I've managed to stay married because my wife, she respects my manhood and doesn't try to reduce me to being one of our twelve kids." Then he dug into his butt, relieving himself of a wedgee.

Respect was earned, not given because a man was anatomically correct. "But did I mention to you"—Jada moved closer so the person beside her wouldn't overhear—"he impregnated another woman?"

The old man wasn't as kind to speak low in return. "So did the Reverend Jesse Jackson, but you don't see his wife abandoning him. And if Hillary can forgive Bill, why can't you forgive . . ." This time he dug deeper into his butt and grunted, "What's his name?" His hand quivered, touching hers.

Frowning, Jada said, "Wellington," for the first time during their discussion.

"Yeah, that's it. Jandra, you're a pretty girl. I'll tell you like I've told all of my kids, 'Pride and love is like oil and water. They don't mix.' The sooner you realize that, the healthier your relationship will be."

He still hadn't pronounced her name correctly; but his wisdom surpassed her logic, so Jada moved ahead of him, impatiently waiting as the exit door opened.

The flight attendant smiled cheerfully. "Thank you for flying the friendly skies." Absent her smile, the attendant resembled one of the girls from

Robert Palmer's rock video "Simply Irresistible": pale face, straight black hair slicked back, and red lipstick.

Jada's lips parted, but she didn't respond. Instead, she stretched her five-foot-nine frame until an arch formed in her lower vertebrae. When her black thigh-high boot crossed the threshold and landed on the walkway, a gust of cold air raced up the front split in her cashmere skirt and kissed her red lace thong. Briskly tracing another passenger's footsteps, Jada wished Candice would be late so she'd have an excuse to avoid reliving her best friend's wedding and honeymoon plans.

Not only was Candice timely, but she was the first person Jada noticed when the attendant opened the second exit door leading into the concourse.

"Hey, girl. I thought you were going to backslide, especially since you didn't call me last night." Candice extended a Holy Names prep girl hug, giving Jada three pats on the back. "I like the sexy style. You look like a woman in search of a new man. That's a good thing." Rambling on, Candice pinched the edges of Jada's jacket and peeped inside. "I'm scared of you, Ms. Thang, a split almost up to your clit. Terrell would never allow me to wear this." She released Jada's blazer. "But what's up with all the black? Are we mourning our loss?" Fanning the wind, Candice emphatically said, "Forget Wellington. He doesn't deserve you."

The little old man slowly walked by hunched over his cane, "She's got that right," he said.

What was that supposed to mean? Jada had taken enough of his insults, and if he wasn't seventy something, she'd tell him to go straight to hell. Sighing again, she thought, *Ms. Thang, not Mrs. Jones.* Maybe he was right.

Jada placed her computer bag in Candice's wavering hand and retrieved the waterless sanitizer from her purse. "Let's stop at Starbucks; I could use an iced frappuccino." Sniffing the freshness on her fingertips, she tilted her head back, lifted her smooth straight hair, and gradually released it behind her shoulders.

"How's Terrell?" Jada raised Candice's hand, tugged at her clothes, and pointed at her head. "Where are your acrylic nails? What's up with the Suzie homemaker muumuu dress? And why are you wearing that pent-up out-of-date hairstyle?"

Candice's flat shoes really made her every fraction of five feet four inches. Her once lavish nails were now nubs so short her flesh protruded beyond the edges. A soon-to-be thirty-three-year-old diva was retired in her prime because the broom she was about to jump had already swept her raving beauty under the carpet. Candice had once dressed so provocatively she stopped everything except time.

Terrell wore muscle shirts whenever he wanted and smiled in the faces of gorgeous women, justifying his actions based on his professional image. The most sought after male model, in higher demand than Tyson, had landed his first acting role starring opposite Morris Chestnut, so he'd immediately postponed marrying Candice.

Jada remembered the days—less than six months ago—when she worked at Sensations Communications photographing the world's finest male models, including Terrell. But once Wellington's wicked aunt Cynthia landed Melanie a job as her boss, Jada typed up her resignation, handed it to the receptionist, and kept on stepping. As long as Candice Jordan catered to Terrell Morgan's needs, he was satisfied. That was exactly what Jada refused to do, compromise herself for the sake of having a man.

The airport was overcrowded. Travelers lined the walls and blocked the aisles. "Flight eighty-one has been changed to gate eleven." Outbound passengers grumbled loudly; some of them dragged kids along. Since Jada had experienced the inconveniences of LAX on numerous occasions, she anticipated the seemingly standard announcement.

Standing in line next to her, Candice replied, "My husband is fine. My husband didn't like the nails or the body-hugging clothes; but my husband loves this hairstyle, and he loves me." Candice fingered the chestnut-colored curl hanging alongside her face. "I have our wedding planner in the car. You've got to see the fabrics and colors. You're going to be the most attractive maid of honor." Candice flipped her wrist to display the diamond marquis her fiancé had recently bought.

Maid not matron. Jada was genuinely happy for her girlfriend. If Candice hadn't invited her to Will Downing's concert over a year ago, Jada probably wouldn't have met Wellington. Neither would Candice have met Terrell. They should have been planning a double wedding and reception. Tension throbbed at Jada's temples, so she pressed firmly, repressing the pain.

Handing Jada her drink, the cashier curled Jada's fingers over the ten-dollar bill. "The gentleman in the tan suit prepaid for you and your friend. What would you like?" she asked Candice, then turned back to Jada. "Oh, and he told me to give you this."

Jada flipped the card over and read, "Don't keep me waiting."

Lowering Jada's arm, Candice said to the cashier, "I'll have a café latte with steamed soy milk." Looking at her friend, she continued, "Terrell says I'm lactose intolerant and shouldn't consume dairy products. See, girl, you're reeling the men in already." Candice peeped at the front of the card. "Impressive."

Jada had already checked out the man with the immaculately trimmed beard. His teddy bear love handles seemed to snuggle under a sheer layer of confidence. He wasn't Wellington, but the brother was tall, sexy, and distinguished. He looked like money. Smelled like money, too, when he walked by and winked. His cologne wafted by her, alluringly fresh and clean; not harsh, bold, or like a cheap bar of soap. His nails were manicured. A watch and a ring adorned his left wrist and pointing finger. Diamonds and platinum. Not colored stones and gold. Casually scanning and assessing a man from head to toe was one of Jada's greatest diva techniques. Maybe she'd call him next week after her furniture was delivered.

Although her coochie, aka Lady C, craved affection, Wellington's semen was the only sperm Jada honestly wanted swimming inside her paradise. His lips were the only ones she wanted pressed against her lips, her breasts, and her clit. The idea of getting to know someone new sucked. New issues. Unbearable habits. Why hadn't she followed her first thought and rented a car. Now she was trapped with Candice for the rest of the day. With a sigh, she left the coffee shop and headed for baggage claim.

Helping Jada retrieve her luggage, Candice recovered the suitcase from the conveyor belt and rolled it to her car. "Stay with us until you get settled," she suggested as they got in the car and left the parking lot.

Homelessness was a better alternative than watching Candice mimic the housewife role of Florida Evans from *Good Times*. "I'd love to, but I can't. I need solitude." Jada paused for a moment, watching the cars in the fast lane zoom by. Lowering the visor to block the sun, Jada sipped her drink and said, "Candice, I know you dislike Wellington because he cheated on me, but you have no idea how much I love him. It hurts me when you brag about how perfect your world is while constantly reminding me how fucked up my situation is."

Candice's head snapped to the right. "Girl, where did that come from?"

Ignoring the question, Jada continued, "I'm not desperate to find another man, to get hitched, or to get laid." Okay, maybe the getting laid part wasn't true, because her menstrual cycle was due, and she was so horny the friction between her thighs could bring her to a climax. "Besides, everything I had planned for my wedding, you're using for yours, including exchanging soulmate rings. And what's up with the marquis diamond ring. That was my favorite cut, not yours. But not once have I protested, and I'm not complaining now. And another thing, you need to stop telling Terrell *everything* I tell you. Am I your daily soap opera topic of conversation? You know Terrell and Darryl are still friends." Finally Jada had said what she'd held in far too long. Slowly her migraine started subsiding.

Jada seldom heard from Darryl Williams, but he called—even if he was on the road with his NBA teammates—whenever Terrell updated him on her latest happenings. Friendships with her ex-men were common and important, but she detested when Darryl delivered a verbatim report to her about herself.

Candice had been her girlfriend since third grade, but ever since she'd met and moved in with Terrell, their closeness had become a triangle when it came to secrets. Candice boasted about Terrell's bedroom skills in such detail, Jada felt as if she'd fucked him, too. The head of his penis was smaller than the shaft. The base of his penis was thinner than his shaft, almost like the shape of green zucchini. His nuts were the size of two mouth-sized gumballs when they shriveled up. And his cum tasted natural, like vanilla extract, except when he drank beer. Now Jada understood why Daddy used to say, "Never tell your girlfriend how good your man is in bed because she will find out behind your back." Fortunately for Candice, Jada had access to dicks through her *reserve* list, to which Wellington had become her newest active reserve member.

"Whew! Girl, you are right. You do need solitude. I'll try not to be so happy when I'm around *you*." Faster than a stunt man on fire, Candice did a stop, drop, and roll. She parked in front of the hotel but didn't get out of her car. "I'll tell my husband you said hello. Call me tomorrow. Bye, girl."

Candice drove away so fast the tailwind literally closed the trunk.

What was up with wearing out the word *husband*? They weren't married yet, and Candice was so blinded by love she couldn't see that Terrell was obviously content reaping all the benefits of a married man while maintaining a singles' lifestyle.

After checking in, Jada raced to her room. Before the frappé settled in her stomach, the chilled liquid poured from her mouth. Leaning over the toilet, Jada heaved repeatedly. She removed her clothes and showered, letting the water rinse the residue from her mouth. Then she turned off the water, stepped onto the rug, and dried her hands on the plush white towel. Admiring her dripping-wet radiant onyx complexion in the mirror, Jada punched in zero zero one on her cell phone, tossed back the floral comforter, pressed the talk button, and sprawled across the white sheets as her skin air dried.

"Hi, ba. I'm glad you made it in safely. It's so good hearing your voice. I miss you already." Wellington's captivating tone made her forget all about her pains.

"Yeah, I miss you, too." If not for the static in the line, their connection would have been undetectable. Dead silence. A million thoughts stirred in Jada's mind, but she didn't know what to say next. She'd terminated her relationship with Wellington. She wasn't going back to him, and she was tired of discussing his infidelity. But she also missed the hell out of being with her man. Exman.

"When are you coming back to Oakland?" His seductiveness drew a prompt response.

"Next week. To get my car." A coochie deluxe tune-up wouldn't hurt either because she loved experiencing those sex-released endorphins, those hormones that made her feel like dancing and singing. Wellington's lovemaking made Jada happy to cook breakfast, lunch, or dinner anytime of the day or night. Hell, sometimes she even vacuumed the whole house or jogged around Lake Merritt, waving and smiling at adults, kids, seagulls, geese, and the sparse flamingos. But Jada also needed to visit Dr. Bates to take a pregnancy test. Her sickness was never accompanied by vomiting, so Jada suspected the worse and prayed for the best.

"Call and let me know when you're coming. I'll help you drive back. And maybe you'll come over for dinner before you leave? That's if you're finished boycotting and egging my place."

Jada laughed. "Cheap shot. Anyway, the last time Chef à la Wellington charcoaled steaks into brittle bits, we ended up eating out."

"If I recall correctly, my Nubian—"

Covering her free ear, Jada screamed with laughter. "Don't say it!" Jada didn't want Wellington to remind her how her quasigourmet meal had been so horrid she washed her food and his down the garbage disposal. The salmon croquettes had been harder than hockey pucks, so Wellington had dropped one on the dining room floor, grabbed the broom, and handed her the sponge mop.

After Wellington's first bite of her pecan-orange bundt cake, he'd said, "Um, you've got to taste this. Close your eyes and open your mouth." Then he'd promised, "You're going to love this." When the dessert hit her palate, each of her five senses had protested. Jada had darted her eyes in search of a place to quickly spit it out because she definitely wasn't going to swallow a lump that tasted worse than earwax. They had then fallen to the kitchen floor laughing until their insides cramped, their saliva exchanged between hungry lips, and their knees became sore from making love on the linoleum all night long.

Jada pictured Wellington's dazzling smile, bald head, thick eyebrows, goatee, and his eight pack. Soft hairs outlined his chest and every crevice in his abdomen. His perfectly erect nipples were five shades darker than his caramel complexion. His gentle touch, sensuous lips, passionate kisses, and orgasmic lovemaking were unforgettable. His firm ass, two-hundred-and-twenty-pound, six-foot-four physique, and seductive mannerisms were etched in her brain forever.

Breaking their silence, he said, "Call me in the morning, ba. I'll talk with you later."

Melting at the hearty sound of his voice, Jada felt the words "I love you" suspend in air and surround her spirit. "What are you wearing?"

Wellington whispered, "A smile and a hard-on that's begging for your affection."

"Wet your fingers and massage the head for me." Jada eased her fingers into her mouth and did the same to her clit.

"Ooh, yeah. I'm stroking *The Ruler*. He's growing an extra inch just for you, ba. Open your chocolate thighs wide so I can taste you."

Jada missed how they used to role-play. Her fondest memory was when she'd dressed like a Jamaican and flirted with Wellington in a Caribbean accent at the Farmers' Market. She convinced him to buy exotic fruits that she'd feasted on, off of his succulent flesh outside by his swimming pool during sunset.

"I'm pulling your face in closer, Big Daddy. Trace Mama's rabbit ears with your juicy tongue. Nice and slow." Jada moaned into the receiver as she enjoyed the external orgasm continuously seeping from her clitoris.

"Damn, ba, all of this cream is for you. Your hairs are marinating in my cum. Rub it in," he commanded.

"I'm flowing with you. Sip in my last drops." Jada caressed the moisture between her inner lips and slid her index finger into her vagina, welcoming the strong pulsation accompanying her internal orgasm.

Deep inside, her pussy knocked hard like an out-of-control, overloaded washer machine on a fast spin cycle. That was the results of her daily vaginal weight lifting. The gold ben-wa balls were no longer a challenge, so one day while visiting the pleasure store, the owner had introduced Jada to the ceramic and smooth wooden eggs. Jada had charged both sets and the instruction manual to her Visa. At first learning muscle control to simultaneously move the ceramic eggs in opposite directions, left and right, and up and down, was difficult. But after Jada started stringing the one-pound weight into the bottom opening of the wooden egg and lifting and holding it with her vaginal muscles, rotating the ceramic eggs was a synch. Jada's clenching drove Wellington so nuts his orgasmic groans intensified, sounding like The

Rock lifting and then body slamming Stone Cold
Steve Austin during a WWF Championship match.

"Say you love me."

"I love you, Wellington Jones." More than he'd
ever know, and at the moment more than she was
willing to admit. Her soul magnetically absorbed
his spiritual energy.

"I love you, too, ba. I'm gonna go clean up this
wonderful mess you've created. Don't forget to
call and let me know when you're coming to get
your car. Good night, my Nubian Queen."

"Yes, it is a very good night." Jada recharged her
cell phone on the nightstand and continued lying
sideways across the jumbo-size mattress. She cried
hard into her pillow so the people in the adjacent
room wouldn't hear her sobbing. Why did she
keep crying over Wellington when she didn't want
him? How long would her head and heart remain
out of sync? The old man on the plane had given
her a lot to think about. Should Jada abandon her
pride in order to salvage their love? Or give up
Wellington and maintain her dignity?

ABOUT THE AUTHOR

Mary B. Morrison woke up one morning in 1999 and decided it was time for her to step out on faith. It was time to stop talking about her dream and start living her dream to become a critically acclaimed best-selling author. From that moment forward, she has lived by the words to which she subscribed—"I'd rather die a failure than to have lived and never known whether I would become a success." Her commitment convinced others to do the same, and she encourages each and every one of you to live your dreams.

After working for the government for eighteen years, Mary quit her job on June 3, 2000, and never looked back. Earning a GS-14 salary of seventy-five thousand dollars a year was no incentive for this risk-taker to continue working nine-to-five. Neither was the GS-15 promotional salary of over ninety thousand dollars a year that she was on a career track to receive. Before she resigned, Mary prepared her foundation and wrote *soulmates Dissipate* in four months—at night and on the weekends—while simultaneously caring for her wonderful son, Jesse.

Mary's motivation to fulfill her dream is driven by a greater humanitarian purpose. She envisions that her hometown high school, McDonogh #35 Senior High in New Orleans, Louisiana, will raise the bar for public schools across America by instituting programs to support the following: (1) a scholarship club to achieve 100 percent college placement; (2) a financial investment club (FIC) for teachers to teach each student how to invest money; (3) a mentoring program; (4) a support system for teachers; and (5) a program which allows students to travel abroad to broaden their educational horizon.

Ms. Morrison currently resides in the Washington, D.C., metropolitan area. To contact Mary, visit her website at:

www.marymorrison.com.

Grab These Other
Dafina Novels
(trade paperback editions)

Every Bitter Thing Sweet
1-57566-851-3

by Roslyn Carrington
$14.00US/$19.00CAN

When Twilight Comes
0-7582-0009-9

by Gwynne Forster
$15.00US/$21.00CAN

Some Sunday
0-7582-0003-X

by Margaret Johnson-Hodge
$15.00US/$21.00CAN

Testimony
0-7582-0063-3

by Felicia Mason
$15.00US/$21.00CAN

Forever
1-57566-759-2

by Timmothy B. McCann
$15.00US/$21.00CAN

God Don't Like Ugly
1-57566-607-3

by Mary Monroe
$15.00US/$20.00CAN

Gonna Lay Down My Burdens
0-7582-0001-3

by Mary Monroe
$15.00US/$21.00CAN

The Upper Room
0-7582-0023-4

by Mary Monroe
$15.00US/$21.00CAN

Soulmates Dissipate
0-7582-0006-4

by Mary B. Morrison
$15.00US/$21.00CAN

Got a Man
0-7582-0240-7

by Daaimah S. Poole
$15.00US/$21.00CAN

Casting the First Stone
1-57566-633-2

by Kimberla Lawson Roby
$14.00US/$18.00CAN

It's a Thin Line
1-57566-744-4

by Kimberla Lawson Roby
$15.00US/$21.00CAN

Available Wherever Books Are Sold!

Visit our website at **www.kensingtonbooks.com**